About the Author

Rebecca McKenzie was born in London in 1980. She was keen on English and Drama and studied psychology and works as a cognitive behavioural therapist. The first idea for her book, *The Tears of Wednesday,* came from the superstitions and meanings that are based around the days people are born. She wanted to amalgamate and capture improvisation written in a way that empathises the mental states of a character's inner person, exploring the spiritual, mental and emotional lives of each character throughout. Rebecca comes from a family background of great sportsmen and is passionate about boxing and literacy.

The Tears of Wednesday

R L McKenzie

The Tears of Wednesday

Olympia Publishers
London

www.olympiapublishers.com
OLYMPIA PAPERBACK EDITION

A CIP catalogue record for this title is available from the British Library.

ISBN: 978-1-80074-576-6

This is a work of fiction.
Names, characters, places and incidents originate from the writer's
imagination. Any resemblance to actual persons, living or dead, is
purely coincidental.

First Published in 2023

Olympia Publishers
Tallis House
2 Tallis Street
London
EC4Y 0AB

Printed in Great Britain

Dedication

To my precious daughter, Chloe. You make every day a reason I live and smile.

Acknowledgements

To my devoted parents for giving me the strength to exist today.

Sigmund Freud proposed the division of the mind into Id, Ego and Superego.
What one feels, thinks and does is the structure model of personality.

    – Freud psychology

"Not everything that is faced can be changed, but nothing can be changed until it's faced"

    – James Baldwin

Written in the memory of our beloved Tracey Bennett, missed but never forgotten.

Prologue

Ruby Anderson's diary:
Summer 2020.

MY DREAM

Listen to me… please, I'm not mad.

They say write down what you feel? Well, if I did that I'd be drugged up on tranquillisers in some psychiatric unit wouldn't I, now?

I would say I'm stable enough to avoid writing journals, besides I'm sure that's what therapy is for.

Well, I don't need that crap.

What I'm going to tell you is real, I saw it before it happened.

I think I'm going to die. I guess I could start with that, maybe?

And no, I'm not depressed, or want to self-harm, you can sod off if that's the psychoanalysis bullshit you're judging me on.

I hear what they say about me. You know that I'm a scarlet woman???

But some even say I'm the beautiful one. What even is beauty? I'll tell you, it's a sexual demon-given curse; all I think about is sex and men.

Beauty is as powerful as a shotgun.

Anyway, I'm waffling, I think it's called short attention span disorder or something???

Sorry, I've not introduced myself properly yet, for anybody reading this, my name is Ruby Anderson, part of the Anderson clan. A family background of strong and successful, driven females. I'll tell you that:

People say I'm crazy.

The one who wants no kids, (yuck).

I like to call myself an actress.

Shit!

Maybe I'm making bad choices in my life? Am I?

That dream last night, Christ help me, it could be sixth sense, a warning, I know I'm not mad though.

Do you believe in witches? The devil? Premonitions?

Well, I do.

But anyways let's move on to my mother, quickly?

No longer married to our black father, there I said it, black! She remarried with my four sisters and I, but kept the surname, Anderson. Most people (OK me) do question this, since the old dear remarried years ago but still goes by the name Anderson. Weird.

I've got three sisters, Betty, Rose and Lily, we all live in Surrey, Virginia Waters, and we are all very different in our own ways.

There's Rose, twenty-eight, the youngest, married, but committed to the dark twisted world of pathology.

Moving on to Betty the uptight snobby bitch, thirty-seven, married, mother (bitch).

That just leaves Lily. The good one.

I never mention that she's adopted, OK? So I just did.

She's thirty-nine just like me, and wait, it gets better, we're so alike in ways it's scary.

Sounds quite like a perfectly dysfunctional family, doesn't

it?

Trust me I'm not the crazy one out of the bunch.

But no, seriously? Where do we go when we dream??

I need serious help.

Pleaseeeeeeeeeeeeeeeeeee

There are others like me out there, the special ones. Did you know that?

Do you believe in premonitions? I do, yeah I know, I've already said that, but it's true I do.

Look! Some bad things are going to happen.

But hey, no one ever believes Ruby Anderson anyway.

Chapter 1

Ruby Anderson – First Sibling
Wednesday's child

DÉJÀ VU

(According to the Mother Goose rhymes, if you are born on a Wednesday then you are a child full of woe)

When you think about how troubled a 'person's' mind can become when the third eye is open, you could say sometimes ignorance is bliss.
R. L. McKenzie

Ruby Anderson, catwalk tall, with a magnifying image, a perfect pout, and branded slightly nuts. Quick-witted and clear-sighted also.

She was known as the beautiful one.

And there she lay, perfectly still, dead silent for a while, quite cold.

She was wearing practically nothing, wrapped bare in just a sheet.

The floor she lay on seemed hostile, hard, making the bones in her body stiffen in lingering pain.

With just about enough strength, slowly making sense of her surroundings, she pulled herself up using the side of the wardrobe door, using one hand to clasp on to the side of her head, it pounded, thumping violently on each of her tiny temples. She had wondered how long she'd been drunk and disorderly for? Her eyelids felt bruised and heavy as they closed, shutting out any light.

She had woken rather troubled so, aware that something had been nibbling away at her cerebral cortex, she had been flat out cold on her floor last night. Yet still she could not quite shake off that annoying dream she'd had.

Newly awakened she stood up deciding to concentrate and focus until she was under some form of hypnosis.

It was rather frightening the way she just so easily drifted, as a small child those abilities she'd been gifted with utterly terrified her especially when she was tucked up in bed alone in the dark. As a child she was always a girl misunderstood. But that had been before her beloved Lily had come into the family's lives, for Ruby there was no other person in the world that got her, someone who really understood her.

From youth the girls had both felt weird, strange things, premonitions. Yet Lily had always ignored her gift, she just kept it to herself, or was the one who would whisper, "You're not crazy Ruby." She had been the one who never judged her mad like the rest of folk, and so it was she felt Lily was her kindred spirit.

Ruby loved to scare the other children. All those times she'd be ranting on about creepy stuff she would see in her dreams, telling all her crazy shit to the other kids in the school playground. That was the thing about schools or institutions, places she recalled as the gates of hell, playgrounds filled with spiteful, nasty mini humans. God help if you were black, poor or a gifted child. How she managed to get through the playground days was beyond belief.

They spoke often as children would, as did Ruby and Lily, whispering about their experiences. Ruby found it hard to imagine what it would have been like if they had been born into those dark malevolent misconduct days, back in a time where there had been immoral acts carried out around the superstitions of witches.

It was hard to imagine really that there was once a time when a woman's toe would be cut off, she would be stripped naked, her feet and hands bound, tossed into a river and if she was suspected innocent the body would sink helplessly to the deep depths below. If she was found floating, then she was proven a witch, nothing more than a lackey of Lucifer.

As Ruby grew older her witch abilities grew stronger. So did her visions, she had been right about a few predictions in the past, but Lily kept up the training in keeping her quiet.

Lily equally was gifted but in a slightly different way. She would always sense something was wrong, particularly with Ruby, in fact it was only ever with Ruby, their connection to each other really had been all rather strange.

Even as a praying Christian woman, Ruby had grown to realise there was no amount of praying that could stop the visions she saw of people.

Even though she had attempted to see a priest a few times to banish any evil lurking around trying to latch onto her good soul, it was only when the last one condemned her as pure evil when he learned of her sixth sense, to think she could be capable of casting some kind of a curse upon him. All she had done was ask if he had been feeling well, yet the priest had banned her from ever setting foot inside of his church doors again, for life.

Although she was still saddened to find out that not long after the vicar dropped down dead with a heart attack. The poor old fool had never seen it coming.

It was only most recently that the vivid, quick flashing visions of their sister Rose had started.

Initially, she was not too worried to begin with. After all, all they were in the beginning were just silly little strange dreams and blurred visions of her baby sister, crying.

Still, it never did take that long before Ruby Anderson came to fear the persistent message she presumed she was receiving from the paranormal world. Yet she had seen her, standing in her bedroom, but why? She needed to know. she needed to know if something bad was going to happen to her or to her baby sister Rose, or to any of them.

Her eyelids still felt bruised and heavy, they flickered but she focused some more until she drifted further, straight back into the dream if she could.

Once she was under, there she focused again until seeing Rose, tearful with frantic eyes, crying hysterically. She could just about make out.

Things had become too fuzzy for her at that point, trying to hold on to any clue as to what exactly it was her sister was trying to say. Yet the more she tried to see, the more vision she lost and then that was it, the episode was over.

She was still standing up, leaning by the side of her wardrobe door when she came back around. Confused as she was, she quickly snapped out of it.

It was always a flustering moment any time she was back in the realism of things.

Her obscene nature at the party she had regretfully attended several hours before had been too shocking to bear as she staggered towards where her phone lay. She desperately needed to check the damage done; whatever hour the time would tell, it would be an hour of shame.

The sun was baking through the glass windows. It was clearly afternoon hours she had slept in until.

Her phone was laid scattered with keys, condom packets with one or two missing from its box.

She had every item from one of many Chanel handbags spilled out across her white marbled floor.

Ruby never did have time to care about the village gossip and keen interest in her love conquest, the pressure of finding a man and settling down was the last thing she had wanted to do, if she was so beautiful enough to have a fair share and pick of any man, then why on earth would she have just wanted to have picked just one? She had already tried that as a teenager which got her nowhere other than a broken heart.

Looking closely, she studied a set of car keys perched on the window's ledge, it was clear they had certainly not belonged to her. She looked across her room, unable to fully see her bed from where she had been standing.

"BMW? What the hell?" She said as she looked out the window.

"Whose keys are these and where the hell is my car?"

A prized possession that car of hers had been, her shiny black Mercedes was missing on the forecourt. Ruby felt puzzled by the other car and questioned who it might have belonged to.

She took in a deep breath to calm down, the fresh morning air was an invigorating feeling.

The morning had been a Wednesday, but she had partied like it was a weekend.

Ruby had a garden bedroom with large shutter doors leading out to the back grounds of her property. She agreed in thinking maybe it was kind of promiscuous the way her invitations were so obvious, the way she would leave her sliding double doors slightly ajar through the warmer nights.

To her, it was just convenient for the strange random men that slid through them in her consent.

Ruby Anderson had a bit of a reputation in the village, make no mistake about it, and on that sweltering afternoon, for a second, she really thought about changing a few things in her life.

There she looked around at the disgraceful state she and her bedroom had turned into. Nervously Ruby grabbed for a top, and turned towards her bed; she walked slowly, already ashamed.

There a man slept, with a smug smirk, naked, on her sheets. She had not remembered much but certainly not enough to know who this strange man was.

She studied him for some time before poking him. Waking him up, he seemed self-assured and probably the arrogant type, or so she guessed for the few minutes it had taken her to decide about him.

"Erm, sorry, but did I invite you into my bed? Or did you just sneak in through my open doors last night, Mister…?" She never did catch his name.

She could not take her eyes off him, as aggravating as she found him to be.

And she thought it extremely odd that she had not fazed him or even startled him as she watched him wake up in her bed. Ruby placed her hands furiously at the side of her hips, frowning hard at the stranger.

"Oh, you invited me, so I thought I'd drive you back, get you home safe and all that. You practically tried to throw me in your car, you know? in fact you tried to do a fireman's lift, I took the liberty of showing you how that's done, and like I said I drove you back here."

"DID WE???"

"No, we didn't, you changed your mind and anyway you were far too drunk for me lady, not worth the risk."

He watched for her quick response. |She was the type to give as good as she got, he had known that at least.

"Hmmm, charming I'm sure," she replied, but he only laughed at her, a laugh that was loud and boastful.

"OK, who are you again exactly?"

She had been right about his confidence, though and she was very drawn to him, she had found the stranger and his nature extremely arousing.

"You know me as Mr Harrington actually, and I do know you Ruby, we met last year, but I think you were drunk then come to think of it."

The name rang loudly in her head Mr Harrington, she thought.

"Hey, aren't you that reporter guy?" She could not place him, other than finding him annoying. "I knew I never liked you." She kind of smiled when she had said it.

"For what reason would that be then?" He pulled the sheets back that barely covered his modesty and stepped out to stand before her.

He made no mistake in pretending to hide his truest intentions. Intrigued by him she pulled him closer towards her, she took his hands, guiding one of them up, underneath her skimpy vest top. Sure he felt her breasts as she had wanted him to do, but he was controlled. Stopping her in vixen mode Mr Harrington chose to resist her advances any further.

"OK Mr Harrington, you like to be the gentleman do you?" She had been sarcastic in her next approach, how dare he be the first man to reject her, she thought?

Frenziedly, she watched him dress back into his white T-shirt and denim jeans.

She adjusted herself quickly as she heard the sound of slight tapping on the outside of her bedroom doors. Ignoring him entirely she watched one of her sisters burst in to her room as they so often still did.

"Ruby, I need to talk to you, where's Lily?"

Rose the baby of the Anderson sisters had burst in, underestimating the fact her sister needed a thing called privacy.

And shameful is what she thought, spotting the strange, rather good-looking man by the corner of her sister's bed frame.

"Oh hi, sorry, you got company I can, see?"

"I was just leaving darling, excuse me ladies." He kissed Ruby on her cheek and nodded at Rose as he picked up his keys to leave.

"Oh, by the way, some chick named Lily has got your car key." And with that he left with not a single glance back.

"My God, the cheek of that guy." Ruby said as she heard his car roar, driving off far too fast on the gravelled stones.

Embarrassed with a dented ego, she said nothing more about him. Instead, she diverted her attention to her sister's shoulder.

"Rose Anderson, what the hell is that? Are you really actually trying to upset me? Is that my Marc Jacobs bag? Bloody put it right back where it belongs thank you, anyway, why are you asking if Lily is here?"

"Excuse me, Ruby Anderson but don't try to avoid the subject of that stranger who just left, who the hell was he?" Lily paused putting her hands out in front to stop any reply that Ruby could have given her.

"No wait don't tell me," Rose quickly added.

"I need to tell you something Ruby, and I can't tell Lily yet, she get all worked up." Rose emptied her own contents out from Ruby's bag and finally put it back in its correct place.

In the line-up of the sibling pecking order, their sister Betty took second place. She was the middle sibling but really anyone would have thought she was the firstborn child, the way their mother had divided her from the others.

Ruby had been the firstborn and baby Rose had come in at third place.

And then there was Lily, adopted in early childhood and raised as Ruby's double. As kids they dressed the same, hair styled the same, she was known to be the fourth daughter of the Anderson family.

Rose grabbed for the cushions hugging one slumping down onto the large bed of Ruby's.

"It's just I think out of anyone you would be the one to know what to do."

Rose was now perching at the end of Ruby's white rococo French antique bed, her cheeks flushed. She wiped away sweat from her forehead.

"I'm pregnant," she blurted out.

"Shit, you're what? Oh, fuck."

There was not a funny moment in that confession, yet she laughed.

"Ruby."

Lily was sweating persuasively, she looked appalled by her sister's response.

But then that's the thing about nerves, they really do seem to have a mind of their own.

Ruby cleared her throat, seeing the desperation in her sister's eyes. She seemed so needy, she looked so helpless.

"No, you're right, sorry, just my God I'm sure you were in

my dream last night. I'm sure it was you."

For a moment they had both looked confused.

"Ok forget that, let me start again, look, are you definitely one hundred per cent sure?"

She moved the topic straight back to where it needed to be.

"I've done four tests and they all say pregnant, five weeks, five weeks sodding pregnant."

"Have you told Matthew?"

Ruby knew her sister's husband Matthew well and if he was anything, he was a powerful man and a rich one that could pretty much bail his wife out of any trouble if need be.

"No, I can't. it's tricky, I've messed up so bad, he is going to flip out if he finds out what I've done. I can't tell him. He can't find out"

"Erm, what exactly is going on? OK, start talking and quick, what the hell is going on Rose?"

Nobody had been a big fan of her husband Matthew. It was true they all saw him as an arrogant piece of work, literally all of them including their mother whose idea it had been for Rose to marry him as young as she did.

But whatever it was that Rose had done, she did not know that it was only just the beginning of all the complications that were to follow.

"I've been so stupid." She buried her hands in her face, her voice was muffled.

"We said we would not see each other again, but then he called me that night."

She could see the irritation in her sister's frown.

"Just get on with it please."

"OK. So remember that night Matthew could not take his eyes off that long-legged brunette, do you remember her?"

"No, I don't remember so cut the crap sis, just get straight to the point please, what exactly have you been up to?"

She had never meant to come across as the blunt cow that she was being, but she couldn't stand it any longer. Maybe whatever it was she had to tell her, she would be able to find a link to her dreams.

Rose burst out into tears. "What a horrible mess, a horrible stupid mess."

She grabbed for the opened box of chocolates, desperate in finding relief from a sugar dopamine rush. The dried coated sugar crumbled, softening into a wet cheek of rolling tears.

Rose always had turned to Ruby; nobody else except Lily ever believed anything the woman ever had to say.

At times her stories all seemed a bit far fetched, but there had been those other times, those times when she saw the way her sister had a way of knowing things were going to happen before they even happened. She only hoped she could tell her something about her future, now she was pregnant.

"This is all crazy. I'm crazy, I don't know what or how you can help me, but what did you see in your dream last night, tell me, tell me Ruby?"

She sat slightly hunched back and stiff. It had been so difficult to shake off the guilt she was feeling, the betrayal to Matthew, this would surely be something no husband could forgive his wife. Betrayal: that was the word that would eternally haunt her, lying in wait at her own gravestone.

After all, Rose Anderson, well she was not the type of young lady to stray with other men, she was the sensible one.

"So basically, there's this guy Eli Bardon, you do remember him, don't you? We're over it now though, we really are, it was a mistake, a stupid night of quick passion, it meant nothing," she insisted, trying to reassure herself in her own sentence.

"What?" Ruby asked half amused.

She had always liked that guy; in fact, she had remembered him well.

"Eli Barden, well that's a blast from the past isn't it then? Wow! So how is he? I could always see the attraction you know, funny, charming, and good looking, so how is he then?" she said again casually, as though it was just normal for a wife to betray her husband.

"So anyway, back to that night sis, at Matthew's work function. I was fuming because I thought Matthew was flirting. Eli called me out of the blue, literally just after I stormed off from him drunk, annoyed. Anyway, why I was on the phone to Eli, I told him where I was and he came speeding down the high street in his sports car and met me on the corner by Bella's restaurant."

The heat from the insides of her body felt as though her blood had been boiled. It was her first guilty encounter and right then she was remembering every part of it.

"So anyway," she said hiding her embarrassment.

"We sat in the car for a while but then we got talking and then next minute we were ripping each other clothes off. Oh my God Ruby I swear it was going to go full steam right there and then, but we went back to his apartment and ten quick tangled minutes through the sheets we were done and I was leaving, the thing is Ruby, there's something else I haven't told you."

The door creaked as it opened wide and, standing at the bedroom door, was none other than their gentle graceful sister, Lily Anderson.

"Shit! I wonder if she heard anything?" she whispered to Ruby before her other sister could get any closer to them.

But their Lily was in plain sight as she stood between her sisters feeling suspicious and agitated with them both.

"Well, well, so what have I missed here then, girls? Does someone want to fill me in?" she said as she entered the bedroom completely unaware of their previous conversation.

"So, tell me Ruby, are you missing a set of car keys? Because they were given to me by some fit bloke last night. If you want a lift to get your car back you need to hurry up because I'm actually too busy for this nonsense today."

It had been at that chosen moment Rose took charge and stood to leave, giving Lily a massive squeeze and a kiss on the cheek as she did so.

"I'll follow you out," Ruby gestured, and as they wandered away from Lily's sight Rose gave one last blank and frosty glare at her.

"OK, OK I won't mutter a single word" Ruby agreed. "What I was trying to say to you before though is that all this has happened before."

"Huh? How is that exactly? You're crazy, do you know that?"

"I'm sure of it Rose, this all happened in my dream last night, you were crying, you were trying to tell me something. It must have been this? It must all be about you being pregnant."

"Sash, Lily might hear you, idiot."

Whatever had happened to her reserved innocent character had vanished, Rose was a rattled young woman.

"My God Ruby you really are such a strange creature," she said turning around to leave.

"Yeah, take no notice of me, text me when you get home OK?" but then she hesitated, dissatisfied with the label of crazy.

"I'm not crazy Rose, you should know that being you work frontline with all the head cases, but it's probably nothing.

"Well, hopefully it's nothing.

"Nothing more than a little DÉJÀ VU."

Chapter 2

Lily Anderson
The Adopted Sibling

THE ACCIDENT WAITING TO HAPPEN

Lily Anderson was a striking beauty similar somewhat to Ruby, with the same glowing brown skinned tone and tall almost to a fault. Her elegance and poise was a distinctive difference between the pair. Intuitive also, she was known to be the gentle one.

Lily was the adopted daughter of the family, her parents were both awfully killed in a fatal, calamitous blaze.

Perished in fierce flames, they had been two devoted parents, she a helpless child, a family residence went up in smoke leaving her an orphan no older than the age of six.

Subconsciously as anyone's mind does in such a case, for herself she tackled each day with survivors' guilt at having witnessed such a tragedy alive and unharmed like she had.

The poor child had heard the screams of her parents' death. She had been found in another room with her tiny hands shielding her ears.

There had been talk, gossip more like of the neighbours complaining it was a sick, bodged-up insurance stunt.

But no one had ever known how that dreadful fire had started.

Ruby and Lily had both met at one of London's top art and drama schools for early girl bloomers. Both girls were approaching five at that time and only in each other's lives for just twelve months before the horrific accident had happened.

Florence, a mother with wings was worshiped and cherished deeply for her generosity and kindness in adopting Lily without hesitation after the tragedy, and although at the innocent age of six the transitional stage to independence, Lily grew with real genuine love as a sister and a daughter in every circumstance, she went through everything with the Anderson family, she could barely imagine any other mother, now.

Finding closure easier with time and age, sharing no familiar memories, nor seeking or gaining any further contact with either side of her biological birth parents' relations, she became part of another family resisting any truth she once belonged elsewhere.

In anyone's presence, enthralled by her petite frame Lily stood with a blooming brown-skinned tone, dark hair and dark eyes like all the sisters, she hid a smile well, and most would compare Lily and Ruby as true sisters, it was more than coincidence that they shared a similar perfectly symmetrical face, skin complexion and hair texture. Lily was the only other mixed-race child in the whole drama school, dubious as that might have been, it was not often in Virginia Waters, a few years back that you would see much of anything if it was not Caucasian.

It had been true that Ruby and Lily became best friends at one glimpse, no one could have predicted the girls would become even deeper connected as their paths crossed together naturally in life as it did. The difference between them was Lily had her act together from her youth. She was always responsible, Ruby was scatty and lived for each day, making her own rules along the way.

Lily sat gazing at her sister. She began staring hard at her thinking if anything, she truly was the one that looked like her the most, not quite as beautiful but more like her than her own flesh and blood at least.

Of course she felt saddened by the fact she would never really know what temperament she had or who it once resembled, and for those who assumed from the outside world looking into the family dynamics that Lily was born as Anderson blood, Lily still preferred not to take anyone's judgment to heart, she only hoped she would never be compared to being anything like their rotten sister Betty. Lily had always been careful not to project any bitter emotions onto Ruby as she knew any of these feelings would influence her in having the same grudge, undoubtedly, the loyalty between them both was extremely amicable and she preferred Lily oblivious to the bitter, neatly tucked-away feelings she held towards Betty, those feelings as poisonous as snakes' venom.

Lily disguised this always though. She was indeed a gentle woman and would often pray for forgiveness, for any impurities to be banished.

She was able to hide things without telling a single soul, Lily used silence and smiling like it was a weapon.

All the girls grew as sisters but Betty in her eyes was hard work, the one she loved the least if she did have to say so, although envy would creep up on her most when it came to Betty, she was not jealous of her sister.

Even in the case of no adoption, had they been sisters from the same birth parents, the unwanted feelings she held deeply for her would still be the same way she felt about her now. Unearthly and unkind were her thoughts, precisely.

"So? why was baby Rose crying then?" Lily questioned.

"For someone trained to be so resilient, she sure is sharing a lot of emotions lately, what's going on, Ruby?" She had always felt her baby sisters' high hopes to do good in the world of forensic was inevitable, she thought Rose possessed such a unique, unusual soul, and assumed she always turned to Ruby instead of her, thinking of her too scared to hear the voice of disappointment.

"Oh, you know Rose, it's probably just a new phase, like you said she's always crying about something these days." Quickly she tried to divert the conversation from Rose being pregnant.

"Now stop fussing over Rose, how did last night go then? Are you actually going to tell me who this big mystery guy is? That you are dating? Come on, who is he?" She became fidgety in her actions.

"No wait, actually don't tell me, I'm going to jump into a quick bath, I've not had one since… you don't even want to know, anyway when I get out, we can have a quick chat before we get called down for dinner, you can fill me in then OK?"

"OK I guess so you filthy cow," replied Lily.

Ruby pulled a silk robe off one of the hangers in her glass double-doored wardrobe, scrapping up her long black straight hair into a high bun, she used loose strands to wrap and hold a neat bun into place, she leaned in towards Ruby.

"Yep, take a good whiff of Chanel when she's mixed with booze, fags and vomit."

"You're actually disgusting Ruby," retorted Rose pushing her as far away from her as possible.

Their mother's manor was always an open door. They each grew, they each left, but it was Ruby who had stayed whilst the others remained close to the family home.

It was home with everything in it, absolutely anything you

might need would be at their mother's house. Ruby had her own en-suite bathroom, a room hosting a double French bed, dressing table and fifty-inch plasma TV with large double doors opening to acres of beautiful land.

Rose's room was identical to Ruby's with double doors also leading outside onto the beautiful grounds.

Betty's daughter, little Ivy had her own kinder suite which Betty demanded to be built whilst six months' pregnant. Of course she was fortunate enough to have internal designers at hand building her own private guest house at the same time.

And although Lily was adopted, she had just as much as the other sisters did. Her paradise was cleverly crafted and designed up on the fourth floor of the manor, with the bedroom windows opening onto a beautiful clever balcony where the view was magnificent.

The snug den which was also built was mainly occupied by the family friends Sue and Paul. Staying over was something the couple became accustomed to over the years.

The old white manor was in fact home to them all. Lying stretched across Ruby's bed she imagined all the different ways in which she could tell her about the man she had been seeing, the one she had fallen in love with.

Their weeks had turned into six strong months with no signs of the relationship ending. She'd always been a cynical type when it came to love, never wanting to know what card she would be dealt. On the chance she would dwell in misfortune and heartbreak. The way love had suddenly developed was not what she was expecting to experience.

Although she was not short of attention, she certainly shied away from it, and hid behind her sister. For the world would always see Ruby first, anyway.

Refusing to believe there could never be such a thing as love at first sight, still, she knew her situation was something Ruby had many dreams about but had given up on Mr Right, the feeling of being in love would be much greater if only her dearest sister would find what had indeed now found her.

"Ruby come on, please get out, I can't go another day without telling you."

Not sure if she was loud enough to be heard, she imagined all the things Ruby would do and say about it, she dragged herself up and of the inviting bed and called out again.

"Fine, your timing in being extra long sucks Ruby Anderson."

She left it a short while before approaching the bathroom door, she banged on it with deliberate intent to disturb and alarm her.

"Rubes we've been called down now anyway, trust you to take forever. Guess our chat will have to wait, won't it? See you downstairs with the usual lot, and you know Mother won't bring out first course without you. I'm starved, so hurry up. You do this every evening.

"YES YES I'M COMING," she shouted back.

Almost suddenly with time disappearing into the hours, the chat between two sisters got lost, postponed for a home-cooked meal sat at the family dinner table.

It wasn't a full house that evening, absent from the table was Betty with baby Ivy, also Rose who had left in a rush. Ruby could not help but feel intrigued mainly about the part she had missed out about Eli.

"I must call Rose after dinner," she announced, preoccupied in thought.

Their mother laid the table as always, but she stood wearing what looked like a new tight-fitting dress. It was certainly noticed and not by just the daughters.

"Your dress is erm nice Mum," said Lily.

"Yes fancy," Ruby quickly added.

Ben was their mother's husband. He stood carving a juicy-looking bit of Beef; almost twenty-three years in marriage he'd had with their mother.

She had already bought the property when she had married him, but it was also Ben who had paid the full mortgage off.

He was of slim build, a nice kind man, quiet, all the sisters were quick to judge him, white privileged and very wealthy, what with Ben's nature being more of a reserved kind for the erratic behaviour of their mother at times.

Of course, this is only what the girls had thought at first, he had been stern in his ways. Subdued with all of them when they had been small, he was a man who believed in discipline and old-fashioned traits with no favourites to be had.

But he loved them well, all of them and it showed in just how much he idolized their mother.

As knives and forks clattered and laugh and cheer filled the dining room, Ruby stopped to notice the detail her mother went to, putting her elegant touch all around, with the silver crusted candle holders. The matching diamante dining sets, the crystal-shaped name tags, the crystal blue Prosecco flutes these were the things they would expect to see at a casual encounter at their manor.

Looking around the table, Lily watched on as their mother and Ben would stroke each other's hands every so often almost as though it was a gentle reminder that they were still one with each other. To her it seemed an almost forced display to her it was an uncomfortable performance.

Sitting opposite was none other than the family friends Sue and Paul, which meant alcohol would be the main attraction to any evening that they bothered turning up to.

Everybody loved a drink, I mean, who didn't in the Anderson household? But then there was just plain drunken, idiotic irresponsibility.

Betty had predicted often in the house Sue would succumb to an outcome of liver cirrhosis eventually if she kept the rotten habit up. The poor woman would get lost in her own vomit on most days and they could all see the strain it was taking on her, seeing it around her eyes. She became tired looking, she was becoming withdrawn, haggard looking, the girls all thought so but it was Betty who could not help but take a dislike to Paul the most. She had made it verbally clear he must never speak to her child and that Sue was just a dear silly old woman, who should find someone richer, better, a man who would help rid of her alcoholism, not curse and abandon her soul. She had wondered why on earth any woman who knew her self-worth would put up with his nasty attitude. The judgment resulted in Betty losing all respect for Sue entirely.

The couple were located half a mile from Ben and Florence, as neighbours lived about half a mile apart here. They had been coming and going from each other's homes for the best of twenty-five years, Sue was like a godsend, when Florence had divorced Mr Anderson, Sue had been with Paul even back then, helping her to raise the girls, and rise back from the dead. It was Sue who had been the one to introduce Ben to Florence and all four of them formed an unlikely friendship.

Sue was never able to have any children. And it had seemed the sisters all imagined or hoped Paul would walk out on her for good, but he never did. Rather, he had stuck around for his own reasons, leading to suspicions that he had only stuck around for a financial gain. The girls became very protective over Sue in the last year, Lily had argued most days that the man had turned into a parasite, treated the poor woman now like she was invisible and took her for granted in every financial aspect possible.

But what could anyone do? After all, she loved him and their mother was always telling each of them things would get better; only deep down they all longed for the time to come when love was no longer going to be enough, remaining hopeful that Paul would one day just disappear out of all their lives for good.

"If you kick me one more time Lily, I swear."

Ruby glared across at her clueless as to why on earth was, she was getting sharp sudden kicks from under the table.

"Sssh, you idiot. Oh my God you're so slow, I'm bursting to tell you who my fella is. Trust me you will want to hear this, you really will."

"Oh, so it can't wait another two minutes obviously."

'NO, it can't, now come on," she said, almost dragging her up to her feet.

Feeling satisfied at the thought of hearing some detailed gossip, Ruby cleared her throat. "Sorry guys but may we be excused? Lily needs to discuss some very important business."

Her mouth full, scoffing the last bit of tiramisu she pulled her chair out to stand.

"Well tell us all, then? Come now, you can tell us," bellowed Paul bladdered and amused by his own drunken display of foolishness.

"I think you should be more interested in hearing about how much you've had to drink tonight, Paul? And look at the state of her already," she said looking straight in the direction of Sue, who was slumped over with stained red eyeballs. She glared at Ruby, continuing to pull at her, leading the way to the conservatory at the back.

"Come on sis, quick. Let's go before we get dragged into hell."

They could hear the roaring sounds from the dining table, alcohol filling the lungs of seeking souls.

The evening started to hype up as quickly as everybody's mood, the hallway clock struck nine p.m. and yet the evening felt as though it had just begun.

"Good job Betty and Ivy never came round tonight," Ruby giggled.

"You do realise the last time little Ivy repeated one of Paul's outbursts she'd managed to say four swear words in one sentence? Betty completely flipped out, didn't she?" pleaded Ruby, anxious for agreement.

And just like that there the foul language filled the house and as the voices continued through the thin walls. Ruby and Lily found themselves in the back part of the conservatory, it was a part to the house only ever used for private discussions and meditation space.

"So then, I'll have three guesses to who your new man is. If any of those guesses are right then you can give me those shoes you never wear, deal?"

"Ha-ha, you're funny, or I could just tell you instead."

It was within seconds before they heard yelling and screaming and smashed glasses. They had both felt it was the start of something menacing.

"We'd better go check everything's OK and continue this little chat another time," Lily said, extremely worried.

"I'm going to make sure none of them drive back, I'll put them in a cab with me."

"Why? Are you not staying home again sis? Wow, it must be

serious, it's like you've moved in with this guy."

"No, not quite just yet. But it is serious and I literally can't wait to tell you about him, I really can't Ruby."

It had become very concerning and inappropriate the way halfway through the week it would become spoiled over a domestic dispute between Sue and Paul. They possessed their coercing nature dragging everybody into their dark and twisted world.

The girls carefully tiptoed over broken pieces of glass from what looked like white china plates and wine glasses shattered into millions of shiny splinters.

Ben was nowhere to be seen and Florence was waving her hands furiously in Paul's face as Sue was lunging forwards at any given chance. Sometimes she could thump the living daylights out of him.

"Give me my fucking keys Paul," she said slurring her words around.

"Shut up you bitch, look at you, damn fool."

Paul shoved her, his hands connected with Sue in such force her body was lifted through the air until it landed hard upon the table. Lifeless and limp, they watched as her body fell to the floor.

She was alive, defenceless and drunk, badly hurt, but alive.

Florence wept, checking and making sure no bones were broken. Ruby and Lily started getting the place back together in shock, adrenaline filled their bodies.

Paul sat silently, gripping a whisky glass tightly. Not daring to take another sip he stood, and he cried:

"I never meant to push her so hard, it was an accident man."

"Just stop talking and help me to get her into the den Paul," sobbed Florence.

He rushed over. Following her instructions he placed his hands gently under Sue's delicate, fragile body which he began to lift through to the guest bed.

"I think you should just leave. Go home alone tonight Paul."

"Florence man, it was an accident, I'm so sorry, I never meant to hurt her, you know that." She stroked her hand across his face, it was not smooth, his beard was dark and thick, touching his hair. It felt like feeling coarse wire.

"I know" she muttered.

Things had become very sour and nasty between the couple. She found it difficult to be in such a devastating position with them both, to see her best friend's life fall into ruins suddenly. The way it was beginning to do so was heart breaking.

With all the foul-mouthed soul attacking there usually was she started to find herself deeper involved than one could predict.

Sadly, it was like immunity. She became so used to their nasty confrontations it almost became normal.

The part their mother Florence now played was denial, gaslighting any incident, blocking out anything that ever happened.

Lily had felt dissatisfied with Paul's apology and his abusive aggressive nature. She made her way back into the den to see if she could be of any help, she needed to double check Sue was going to be OK, but how angry she felt catching sight of her mother offering sympathy to the same man that just pushed a woman they loved violently across the room. She was impulsive in her words as she spoke:

"What happened tonight was just an accident waiting to happen Paul."

"What are you trying to imply?" Paul shouted out.

"Exactly what I just said, it's bound to happen at some point the way you are with her these days. I can't believe you don't think so Mum, or do you?"

Lily felt furious and just as baffled as to why her mother's mouth stayed shut at the point of questioning it was hard to understand.

"Let's just leave Sue to sleep, and were discuss this another time Lily Ann, but yes your right, it was an accident."

"Well, that's not exactly what I meant Mother. Accident or not, he should be arrested right now. And why is it always a sodding accident, anyway?"

Not being able to bear looking at him or her mother a minute longer, she turned her direction to the door.

"My cab's outside Paul, unless you want to be charged with battery as well as drink driving?"

She was disappointed in her mother when she left. She never spoke to Paul in the car or even said goodbye to him once he stumbled out of the cab. Whatever the case, whatever the emotion, she knew this was abuse and aggression, instinctively she was beginning to see a pattern with Paul and Sue, and easy as it may have been for Paul to stick by his words, she knew it was not just a black and white picture as it would seem.

She had known that what she had witnessed had not been any accident, it was his choice.

Every hour after that incident Lily became more uncomfortable about it.

For Lily Anderson had known far too damn well that it was just not good enough to have fobbed off the violence she witnessed on a defenceless woman and one she loved so dearly.

She knew deep down it would not be the last time because it was much more than just some silly little accident, waiting to happen.

Chapter 3

Rose Anderson
The Baby Sibling

SECRETS

Rose Anderson, an innocently pretty girl with an ample-framed figure, although the youngest sibling, wore youthful skin far younger than her actual age. Innovative and observant, she was known to be the sensible one.

Rose had practically every room filled with a large free-standing mirror, reflecting a masterpiece of fine art on every back wall. Painting was a regular way of releasing trapped emotions, it was her deep connection to the earth's energy.

In the sensitive nature of her duties, she needed distraction from the intensity of each murder, death and decomposed body seen in a day's work.

She loved to stand and gaze into a reflection of captivating colours and shapes, but this time she watched her own reflection and visualised a bump that would be appearing in about seven to eight months' time.

She placed a pillow under her fluffy pale pink jumper and stood from side to side forwards and back. Disgruntled at the thought of becoming fat, she took a long sigh and pulled the pillow back out from underneath her.

Perfect though it was in size and proportions, she hated her figure but wore an extremely daring short dyed blonde hairstyle. complimenting her tanned skin tone and dark brown eyes where the pupil was hidden in darkness.

Rose and Matthew had brought and moved into a quirky, tight fitting three-bedroom detached house three years last summer, located with easy access to all routes into London, which was the main reason they both snapped it up when they had the chance.

Matthew proposed in the month of September on her twenty-first birthday.

A surprise cake had been designed into the shape of her small pretty hand, and painted fingernails, but carefully placed on the important finger of the luxurious cream cake was a sparkling, sapphire stone engagement ring. When the cake came out, she instantly saw it glistening and screamed in delight.

In that first winter, putting up their first Christmas tree together in their first home, newly engaged went down as a confusing overwhelming moment, she was wed by the next spring and it made everything suddenly feel so serious in her life.

Rose had been keener in keeping her family name Anderson, and Matthew was never bothered enough to show it mattered whilst that had suited her just fine.

She dashed out from one of the dressing rooms hearing howling and clatter in the front porch. She raced down the spiral staircase thinking how unpractical their house was if there was ever going to be a baby. Recently there had been many discussions raised around the topic of babies, although Matthew seemed to quickly brush of the idea more recently in the last few conversations they'd had, the couple both had busy work schedules between them but it was Rose who would often ponder the question of when would there ever be a right time to have a baby? When it happened it happened she'd thought but now the sick feeling of Matthew never wanting any children was just one of the outcomes Rose had been dreading in her current scenario.

"Shoo, shoo, get away you horrid little thing."

Rose went back in to grab for the mop before making her way back out to the front porch to confront a stubborn fox.

There was something mysterious about foxes, there was uncertainty about them. Well she had always thought so.

As the fox froze in a sunbeam and glared, they both stared at each other deeply for a minute or two, before Rose again flapped her arms about yelling and directing the mop towards the mammal. With a quick step forwards the fox was gone.

Rose looked around to see if any of her neighbours had noticed the disturbance. Deciding to clear up the mess, she put the plastic bag of rubbish inside the big recycling bin, something she knew her husband would complain to her about, but regardless she did it anyway and went back inside.

The walls glowed in an antique creamy white, bringing warmth and relaxed energy throughout the whole home.

The kettle whistled and there Rose sat herself deeply into a resting armchair. Where her thoughts deepened leaving a heavy attack of feeling deflated.

If ever there was a time she needed her big sisters it was now, but she needed to speak with Ruby again first, properly this time, with urgency.

Matthew was a good husband, that's the impression people would give. Frequently she would wonder what most husbands were like? At a modest age of twenty-eight with everybody stating how lucky she was to have been picked by him, that they were childhood sweethearts, all felt like absolute rubbish now, surely everybody could see the way that man just loved himself, even if he did not know how to be romantic, it was a shambolic display of affection. Her husband's arrogance was of an extreme level that it was not possible for him to care about anything other than his himself.

The possibility of Eli Bardon at that point excited her. What if he too had managed to work in law and criminology? Invested smart, what if he too would wear an expensive watch to impress her mother with? What if he too would have been the perfect pick, the perfect guy to marry?

Feeling like a tortured emotional wreck, taking a slow sip of tea, she began feeling a little tense, wiping away more tears.

"How did I let this happen? What have I done?" She could hear the echoes of her shaken and distorted words, suddenly and quite frantic she got up and rushed upstairs into the master's room, remembering the pregnancy test she had left lying casually by the dark grey drawers. Matthew had more say so on that room of the house and decorated it to suit himself with no thought of anything feminine, almost a loud message to say if she didn't like it there were two other rooms she could sleep in kind of attitude. She smelt his aftershave still wafting through the air, Roses eyes scanned the bedroom where she caught sight of Matthew's suit jacket, it had her full attention, she was curious as to what was poking out of his pocket and with no hesitation, she quickly hunted out the answer, pulling out an envelope that was screwed up, unwrapping the crumpled paper she read out loud:

Dear Dr Ashley,

I reviewed your patient Matthew Townsend in my clinic on 23rd February 2019. Mr Townsend is to be referred for further investigations leading to possible cause of infertility.

Rose took in a deep breath as her lungs felt suffocated, she clasped for air.

"Oh my God, but this can't be true," were the words rambling through her brain. The month was now May 20 and Matthew had not said one word to her about it. But why, she asked herself? She tried going as far back in her head as it was possible to go over the last conversation she could even remember having. She had been moaning about the side effects from the contraceptive pill. But then another sharp knot twisted away at the details she now remembered she had left out, had she not been taking the pill for quite some time now? And she had not bothered to inform her husband about it either, there had been no reason before now. She had never fallen pregnant by using natural cycles but now all she thought was horror, the more she looked at the other reason she never became pregnant, was her husband shooting blanks? My God, was what she thought next, imagining it could actually be another man's baby? Totally mortified Rose grabbed for the phone.

"Damn engaged," she cursed, rolling her eyes, hitting the redial button to Ruby's phone. She knew Matthew would be home any moment, she was feeling truly mortified.

Downstairs the front door knocked loudly. She jumped in fright, rushing at the same time to see who it was.

"Hello dear, sorry to bother you." If there was such a thing as a nosy neighbour, she'd certainly found herself with one of those.

"For goodness sakes Ethel, you scared the living daylights out of me knocking that loudly, silly woman," Rose moaned a little before letting the old dear have her say.

"I noticed you been having trouble with a little friend."

"Huh? What do you mean"

"I was watching you from my front room window just now and I saw that blasted pest. Anyway, I've been talking to other folk, and they say the fox has had most of us up all through the night howling and trying to get into our bins."

"Sorry, but this really is not a good time," Rose said abruptly, flustered, wondering that surely whoever Ruby was on the phone to must have ended by now?

"Sorry Ethel, I really must go" and with that she shut the front door behind her to leave the lonely elderly woman alone with her busybody good doings.

She tried ringing again, this time Ruby answered.

"Sis, can you talk?" Rose pleaded down the other end.

"Not really Rose, I'm in a shoot, I got five mins, I've been thinking about you all night though, how are you doing?"

"Like shit," she replied fretfully.

"Look not that it's much but try do the maths? It's bound to be Matthew's if it was just that once with Eli anyway?"

"Oh my God, listen to yourself, that is utterly bullshit, what do you mean, do the maths? The fact is there are two men, one woman, shared bodily fluids, no protection, what maths is that? God, what am I going to do sis? Help me!"

Rose paused, questioning herself whether this was now the right time to speak about Matthew's suspected infertility letter, what if he really couldn't even have babies, she thought? Her words were on pause as more wild thoughts ran away. If she would simply just assume the baby was her husband's, would that make it all OK? Make the mess all go away? Rose continued to remove the envelope which she imagined had been screwed up ready for the bin, the state it was in. She pulled out the letter and read out loud the note. Unless Matthew had already been told he could not father a child? There should have been no reason for him to suspect foul play. Particularly if no one ever new about the affair, after all it was only Ruby she had told, so far.

She took a deep sigh, wondering if her husband planned to tell her any time soon he was having infertility issues, and with thoughts still running loose Ruby interrupted by pulling her back into the phone call

"WELL? Can you hear me?" What was that other thing you was going to tell me Rose? When you rushed off before telling me, I'm surprised you've not spoken to Lily yet. Or have you? Anyway you said there was something else?"

"It hardly seems important now, and no I've not told Lily anything, she won't even be able to look at me right now, so don't you dare go telling any of them, not to Betty, not to Lily and not to mother sis? I bloody mean it."

However, much Rose had wanted to tell all about Eli, besides being pregnant by either him or Matthew, there was still something else playing on her mind that she needed to discuss.

"Look sis, I promise I'll call you later, I'm getting filthy looks from every corner backstage, hold on Rose two secs, let me just deal with this idiot." She removed her phone from her ear and looked straight ahead.

"Yes, it's an important phone call mate," Ruby fired out.

"SORRY about that sis, bloody idiot," she lowered her tone and whispered,

"Oi sis, this director is a real power-tripping prat, bit of a perv as well, anyway look, as soon as I get out of this studio I'm all yours with ears, promise."

"OK, call me later, bye sis." The call had been disconnected before she heard a goodbye back.

To herself Ruby was confident, there was nothing else to it, her guesses were that sexual promiscuity came from within the person, usually involving a vulnerable woman. However, she felt Ruby was far from vulnerable. She always made sure everything she did was suited and beneficial to her in some way or another that nobody ever worried to much about her promiscuous traits or wild stories.

Exhausted she was, feeling the strain of pregnancy, fatigued also.

Right now, she felt even more confused than she had ever done before. She went over everything in her head, being pregnant, the one-night stand with Eli and a husband dilemma? How dare he keep this from her, she thought? Furiously she reached for her phone to call him, to demand answers. Yet just as quickly, she came crashing back to reality, guilt ridden.

Her own double standards made her cheeks blush with shame and humiliation.

He would be pulling up onto the drive and coming in through the porch doors any minute, everything was suddenly beginning to make her feel queasy.

She pulled herself up and fixed herself back together.

As Rose Anderson waited for her husband's return, she could not help but dwell onto the dirty little secrets she was in fact now holding herself.

After all, their mother had always told them,

A secret held is better than a secret told.

Chapter 4

Betty Hughes Anderson
(Middle Sibling)

HARSH LESSONS

Sometimes in life lessons can be hard. Sometimes in life the lessons come too late.

R.L. McKenzie

Betty Anderson was a woman of fine cosmetics, attractive by sight, thin by strict dieting.

Shrewd and astute.

She was known to be the stuck-up one.

Betty and David had met at the family GP's clinic when Betty was a practice nurse.

One of the doctors had taken a placement in Uganda and David came in as a fresh new replacement. It was instant attraction and after a few months of long pauses, eye gazing and a few whispers from the other staff Betty and David became official. They were deemed to be the hottest couple in the village.

Betty was very different in her appearance to the other sisters. She stood unique, with a straight, waist-length mane of auburn hair and hazel eyes that came from their mother's great aunt apparently. Something she was told was seen as rare, even odd in white and black Caribbean children.

Betty was now a practice partner with Matthew in the world

of aesthetics, cosmetic surgery to the finest. When baby Ivy had been announced it came as a massive shock to everyone, after all it was Betty that had always said she was never ready to disfigure her silicone breasts and was more likely to have paid for a surrogate mother than to have gone through the real thing herself, but their baby Ivy came, and although motherhood did not suit her well, she had no real regret in being hers.

She had been working remotely from home most of the time whilst David was still very much a plastic surgeon, correcting noses and reconstructing jaws. Yet the handling of breasts were long gone, once Betty became pregnant she could not bear the thought of her husband being around other women's bodies that he immediately focused his skills on other important parts to make the human more attractive, and you could pretty much say certainly mostly everybody did envy Betty Anderson, leaving the very few that pitied her for being a cold-hearted bitch that she was.

She was married to a good, handsome, honest rich man adored by all. She saw the way all the other women would lust after his money, but they had only seen for themselves that his eyes were only ever set on Betty, wherever she was, or any room she was in, his eyes met every time in hers.

It had been widely known the pair were a solid devoted couple.

The village was small, and the Anderson women had a bit of a high reputation with powerful influences. No woman in the village would have been stupid enough to cross any of them particularly Betty. She was deliberately spiteful, she was naturally skilled in using words as savage as a spit roast, inflicting pain and harm to anybody who challenged her.

Yes, Betty Hughes Anderson was extremely happy and

grateful for the man she had married.

In her eyes her husband gave her the world she'd dreamed of, everything, and to the outside world looking in their love was pure genius.

To David and Betty however, it was nothing more than easy and true love.

The cottage they shared stood alone, the last cottage upon the hill, a few miles from the village centre.

Their mother was not shy of making it perfectly clear that Betty was the perfect example of a fine powerful woman. In a way all the sisters felt she had favoured her most, she was put on the highest of castles and, as hard as the other sisters would try to build their status, it was always Betty that seemed to impress their mother most. This did seem to cause quite a bit of friction between the girls growing up, the loyalty continued to lie deeply between Ruby, Lily and Rose, excluding Betty from practically anything and mostly everything. Even so, Betty knew she was the outcast and the only type of revenge she could throw back in any of her sisters' faces was of her being more rich and more successful than any of them.

It seemed an English cup of tea could calm any mood and bring the joy back into oneself, only more irritated in making it herself. She poured out the hot steaming beverage from a meadow porcelain teapot, she blew over the cup breathing in the steam taking a few sips but finding it too bitter to continue.

"I can't believe I'm making my own teas these sodding days," she said out loud, emptying the rest into the sink. She slid backwards over a pile of toddler crap, pens, dolls and more colouring pens.

"Ivy, Ivy, come and pick up all your pens right now!" she screeched. "Right, this second young lady"

Ivy even at four had a raw talent for art, it was more than likely she had taken after her aunt Rose in that way.

Throughout the cottage the little child monster had managed to scribble, paint and colour practically every room possible to her own taste and to Betty's horror.

Hearing her own words, feeling tense, anger evolving quickly, Betty scooped all the mess into one. She would not be cleaning up her own kitchen and making tea if that's what the housemaid had in mind. She would demand for Magda to remind her of why exactly she was paying her so much damn money.

Magda was the housemaid and nanny. She'd been with the family since Betty had been early pregnant to keep orders of the house whilst allowing her to keep her feet up.

"As if I've not got enough to do already guys," she said and, feeling like a volcano erupting, she fiercely shouted after them both again.

The cottage was completely renovated inside but kept its traditional outside looks with its thatched roof and endearing character.

Inside was all open planning, a spectacular kitchen, featuring a large white glossed island, an exact lookalike to the one that stood central inside her mother's kitchen. There was light marble flooring creating a welcoming dining area. Once stepped inside everybody would confess to have felt tricked, almost as though they had stepped inside a palace, not a cottage in Virginia Waters.

Between Betty and David their net worth was in the millions, Betty married into a man with inherited wealth and money was something she made sure was visible to anyone and everyone that knew them. Most would have it that Betty and their mother were stuck up, looked down on others for their misfortunes, of course gloating and being boastful about all things material, expensive watches, designer clothes, Botox and fillers were not the most tasteful traits to share in common but Betty did exactly that, her views remained to be known, to her people should keep up their appearances, if you got it flaunt it, and there were too many lazy people with ideas but no follow through plan, quitters, the weak characters she implied.

She became a little distracted admiring the rare Indian vase she walked past. She continued going from room to room in search of Ivy and Magda.

"Magda, this is the second time I've called you now."

'Ivy, where are you little madam?"

Her voice was growing louder.

"Boo, I got you" screeched and giggled Ivy, clinging onto the long trails of Magda's dress.

"Forgive me madam, Ivy wanted to play let's scare Mother," she paused in her sentence, "I don't know where this one gets her imagination from, Ma'am." She admired Betty for the time spent in correcting her pronunciation and widening of her Portuguese vocabulary to practising words from the English dictionary.

"Well yes, who knows? Well anyway enough of that, the kitchen and lounge need seeing to at once, and Ivy needs to change her dress, were off to my mother's for dinner tonight and don't forget my friend is arriving later, no dinner but I expect evening tea."

Already dismissing the pair, making her way down to the mini spa, she poured a large glass of red wine, flipping through the pages of *Vogue* as she did so.

Betty was always groomed and nicely presented. She wore a wealthy look, she was attractive and photographed well.

The spa was built in the back of the cottage, which before was a huge wasted utility space. Once the building and reconstruction of the whole area was complete, the end project satisfied her immensely.

She had it filled with a mini jacuzzi, a bar, and a three-metre heated pool, gym and dining seating patio area.

She looked across at a half-drunken glass of wine she had poured and lay impatiently for Georgina Blossom. Georgina, was the perfect best friend any woman could have in her eyes, the only female besides her mother she had admired. She was never one for having lots of friends.

Georgina was leading a National Health psychiatric team based in Scotland and, when the month of July arrived, so did Georgina. She would routinely stay with Betty and David and usually she was the type to be proactive, en route or on time. It was not like her at all to not call, she thought, becoming more concerned by the hour.

Georgina and David had done a spell of multidisciplinary meetings at work discussing a mutual patient together a few years back. Once Ivy had been born the women would spend six weeks annual leave together like clockwork, she would be put up in the guest house for six whole weeks, and in the second week of her stay, you could rest assured Betty would have also moved into the guest house for the rest of her duration.

The excitement, the gossip, the female company made her feel youthful. She could not remember life before Georgina and she would never want to.

Georgina had never settled down or committed to any one relationship and part of Betty always envied her friend for the wings she flew with.

She had no time to stop and wonder why any one person settled. All the thrill and filthy lust, the hits and misses and the freedom to go and be whoever she wanted to be at any given moment.

There was only ever one man that came close to stealing that woman's heart. Having said so it ended pretty quickly. It got sour when his business went bust together with her loss of interest in him. Georgina never showed a particular type or taste in men, she would have the occasional female fling here and there. It was true Georgina scooped up more men than a dessert spoon would scoop up some trifle.

David did not try to pretend to hide what he felt towards Georgina. To him she was a lost cause, a bad influence on married women. But Betty had never once believed any normal woman could be capable of adultery through someone else's suggestion, that women cheated based on temptation, being negatively selfish or usually seeking something they felt they were being deprived of from their own husbands. For herself she was overly satisfied and deeply in love with him he would never have to worry about any bad company she kept.

She knew it would take more than Georgina's lustful games to make her stray away from her marital home, that was for sure.

After many failed attempts from Georgina's meddling over the years she eventually backed off, keeping to herself her strong opinions towards her friends' insistent faithful ways to one man only, and whilst Georgina had once tried to tempt her into a lustful world, but it never made any difference to the way David always made her feel welcome in their home and Betty cherished him dearly for it.

By this time Betty used the intercom to call up to the cottage to Magda. On Thursdays it was a day of indulgence, no work, no emails, a very missed husband until his evening return and as spring made way for the new season, it was a perfect afternoon to destress. She settled into the jacuzzi, the bubbles came soft at first, gradually becoming more forceful, releasing trapped nerves from her week before.

Headphones set, she lay back giving, completely tranquilized and at peace. She pitied no women that worked every hour God sent, she felt she deserved to have a good unwind before a visit to her mother's house but, still with no sign of Georgina, she made a second attempt of requesting Magda to call her, and as the minutes slipped away so did the sunlight and day, she thought maybe Georgina would go straight to her mother's manor instead. She finished the last bit of red, followed by a deep sigh, it was time to vacate the spa and change for the evening ahead.

The table was set as an Alice in Wonderland theme at their mother's courtyard, a special occasion for a spoiled grandchild, they were all to celebrate Ivy's first ballet performance, twirling and pliéing. Little, petite, almost a doll come to life she was on that stage, everyone in that hall had the little girl's full attention and as the other mothers watched, some in bewilderment some in complete dismay, Betty took all credit. After all, of course she would bear the perfect, prettiest, most talented girlchild there could be in town.

The manor was a full house with roaring familiar sounds and voices. Ben was laughing in all gears sitting with the family friends, Sue and Paul, then sat Ruby, Lily and Rose and of course placed at the top end of the table near their mother, as always, was Betty and Ivy,

"It looks lovely Mum, doesn't it Ivy? Say thank you to nanny."

Ivy, fascinated by glitter and all things wonderland, ran impulsively at Florence. She hugged and kissed the woman dearly.

There was no mistaking how besotted Florence was with her granddaughter, Ivy was certainly God's perfect creation in her eyes, insisting she was more than a product of good genes.

"Thank you darling, yes I think the maids did a good job."

And just as one of the housemaids began bringing out the main course, one of the new girls approached Florence with a deep frown, lines that made her look older than she probably was. She had seemed very confident for someone in training Betty thought to herself.

Trying to carefully listen in on the urgent interruption, Betty cast her eyes upon the young maid's lips, that almost seemed like playing a hard game of Chinese whispers, all the words. Abandoning their conversation, Betty gazed around the table finding Ruby's glare.

"All right up there sis?" barked Ruby. "Why don't you come down this end, join the common lot?" It was always typical for Ruby to pass some snide comment, but she was right. Their mother had always been so superficial, she was blindsided to the needs of her other three attention-seeking daughters.

"Richest first," Betty sniped back sarcastically.

Just as she was about to enlighten her sisters on where they were going wrong in their lives, Florence's voice croaked. she spoke with a voice of concern:

"Betty darling, Matthew's on the phone, he says it's important."

"Fine, don't think I'm finished with you Ruby Anderson." She got up in a quick second and rushed to retrieve her husband's edgy tone.

"Honey, I don't know how to tell you this, well I shouldn't be, but I just have to."

"David what is it?"

"It's Georgina, there's been word about, and I'm afraid it's true. I can't say I did not tell you something like this would happen darling."

"David what on earth are you talking about? Has she called you? I thought she would be here by now."

"No darling she hasn't called, only I, well Doctor Maddy has told me something, but maybe I should just wait until she comes. This will be the reason why she has not called you yet."

"Tell me what, David? I'm getting bloody annoyed now." Her heart was racing to hear whatever it was to be heard.

"Well look, OK, but I'm in total shock, I don't know what to say, I'm so sorry, but Doctor Maddy as you already know darling had been romantically involved with her."

"She was having sex with him David; you can just say that you know."

He cleared his throat.

"He has some results back from a scan she had recently. She has cervical cancer Betty. Darling she's riddled in it, I'm not sure what stage, Dr Maddy said it's just devastating that the HPV vaccination was not licenced for use until 2006. This whole thing could have been avoided for many women like her."

It was true she was extremely sexually active; contraception was in place for pregnancy prevention, but Georgina had in fact underestimated the power and glory of condoms. It seemed the price of not using one was severe. She was battling cervical cancer unknowingly until it was too late. Incurable it was going to be a cruel debilitating disease.

Betty's hand shook as she dropped the phone from her ear. She could hear her husband still talking through it, repeating the same words over and over again.

"Betty, can you hear me? Betty are you there?" David felt

desperate to hear his wife's voice. She stood still, in utter disbelief. Fear struck through her as though a death sentence had already been written up for her best friend.

And now with such a frightening thought, Betty could not help but think for a second. Had her husband been correct in what he always said? Had the lustful, casual encounters finally caught up with Georgina Blossom? Surely not. It couldn't be too late?

Surely life would not be so cruel?

Surely there could be no such thing as a harsh lesson to learn?

Chapter 5

Florence Anderson
The Mother

A RECIPE FOR DISASTER

Florence Anderson portrayed a curvy silhouette, a sharp black short styled sophisticated bob, a mother to four daughters, two marriages, divorced once. She was a woman grown into class and elegance, money and power, along with a topless Porsche, and six-bedroom manor. Florence grafted in youth and blossomed in age, invested smartly.

She was once a young divorcee clinging on to prime's youth pulled into a world of escorting top-end clients, such contacts that eventually led her to the fashion world with a dazzling paycheck.

Florence was only sixteen when she married Mr Anderson, at seventeen a mother to Ruby, she had always spoken of how ridiculous it really was back then, how women all just married young and were mothers just babies themselves.

It was a daunting error, a time of undignified childbirths, birth torture was the only way she could create the experience, children who were born only to be seen but not heard, she described the stigma attached to being an only child as spoiled or shunned isolated brats. She would relive her past describing the miserable days of walking past familiar neighbours' homes, hearing the piercing screams from open windows that would make the hairs on your arms stand up, you would know it was a man beating his wife to a pulp or a child receiving a complete hiding from its mother of father, the cries from young girls no mistaken were being or had been miserably molested, blind to their own mother's eye, yes back then the days had been very dark and very different for women, but even more so if you was poor, Florence came from a family background of white middle-class wealth, beauty and education, both her parents were still wed in which she grew strong contempt over the years towards her father, he was still to this day a bone idle lazy man who was gambling and drinking his and her mother's whole lives away.

He was a father she put the sole blame on for the way her own mother wore wrinkles thick and grated very early on because of a man's studious plan to control and dictate. Florence, from a young age swore she would choose death before taking a broke and lazy man in to ruin her.

For herself, well, she welcomed romance that only grew stronger, it was a love hopeless and doomed in her first marriage To Mr Anderson, although it ended with no love lost between them both, it was only the fact she had fallen in love with a black man why the relationship had come to an end.

The world Florence had come from was too heart breaking to bare, after the degrading childbirth of Ruby followed by Betty, birth was very much on a whim, it was either natural blessings, or natural misfortunes, and then just like magic itself when baby Rose came along, so did the newly invented drug on tap doctors, technology brought to women was portable gas and air, the kindest gift from man.

Florence had always held on to her morals proud of the fact that at least her girls were born as no bastards, but it never made a difference to the backlash of birthing yet another black child with him, that had been her father's last straw, Florence was cut off on baby Rose's arrival, but Mr Anderson's side of the family took them all in.

They had never mixed with an interracial couple before and it was shortly after Florence moving into their family home was when a few smashed windows had started, 'negro lover' graffiti smothered over the front walls of their home, firework explosives sounding of in the late nights. Maybe if it had not been for the fact that his father was also a strict Christian man who felt nothing but shame and disappointment his only son had broken his bloodline, the stress took toll on the whole family his mother condemned the life they had chosen for themselves eventually asking them to leave with a bundle of cash and out onto the cold streets of East London the young couple became poor overnight.

Eventually all the hate, spite, abuse and fear drove them to divorce a few months later, even after woman's civil rights and the change of law on black segregation, the financial woes and the colour of his skin was almost impossible for any women to live peacefully, happily even.

He had come from a background of family wealth himself, privileged also but no money in the world could have changed the venom that came from her own father as well as his own and every street corner turned, in wait for the young couple was verbal abuse, violent threats, there was nowhere to run, nowhere to hide.

Rose had just been a baby when Ben came on the scene. Ruby, Lily and Betty were completely torn apart with their father leaving it had taken them a while to adjust to a new father figure and accept they would never see their own again, for he had vanished.

At the beautiful age of twenty-seven, and whilst Florence

felt indebted to her new husband by removing her from a seedy world into an honest one.

Some would say she was just plain lucky to have married a rich white man who had accepted her as good enough with four mixed-race daughters, that was just one of the reasons she loved and stayed with him, it was more law of attraction, rather than attraction. Neither was there a need for his money, as she had enough of her own. It was not for the excitement because she had lived better days, it was more knowing when a man was kind enough and worth sticking around for. Ben was kind and giving to everything he did have, maybe not entirely compatible but she loved him, sure she did, although quite often she would long for the hands of her husband to touch her, it seemed easier to make an excuse and neglect the idea of having any pleasure or play between man and wife all to easily with Ben, the reserved prudish type of character he was. It was not hard to see that she became to feel increasingly lonely, alone even in his presence, and once all the Botox parties, shopping, and trips to the hair salon were done, she found herself restless most of the time, unaware that things were about to get very messy indeed. She was always finding an excuse to leave the house as soon as Ben set off for work for the day usually until late hours, on most days, the manor was huge just filled with empty rooms most nights unless the family had been around, she became restless as time went by.

As soon as the maids would have their break until returning at dawn. Florence's front door would close shut and the afternoon would usually involve an action plan for the Jekyll and Hyde, she would prepare for Sue's unpredictable mood.

The best friend who had become dependent on any form of alcohol, it was a way to feel any wanted existence to life, Sue on some days could be a bundle of joy, be the woman she once was, on other day's she was the sick patient and whatever was left of her after that she was a woman possessed.

The day was Sunday. There was a calm, gentle feeling to the morning and if you listened carefully, you could hear all but the sweet sounds of nature, the air was close, a humid day with just enough breeze from the light wind intervals. The summer was in its final stages as autumn would soon approach.

She set out in a cream-linen fitted dress, the slight obsession for her clothes to be tight fitted these days became more of a blatant stunt to get any reaction she could even if it was not always from her husband.

Being that Sue's house was only half a mile the drive seemed as though it was seconds before she was pulling up onto gravel stones and on to sue and Paul's place.

"Only me," she announced as she arrived waiting at the security gates., the stones and drive went on for at least another half mile before you approached another beautifully well-kept manor.

She pulled up next to two flash cars and a shiny looking jeep.

"Come up"

"Oh, hi Paul, thanks, see you in a tick."

'Hello darlin'. Sue's taking a shower, don't know if she's coming down after though, want a drink?"

He started heading towards the garden bar, Paul and Florence new exactly how to fill the time, they both shared the same humour, drink, in all the years she had known of him.

For himself he showed no signs of being a heavy drinker with a problem unlike Sue who had started to suffer from a certain redness in her face. She had blood vessels bursting through like raspberries, there was a distinctive yellow tone and awkward puffiness in her face starting to show the devastating effects, leaving her unrecognisable.

But Florence could see what it was that Sue was drawn to about Paul, he was tall, dark, strong and masculine.

He had a deep Jamaican accent which had always appealed to Florence from her memorable days with Mr Anderson, Paul had always preferred women of a slim build, petite and very pretty, exactly like sue use to be and the complete opposite to what she was now and to what Florence was herself.

Some folks would humour that Sue had been the complete opposite to a typical black man's woman, there was not enough of anything important, whilst Florence was well rounded, oozing love handle hips, large breast and had been lusted after by many ethnic cultured men in her time, she was famous for her larger buttocks and curvaceous frame. Sue on the other hand was slim, breast done by Betty's husband, she had long blonde hair, blue eyes, the typical Miss Californian type of girl but that had been Paul's thing. And for that reason alone it would not have been an obvious conclusion to anybody of there being anything more than just a friendship between Paul and Florence but yet any time of recent, any time she found herself around him, she found herself competing for his attention. She could remember exactly the first time she began to feel curious about him. It had been the day he had popped round to see Ben, passing detail of the most romantic encounter he was arranging for Sue, she remembered feeling overwhelmed with envy, wishing for the same exact life her best friend was living, but what a difference a year could make. Sue these days was living a true nightmare. with toxic arguments, empty threats and degrading tactics, purposely used for soul destroying.

And with Ben being well reserved, he was never an impulsive or daring man, Florence happened to fall into a classic case right time right place scenario, fooled by an illusion, she was a bored housewife in the making, she replayed the memories back and remembered the way Paul had looked at her as she came in interrupting them with grocery bags, he had said that she looked really nice that day as though the other day's she could only assumed she failed. Yes, ever since that hot summer's day last July, Florence went on buying tight-fitting promiscuous outfits, enjoyed lustful dreams of Paul's hands touching her, but as a loyal friend she considered herself to be to Sue it was a fantasy kept safely locked away. After all, she was not even Paul's type she had told herself many times.

"Here you go Flo it's just how you like it." Paul handed her a large Martini-poured glass.

"How's your day been?"

"Oh, you know? Lucky for another day as they say, just shopping really, eyeing up a few things."

"Did you buy anything nice?" I like what I'm eyeing up now, your dress I mean, it's nice, is it new?"

She blushed, hiding behind dark Christian Diors she made sure the expensive glasses stayed right on top of her nose, pushing them up higher, hiding the truth in her eyes, her take me to bed Paul and lose me forever eyes.

She shrugged off his comment.

"Oh, flattery won't get you anywhere Paul, save the compliments for you wife. How's she been since the other night? have you both spoken yet?"

"Your friend, my wife, man I tell you she's not muttered a word, put a dress on or painted her nails in I can't even remember the last time, the damn fool. The woman lives in pyjamas."

"Give it a rest," she said but underneath she could not help but agree that sadly her best friend was not looking like the

Barbie doll she once was, she'd became fearful that there was no going back for Sue now, having no children would mean no effort all round, no cooking, no cleaning, no feminine outfits, no grooming the list went on but yet Florence could not help but pity him more so and she became drawn to him. Of course it would never be her intention to want to hurt Sue as though the poor woman had not been through enough already, yet to discover her best friend having an affair with her husband, deep down she knew that would surely be the final crack it would be practically her friend's suicide.

Paul's other fascinating quality was his cooking skills, his dishes would leave you with an orgasmic experience, taste buds bursting inside your mouth with Moorish succulent flavours.

His West Indian roots did him well. Sue had met him the same school days around the same time Florence had met Mr Anderson, but Sue in her own wealth and family fortune experienced only kind wishes and support from loved ones she went on to live a happy marriage full of promises fulfilled she spoke of having a great sex life and shared lots of music laughter and fun times up until last year when everything dramatically changed.

It had got to the final stage, the last attempt of IVF treatment, Sue hit a nervous breakdown after learning the unsuccessful outcome, the strain and torture of not being able to do the one thing they both desperately had wanted together had struck a consistent detachment between them both. It turned out to be a nasty bitter end to a true romance that was no more.

Florence recently noticed Paul's flirting behaviour and subtle confidence around her more and more, and even though she deliberately fought back any inappropriate desires for him, she found herself dressing to please him, to entice him more and more, she became to like the flattery, the attention. she started to notice the way he always tried to get full eye contact with her which she would never give him.

An affair was not something she ever believed she could do or want to do now in her life, especially not stealing her best friend's husband.

She hoped the fantasy was just in her own head, the thought of it was enough for her, but as the days passed by as quickly as they already were and with Sue becoming fixated on a take me how you find me look, she could feel some heat stirring up and if there was a signpost signalled ahead it was one clearly reading danger approaching on all levels...

"Do you want me to cook you up something, I got a new recipe for you to try."

"Oh do you know what Paul? I've eaten." She panicked but recovered quickly reminding herself it was all in her head and no more than a silly bit of harmless flirting.

"Oh, what the hell, a small plate though OK? After I'll try and get her outside for some fresh air, how's she been since the other night? Seriously have you both spoken?"

"We don't talk." Paul replied becoming serious, his eyebrows creased his voice sharp.

"Well, I'm going up, wish me luck," she said leaving him in the kitchen to cook.

She looked up at the stairway in the hall, Florence whispered out the repeated affirmations she used to pluck up the courage to face Sue. She used different tactics to help defuse her best friend's Satan-like ways. After all, it was called the Devil's juice for a reason.

She repeated the loud and strong her chosen words.

"I am going to get sue out of bed today."

I am her best friend, and she needs me.

I am going to keep calm no matter what she says or does."

With her voice changing to somewhat empathetic to whispering disdainfully.

"I am not going to bed Paul."

"Sue darling, I'm coming up."

"Go away," is what she could just about make sense out of Sue's slurred words. she hurried up the stairs to rescue her friend from climbing back into her bed in the middle of the afternoon bright with sunshine with a bottle of Jack Daniels plunged under each pillow. dreading what the outcome was already she walked in calmly to sue and Paul's bedroom She looked around noticing Paul's wardrobe had been cleared out and his side of the table was empty when usually it had an ashtray with a half-rolled spliff, a book and his glasses. she had remembered Sue mentioning they were sleeping in different rooms, but she had thought that was for just a few nights nothing permanent.

"Hello gorgeous, how much you had then? And come on, let me do your hair and let's sit out by your gorgeous lake, Paul's put some new fish in there, I've seen them, just please Sue, get out of bed today yeah?"

"No, I can't I'm too tired, piss off Flo, seriously, you're here winding me up every bloody second. I just want to sleep, and no I'm not drunk," she said, and already asleep there she lay next to a stained pillow of drunken, spit and vomit, Florence took the bottle from underneath the covers she knew she would be hiding, She stripped the pillowcase bare, replacing it with a fresh one, she stroked her best friend's cheek and replaced her bottle of whisky with a small picture of the way she once looked and kept faith that it would give her a kick up the bum to get up and get sober.

She closed the door quietly behind her and went back to join Paul who was ready for them to indulge in his exquisite dish.

"Want me to do anything?" she said smiling and reaching for an apron. She crept towards him, she felt nervous, sexy, maybe? And because of that reason it had felt naughty, it felt very bad.

Sneaking a quick glass of Martini, she noticed Paul silently watching her, nodding his head in beat to the soulful sounds of reggae. The music filled the kitchen floor.

She pretended she had not noticed, but she could feel his eyes undressing her, the back of her neck felt hot, she never wanted to turn around to face him, but she could hear him approaching her. Florence wondered if Paul could feel her body yearning for him, wondering if the hot flushes were anything more than menopause, and the unwanted feelings of Paul was no more than a selfish and dangerous game between them both, a harmless bit of fun.

Paul brushed past her reaching for spices and herbs from the cupboard, smiling as he always was. And it was now Florence who was standing and watching him move around.

Florence tied a knot to the strings at the back of her pinny, fumbling around for a couple of seconds, he walked straight towards her.

"Turn around, let me help you with that," he said as he spun her around to help tie the knot she had hoped to do with still hands. she felt him push in towards her and she felt him breathing on the side of her neck that she left tilted and exposed.

She knew he was doing this on purpose, she knew he was.

"Right then, come now, you ready to try a lickle flavour of something sweet like you?"

He turned her back round to face him.

She felt embarrassed, like a silly teenager, she felt him

breathing on her neck. She could not bear to feel at his mercy or planed on revealing the unfaithful demon inside of her begging and desperate for him.

"Hugh," she said. "Sorry I think I've got to go."

"Ten minutes Flo, come sit down and try this."

Although at that point the focus of the evening was indeed a new recipe, he had wanted her to have tried, Florence new as bad as it might have looked, as naughty as it might have seemed, it was going to be a guilty pleasure she was about to taste and the only dish on the menu was a recipe for disaster.

Liz, Sep 2014 – hello poetry

On a Wednesday

On a Wednesday,

I want to tell you the truth. listen to me as if it's the first time you've heard a voice.

On a Wednesday,

I want you to understand. because I don't want to hurt you, you see. I want you to hurt me.

On a Wednesday, at this table I want you to realize it was meant to be like this all along.

To be on opposite sides of the table with different worlds as plates, different wants and needs as different tastes.

On a Wednesday,

I want you to taste what I taste. the sour taste of our expired time.

Chapter 6

Ruby Anderson
Wednesday Child

ALWAY'S THE POSSIBILITY

Audition checklist:

: Monologue

: portfolio

: glasses

: packed lunch

: lucky lipstick

She grabbed for her gold-buttoned blazer hanging from the back of her dressing table drawers and took one last glimpse at herself, ready to bare a stage full of fame-hungry females.

Although she had rehearsed with Lily a dozen times, she knew her lines inside out, but new her performance was weak, Lily had in fact blown her away when she imitated the exact same character only acted out in a more believable way, she noticed the power and influence her sister spelled over the same audience.

But again, when beauty strikes it strikes as gold and that is exactly what she felt when the casting directors gave her the call to audition instead of Lily, she had left that morning feeling empowered and determined.

Setting the mood to fit her character she waited silently

backstage…

"Ruby Anderson, centre stage please."

There was a final stroke of a blusher brush with an approving nod here and there from both make-up and costume team before one of the runners came beaming in with a swinging ponytail, mouthpiece looking all official.

"OK Ruby, all set?"

"Yes, I'm ready," she said making her way to the front centre of a very large stage.

Already feeling the anticipation, any nerves was good nerves was something she trained herself in believing, looking down into theatre red velvet seats she noticed one of the directors already refreshed by her entrance and femininity, Ruby gave her signature one wink which she did as a sexual stunt of distraction.

"Erm, sorry could I just have a quick second." The two male directors both now gave Ruby the attention she requested, and the female casting assistant raised an eyebrow, intrigued by her also.

"Sure, take as long as you like, we would like you to read a piece of your own work first."

Topic – love.

It's RUBY isn't it?"

"Yes," she said watching his expressions carefully for any signs of weakness from red-blooded male syndrome.

Ruby pulled out a pocket mirror and a red lipstick, slowly, seductively, she applied dominating red lip paint across her pouting lips. with another second she cleared her throat.

"OK. Ready."

She wore a black opened blazer exposing the side flesh of her natural, cupped breasts. her long straight black hair wore down which she flicked to one side.

Ruby began to read her work. she began and read out loud.

"A Perfect Dream. an idea of Love." Getting into her stride, she continued:

> *To love is to hurt, to hurt is to feel,*
> *To feel is to believe your love is for real,*
> *Nobody can touch you in the unique way that he does,*
> *Nobody you thought you could love so much.*
> *To love is to cherish, to hold and respect,*
> *Love is not to say sorry, just simply forgive and accept.*
> *Accept who you are, who he is and what will be.*
> *If you walk a long path, don't give up:*
> *You will achieve your definition of love, your perfect dream.*
> *A dream of which will remain to be.*

Ruby shuffled and placed a hand on her hip. "That's it," she said.

Surely impressed she'd imagined they would be she was asked to read a couple of lines from the script given, if successful the part would lead to a short, pre-recorded BBC series and would be her highest paid job her agent had struck so far to date.

Already thinking of Lily and how much she also wanted the part and how much better she was in character than she was made Ruby focus on everything she remembered her sister telling her what to say and how to say it, she did exactly that and for a minute she was alone only with Lily back in the bedroom practicing the lines...

She stood silent for a while as she finished quite perfectly, other girls were lurking around waiting to be next, she could hear sounds from backstage and all sudden she was back looking at the red velvet seats and in the eyes of both directors.

"Thank you, Ruby."

And just like that it was time for the stage to be accompanied by another actress.

She pulled back the thick stage curtains, as she did, she was interrupted by a tall Russian girl smirking as she was about to pass.

"You did good, he liked you."

"Oh, thanks. You up next? Which one liked me?"

"I'm sure you'll find out, red lipstick girl."

The Russian laughed and tossed back her thick mane of blonde hair.

The casting was open to diversity, and it seemed that a few of the girls had known these directors on a personal level, she knew there were very many favourites with these directors, so she had better of done good.

She was back in the dresser room, grateful for the freshly poured lemon water and the sweet smell from the flowers arranged beautifully on one of the glass tables.

Ruby was in a score band that rewarded her with real perks of the job, and today was no different she thought placing a bouquet of flowers in her bag as she left content.

Back in Virginia Waters at her mother's manor Ruby immediately diverted her attention to food. She had already put the audition to the back of her mind and what would be would be with no details given of when any of them would be notified of being offered the part. She knew nothing was likely to be decided until after the audition date closed and that was not likely to be any time soon. She checked her phone to see if Rose had called back. Aware she would not have been able to have reached her in the audition but expecting her any minute, she was due to turn up and carry on with her unfinished confessions. She longed for the need to have a rest before any talking session. she began thinking of her sister's frantic state of mind, she could not quite believe her little sister was pregnant and by who was the next question they needed to find out and quickly.

Ruby's stomach began to rumble, the lunch eaten way before it was due left her feeling starved, but she felt too tired to eat, she lay on soft satin sheets and lay still like veg.

She considered all the possible outcomes. A possible abortion? Attempting a stunt at pulling a strand of Matthew's hair for DNA testing. Divorce? what their mother would say? Ruby's brain just kept on spilling out little episodes of disaster.

Feeling a draft of cold air coming in she pulled the covers over her drifting off into a tranquil sleep focusing back to an image of a man in jeans and a white vest top, the surroundings were familiar, yes as she focused some more Ruby became to see her image more clearly, it was of that strange man she had woke to find in her bed.

As she lay, she fell into a sedated sleep, peaceful and somewhere else for a while. What felt like seconds of sleep she then heard a soft-spoken voice.

"Hi sis, oh I'm sorry I should have known you would fall asleep. How did the audition go earlier?"

Rose kissed the top of Ruby's forehead waking her.

"Hi beautiful, how are you?"

Instantly Ruby dragged herself up altering her position. She grabbed for her bottled water and chocolates, she had felt ravished by that point it had been difficult to concentrate on anything else than her appetite.

"Mother's not back home yet? And the maids have not cooked, they said she left no kitchen orders, what is she playing at these days I just don't know."

"Oh my God, you sound like Betty. God forbid you'd have to cook your own food, hey?"

"OK so forget about me, what will Ben eat when he gets home? If he gets home? I'm ordering a pizza, you having a slice?" She asked picking from the menu.

"The thought of a pizza is turning my stomach, I'm struggling to keep anything down right now, and the smell of anything is just cracking me up, I'm not staying long anyway, Matthew says he wants to talk."

"That sounds ominous." And there in conversation between them both, they squealed and shrieked, the two women talked, and discussed the issues of Matthew's possible infertility, who the father was? planning and plotting? the hour passed so quickly as it always did, a light flashed up on Ruby's phone distracting the girls from the discussion.

"The pizza delivery will be arriving in seven minutes, will you still be here sis, are you sure you don't want to just pick at a tiny bit, it won't do you any harm you know? There's nothing worse than not eating in your condition, this baby is going to steal all your nutriments and nourishment, that sort of thing?"

"Oh my God listen to you. Who are you right now? All responsible, you know nothing about pregnancy or kids." She quickly thought about how insensitive that came across and corrected her outburst.

"Look thank you for the support sis, but you got no clue what this feels like, I'm sure I got an omen inside of me, I feel sick every minute, I throw up every hour, my taste and smell has gone crazy and if you thought I was emotional before my God you will be crushing up Prozac and slipping them in my tea if you see me even on a normal day."

"OK, I'll let you off, I just worry about you that's all. How you going to cope with work?"

"Good question, but I'm going to have to tell them, or the

team will think I've gone soft."

"Good, well anyway before you go, what is this other thing about Eli Bardon."

"Don't worry, I really got to go sis, I'll be late for Matthew, but just quickly?" She felt keen to get it of her chest anyway.

"Do you think it's possible that another man could love me and be right for me?

"Eli has told me he is in love with me, sis."

Everything she had supposed to have continued feeling such as guilt, regret, somehow it was all heading of in a different direction she could not understand.

"And well? Do you love him back?" Ruby questioned her.

"I don't know what I'm feeling or what to think sis I really don't." She made her way out to the front entrance doors of Ruby's bedroom

"Sis?" Ruby said just before her baby sister was about to depart.

"Yes?" she said tuning back around to face her.

"Wherever there is true love, there's always the possibility of just about anything."

With those final words from her sister, she smiled and cried at the same time walking out the manor.

And as the echoes of Ruby's lasts words followed her out, they had seemed to fit perfectly for Rose.

"Always the possibility."

Because sometimes that's all a girl needs.

Chapter 7

Hollywood Baby
Lily Anderson (Adopted Sibling)

Being in the wrong time at the wrong place was exactly how she felt waking up, sharing the cab journey home with Paul when they had left their mothers that Sunday. Sue was in an incapable state and very much the victim, he never said much, but to her the journey was awkward. He had drunkenly stumbled out of the car dropping his phone,

It would seem rather rude she was being invasive sniping through it the way she intended but she mimicked an old saying "If you search you find." But what Lily was going to find out was going to change the dynamics in the family indefinitely.

Yawning and stretching Paul out of her mind her she turned her attention to something else.

She picked up a newspaper reading a print from an article on the production Ruby was hoping to get the call for.

"They've already made this sound like another BBC success." Her voice sounded excited.

"It will be set with a great cast, should be good." Lily did not show her sister any disregard to have been called to audition She gave the paper to her boyfriend. She had managed to keep a low profile so far dating him all through the spring and as summer was sizzling up, it seemed both Lily and Brandon became a tight fit, a solid knot, the relationship continued to soar high and fast.

Bran was tempted to make an official statement to say he was of the market, but Lily preferred they take as much time enjoying themselves before they were public interest.

"How ridiculous, I'm sorry, no disrespect to Ruby babe but that should have been your audition, if she gets this I'm done, you're coming with me to America, baby I'm telling you all your dreams will come alive, Hollywood only wants the best, and you're the best and being that it's all # me too campaigns you'll be safely assured the directors will not be an issue if you know what I mean."

"I know what you mean, babes."

They both shared a subtle smile, sinking and lying back in his enormous bed. His apartment was in Sailmakers in London's Docklands. One storey below the penthouses, it boasted a giving a panoramic view of the Thames.

His American property was just outside of Hollywood itself and was equally an intriguing establishment.

He rolled on top of Lily, he lied gazing deeply into her eyes.

"You do know how beautiful you are don't you?" He kissed her gently and sincerely.

"I love you Lily Anderson," he said stroking her face.

"I love you to," she said pushing him of in a teasing way.

"But I'm a busy lady." She rushed up pulling the sheets over her naked figure, he could see her nipples piercing through the white cotton linen.

"Come with me to Hollywood."

"What? That's so silly, I'm not seventeen, Bran. Just running off with you based on a ridiculous fairy tale"

"Cynical," he firmly snapped back.

"I got the connections, and you got the beauty and the talent so that is already a fairy tale."

Lily laughed again, she was always laughing at him, he bewildered her, he excited and reassured her into a world of hope, positivity and confidence and she loved him dearly for it.

"We should discuss this later if your serious?" There were still times she very much pinched herself to believe he really was real.

"Well, I am, I am serious baby, come back with me Lil."

She kissed him.

"Well, I'm serious about something else right now as you know, so let's talk later, OK?"

"Yeah, yeah OK," he said smiling sheepishly.

He reached for the remote control flicking the channel straight to CNN's American news for the latest catch-up. His idea was to spend the rest of his morning in England Town watching British movies, expecting his cosmopolitan breakfast to arrive up to his bedside.

Bran's apartment was in Kensington, set in an exclusive building with a star clientele.

It hosted a private kitchen providing chefs on hand and foot twenty-four hours a day with exquisite Michigan menus catered to detail. He was your typical American dream movie star. Recognised for leading many blockbusters but better yet for his reserved ego green style of nature, only ever giving small details of his personal life and never a wife on display, he was a selective man to who he allowed into his circle and into his heart. but Lily had managed to do that without any entrapment or financial aid, although, she adapted well to celebrity life just fine, she had always shown willingness to sign any pre-nuptial should their relationship deepen to anything like marriage. and as satisfying as it would be for her to wipe the smug smile of Betty's face, she would be patient and allow it to happen naturally, Lily struggled on many occasions about the uncontrollable urge and mission of having as much as her, being more successful than Betty was now in fact an asphyxiation needed to be worked on in psychotherapy.

"Oh babes, don't order any food for me later, I've got to go over to mum's and see Ruby, I know what you're thinking but I just have to tell her about Paul?"

"Only about Paul? are you kidding me? Is that the only serious stuff then? she must notice your wardrobe is cleared out and most nights your here with me."

"She knows about you silly, just not the huge A-list celebrity part," she laughed. "I'm telling her later as well, she's just going to explode, you know she be round in a flash from tomorrow don't you." There had been endless conversations about their fate, the secretes they shared, the solid pact made between them from young infants, the scars that remained from deeper wounds, a scalpel once used to slice a small deep incision on each of their palm, saliva rubbed together, with the final shake of their hands cursing any day that would part them, was the way they insisted nothing or no one would ever come between them, sisters first and best friends second for life, forever and always.

"I do know how much she means to you babes," Bran said. "And if your sister is a part of you and your happiness then she's a part of me and mine."

Lily ran straight back to the bed and jumped on him smothering him with the pillow before kissing him and arousing him, leaving herself to be his last thought for the morning.

They had met in convent garden, for many months she stared in a West End production. He was drawn to her from the start. He instantly requested to meet her and from that moment love struck between them.

Bran had been sensitive to Lily's trauma relating to her

parents' death, he felt she deserved his protection and security. He was fascinated with the stories she shared about the strange likeness she'd had with Ruby, both had white mother, and black fathers, Jamaican descendants. Brandon was a proud white American who believed in not seeing the colour but the person, instead.

It had been a good while she had not stayed at her mother's, for three weeks in a row now she'd been completely absent in the old white manor, she had noticed change in her mother recently, the same weeks shed been gone, and it did not seem as though her mother was sad but more distracted if anything. As she approached the large stunning property, pulling up in a prestige show driven car back into Surrey, Bran insisted she arrived at her mother's looking like new money, he had also learned quickly of Betty's judgmental character towards Lily and wanted to give this sister something to talk about.

"Mother dear, I'm home sweet home," she said, bursting in with an instantly welcomed feeling, she was home. And as much as she loved being at Bran's there was something magical about her mother's house and she could not wait for Bran to be a part of her family home.

"OH DARLING, I've missed you so much," she rushed over to her, giving her thin looking daughter a full inspection,

"Hmm, you're looking a bit twiggy and skinny. You starving yourself or what Lily Ann?"

"That's not how a woman's body looks when she's in love."

"Or are these new bones protruding for a new role you're filming." Florence asked concerned.

"Yes Mum, I'm actually starving, so you can feed me now and watch me eat it all," she said, mocking the cause of concern. With no hesitation Florence sat her daughter down and straight to the stove where she produced a mouth-watering casserole and as the smell lingered on and through the rest of the house, the inviting smell, called the rest of the Anderson clan hungry and expectant to the table. Before long the family laughed and joked, with seconds served and desert demolished. Each person at that table looked at an empty plate in regret, guilty pleasures had certainly had its greedy way that evening. It had been Lily who had discussed on many previous occasions that people would be a lot richer if they learned how to clean up after themselves instead of hiring the help. She had always asked from a young inquisitive age, what was it about money that made people become incompetent and lazy. and rather yet, plain stupid?

"Shall we clear up that wonderful feast then? We all enjoyed it" and up on her feet, Lily juggled cups, plates, shooing and encouraging their mother to start unwinding, relax from all chores, Rose and Ruby followed Lily's kitchen orders.

"Is that not what the maids are paid for? I'm joining Mum with feet up girls, thanks though for the offer Lily? but cleaning's not really my thing."

"Bitch," in the defending corner as always was Ruby.

"Ruby, your sister has had some extremely bad news about Georgina so please just ignore her outbursts. She's just upset deep down, so just all be kind to each other."

Lily could see the way Betty was dying to start more aggravation whatever was the cause to her irritating diva attitude She always needed to be centre of attention, she wanted to be seen as to good to clean up after herself, it would have come as no shock to Lily if Betty had got her way and paid Magda a little bit more money to dress her and not just get the dresses ready.

And seconds later Betty and the grand inquisition began, in every attempt she tried publicly shaming her sister with whose bed had been left? And questions to who was the unlucky man in her life?

"So, what you hiding then Lily who is he? Furthermore, how much money is this one supposed to be earning then in the world of actors? Don't be shy Lily Ann tell us where your sisters aren't we?"

"Give it a rest, why do you always have to be a sarcastic bitch? That's what you can tell us, we'd rather hear that instead actually Betty." Ruby snared back.

The girls were all dissimilar contrasting different female opinions, and any time together was when they would all let go and explode on one another.

"That's enough girls, now come on, don't ruin a lovely evening, please just leave the kitchen and its mess, it is the maid's job Betty's right and I do bloody pay them enough."

Marching all her daughters off into the lounge room Florence dimmed the lights and closed the double French kitchen doors shut.

The rain had pelted down hard, repetitive thundering spells had continued to early evening. Rose grabbed for the fur throw whilst Ruby set the coal for the fireplace, the house became cold in the evenings, Lily nestled between them both, three sisters all snug and cosy.

And with her feet up in the air as declared she would have been Betty was trying her best to enjoy the quiet time without little Ivy, as usual she was safe in the hands of David for the evening, and just hoping and waiting to hear from Georgina there was still no sign of her, and David seemed certain it was definitely a serious case.

The women each moaned, nagged, bitched and laughed amongst themselves, wine and hot topics filled the room with

Lily being the focus of the evenings subject.

"All you need to know Betty is that my man is perfectly happy in his skin, who needs no plastic fix or your husband's genius attention."

"Well, that's what's wrong with him them ha-ha or he's just as broke as you, can't afford the cosmetics."

"Betty Anderson be prepared for me to wipe that silly smile of your face your see soon enough." Lily tugged at Ruby's arm.

"So, you ready for our chat."

"Let's go," Ruby said.

They raced to the back end of the conservatory space as they always did, Lily staring hard and smiling harder at her as she watched his eager Ruby had become.

"So, you know when I made you watch that film? The one about the writer?"

"Oh yes, love it, loved the actor in it more, his hot, what's his name again? No wait, It's Branden Glassier? Yes, that's his name, I googled him after we watched it," Lily laughed, "yes that's the one sis, Brandon Gassier." She took a long breath. She clenched her fist together.

"Well guess what? Your never guess, but anyway, tahdah, that's my boyfriend." Lily stopped herself in her own words to hear them out loud, thankful for the pace she took in telling her because if there was ever a moment when things were too good to be true it had been then and she had wanted to be sure a true romance had definitely begun between herself and Bran before sharing any details of it.

And now was that time, herself and Bran were in love and, well, it would not have been right to keep it much longer from her devoted sister any longer.

"Are you joking," Ruby said in utter shock.

"Please tell me this is some kind of windup."

"No! Ruby Anderson, sis I'm serious, I'm dating the actor Bran Gassier." Lily screamed childishly, weirdly doing small jumping movements as a result from throwback excited nervous reaction.

"OH MY GOD, OH MY GOD, I CAN'T, I JUST CAN'T," Ruby squealed joining in with the peculiar jumping, and at the top of her lungs she screamed out "Mother."

"SSSH you loudmouth, shut up, I'm not telling her yet, none of them."

"Hugh? Why not, oh my God, I can't wait to see the look on Betty's face, it's going to be classic."

"Look sis, the other reason I came round to see you is because of some other stuff, horrible stuff obviously I've been meaning to talk to you, just not been able to find the right time, but I'm sure somethings up with Mum? I wonder if she already knows."

"Knows what?" Ruby said.

"Stop it Lily, you're scaring me."

"Sorry, sure, OK look at this." Lily took out her phone and went straight to the phone's gallery, willingly she passed over the device to her fretting sister.

Although the screen was clear as crystal and the image, she saw had been snapped in full portrait, there was a long pause before Ruby demanded a voice, an opinion from Lily, her words, her sense, just about anything other than the silence.

"Well? Ruby said." Lily glared at her, cheeks feeling blushed All the bones in her body began feeling stiff so suddenly.

"What the hell is Paul doing kissing this bitch? Who is she, that's not Sue?" Furiously she demanded answers.

"No, you don't say? Obviously, I know it's not, Sue I think

89

he is having an affair?"

Well yes, I can see that and with a kindergarten it seems, disgusting."

She hugged Lily and for a while they sat in deep sunken sofas, they both never said another word for what seemed like hours.

"So, what do we do? We should tell Mum immediately," Lily questioned.

"She's been acting really strange, maybe she knows about Paul's affair already, and does not know what to do or say?"

"OK, so let's call Mother down here right now." Ruby rushed impetuously for the intercom and dialled through to the living room area where she knew the beeping would alarm their mother and would be the quickest way to get her attention.

"Is that you girls?" Florence spoke into the receiver.

"Mother, can you come down to the conservatory? You can bring the others with you."

"Why can't you come back and join us here?"

"For goodness sakes Mother, fine, we'll come back in."

Out of all of them Lily had a special connection with Sue. From a young age she would read her stories and she was the one who had always been there for her from the start. And with the toxic abuse she started to pick up on together with an affair, Lily was not sure on how to handle any of what was going on she had desperately hoped their mother would know exactly what to do?...

"What's this all about."

Betty spoke first standing up crossing both her arms together.

"Sit down Betty and let your sisters speak, please."

Florence urged the girls to hurry up and get on with it.

"OK, so Paul's cheating on Sue."

Ruby started the confrontation.

"What are you talking about Ruby? Is this one of your wild stories?" She had wanted to sound confident she had wanted to be convincing; her hands were shaking as she looked at her daughter hoping Ruby was being melodramatic.

"HE'S HAVING AN AFFAIR," Ruby rephrased the comment.

"It's the same thing, isn't it? don't try paint a pretty picture with this one sis, talking of pictures," Lily quickly pulled out her phone to prove her sister's accusation.

"Here you go, take a look at this," she said.

White as a sheep and cold as the deceased, Florence's world felt like it was spinning. Not quite sure of what the guilt-ridden feeling was about, for she was not the mystery woman in the picture, but what she was feeling was uncontrolled jealousy, a raw rage and not for or on behalf of the betrayed, more that she could not believe Paul would do this, it had been bad enough he had been teasing and flirting with her. The thoughts of scumbag, piece of shit came into mind Florence froze as she stared into a picture of a young women sitting on top of some tabletop, his hands on the inside of her thighs, the girl had been wearing a mini skirt. The photo had been provocative, it was explicit detail with Paul stood between the girl perched with her legs wide open.

As Florence looked further into the picture, she felt like an old pathetic woman to look at girl's youth, her long hair brushed over to one side completely covering one of her breasts, exposing the other one that Paul had his mouth around.

It was not clear as to who would have taken such a private intimate photo and the young woman was not recognised by any of the Anderson women, they had all stared hard, asked questions, and none of them could say who the young woman could have been.

"So, when will we tell Sue? This is going to finish her isn't it Mum? It's bad enough he's violent with her and now a cheating rat as well and has anybody thought she could be really hurt and just too drunk to say."

Lily cried along with Rose and Ruby."

"I knew this would happen at some point," shrugged Betty.

"Not now Betty," Florence snapped.

"But you did give her a check over though, like I asked, didn't you?"

"Yes, let me remind you that I was a nurse before I was rich, and well it's hard to say without any scans and a doctor how bad anything might be? But she just seemed drunk the last time I checked. Do you want me to tell Paul I need to assess her?"

"I will talk to Paul first myself, Sue's in a bad way and I just don't think her body or mental health can take the strain of this crap girls, I will talk to him, I'll go over first thing in the morning."

"Do you want us to come with you, Mother?" Ruby asked.

"No, I'll do this alone."

Florence scurried off out of sight from her daughters, straight to the cabinet for something strong. Lighting a cigarette she stood still, numb; how on earth could she wait until the morning? She needed to see Paul, tonight.

As the girls all departed their own ways feeling extreme emotion and anger, their dear beloved Sue who had helped raise and love them since they could all remember, the sisters all agreed with something that evening and that was they were going to make sure Paul was history, some way or another.

Lily had gone to her room collecting a few more items from

her wardrobe, she wanted to run straight back into the arms of Bran.

"Do you know what Rubes? This is probably bad timing but the more I think about it the more I'm just done of this tired boring little village, same old same old Virginia Waters, the predictable daily routines, the lack of acting roles, and now all this drama with Sue, I just can't bear it. I really can't sis."

"What are you saying? You're scaring me again."

"Ruby, Bran's asked me to move to Hollywood with him, just a trial for six months probably at first, just to see what it's like, the opportunities are wild sis, he's got all the connections too, I could bring you over once I settle."

Ruby instantly burst into tears.

"Oh sis, please don't leave me."

"I will never leave you Ruby not permanently, but I need you to let me do this. Look, come for dinner tomorrow and meet Bran." She wiped away her sister's tears."

"Nothing's decided, we've not even discussed anything properly, it was just some flying comment, it probably won't lead to anything and I probably would not go anyway."

"What? Yeah right, you must be crazy not to go, it's a once in a lifetime's dream come true. I'm totally buzzing for you sis, I really am."

They both smiled and hugged each other close and as the evening kept on creeping by, the Anderson household became quiet and dark.

Lily stepped inside the chauffeur driven car with the destination to Docklands' penthouse, she unwound the side of her window.

"Sis," she said poking her dainty head out of it, "I'm going to Hollywood baby."

The black jeep drove of the manor's dark surroundings.

As Lily looked out of the car's back window waving goodbye to her beloved sister. She could not get the idea of Hollywood out of her mind.

The answer to Bran was yes.

Chapter 8

Rose Anderson
Baby Sibling

THE WITNESS STAND

The evenings were always the coldest, but as the new month settled, the temperature was above average which always seemed the most appropriate weather for the types of phone calls that awoke her breaking the silence in the middle of the night.

Any warmth in the air made the distasteful events feel less chilling.

As professional as any one woman could be, Rose felt that winter made it all so much more intense, any warmth in the air and any brightness from the sun, seemed as though it snatched the darkness from the perverse truth that awaited her...

The call came in just after midnight, two forty a.m., a murder, female, immigrant, was all the information given from the crime-scene investigation team. As most wondered why such a beautiful warm woman chose a sinister path as a forensic pathologist, but it was just that what made Rose the unique one. As morbid as it might have seemed each death she handled she did with compassion, each body investigated she treated just as important as the last and the next. She worked believing she would help make sure the unsuspicious acts were precisely solved and that the lengthy trials would eventually lead to custodial sentences and with each sole taken she would be the one to make sure the victim's obituary and personality was captured to real likeness.

If there was any good in any soul once lived, she would make sure they would be remembered not only by the horrific, malevolent ordeal in which they faced death but for the moments of each life with what and with whom they once loved.

The season was autumn which she admired most, paying particular attention to the chemical in the leaves that made them the stunning colours of yellow, reds and brown shades. She pulled over a polo-necked top, scurrying to the drawers for underwear she dressed into black trousers, black socks, black plimsoles, it would be a quick effort in slipping into the protective gear for attending the crime scene.

One of the hangers rattled from the wardrobe making her turn towards Matthew and there he lay like a baby as still as the night himself. The couple's working patterns left them isolated from one another, whilst she was banging the world to rights, helping put the guilty murdering perverted criminals into captivity, Matthew was standing with them, defending them, hustling a court system and jury into absolute trickery.

She was never quite comfortable with a fair outcome, to Rose it seemed it only meant good people were left sharing their world with all the psychopaths and serial killers just roaming around in hiding with new identities.

The noise from the hangers made no disturbance to her husband, she continued through to the bathroom, brushing her teeth, she began to stare at her sleep-deprived reflection, the skin under her eyes still young enough to recover quickly, remaining bare faced as she applied no make-up just a moisturiser.

She hesitated at first before flushing the toilet chain, once she did she focused only on Matthew's expressions, watching for one twitch one stir from him but again there was nothing from him, if there was a hurricane or even assault right there in the house, she imagined he would be that type of character to sleep through the whole thing, "I never heard or saw a thing officer would be the only recording you'd get from a man like him, she told herself. When most women would kiss their husbands goodbye even as they slept, Rose would not have dared to have disturbed him.

They never did speak in conversation even though he had summoned her home

The night she rushed off from Ruby, the sudden demand was soon replaced with an important business call, one that caught his full attention, she had felt relieved as she never planned on informing him of the pregnancy either, even more so that she doubted him to be the father, the suspicions lay with her husband's outcome. That if he was infertile and she was pregnant, the reality of what she had done was beginning to kick in. Even if she was unhappily married, she should never have had an affair, she should never have created such a situation, but it was too late a new baby was on its way. She needed to be practical, and she needed to do a lot of thinking, the only solution she suggested to herself was of one to try and hold off the talk to her husband for as long as possible. Well, at least just to see if Matthew was going to come clean and spill the truth about his manhood.

She left that morning muddled, her head felt chaotic but with any further distasteful thoughts of Matthew and the unwanted pregnancy she knew the body of a young woman that lay in wait for her, was far much more significant. She remembered the first murder case she had worked on, she remembered the feeling at the pit of her stomach, domestic, premeditated first degree murder, of course this was before any plea bargains were made before the judge, the bastard attorney settled for fifteen years voluntary manslaughter, had it not been for the sheer incompetence from her side of the camp, the officers first on investigation lost the vital lock up and throw away the key evidence before the trial, And possibly producing such evidence as a front door key and hand written threatening note from the accused to the victim could have been presented to the grand jury as a final clue to how one plots to kill his girlfriend in cold-blooded revenge to staging an accidental incident, killing her in a crime of passion.

The beautiful woman who once walked on earth had almost escaped her abuser, she took her final steps in recovery, she had entered the road to bravery and pursued a new healthy relationship. Well at least for a short while the women lived a new healthy happy life.

But on the other perspective it was bludgeoned revenge, for she would face her death.

He claimed he loved her so much he lost control. The despicable subliminal manipulative words she could only hear loud and clear in her head was that if he could not have her then no one would.

Rose became a mute, silent for two days straight after observing the victims cold lifeless disfigured body, twenty-one years old, twenty-one knife wounds inserted, punctured and cut her to an untimely death.

They had matched the same knife to a purchased receipt, his fingerprints and DNA were captured all over the weapon, body and crime scene.

But the Devil's advocate as she knew came with twists and

corruption, lost evidence meant it was just a powerful white man's word against a dead woman.

It was early hours of the morning as she waited for the senior crime scene manager to arrive.

The instructions were to wait before entering the property, it was a private road, a quiet street, with not much lighting and to many alley ways, the scumbag could have fled the scene spoilt for choice she had thought looking around.

The house was an Edwardian building about four storeys high, like many other of the properties it had not been converted, the occupant would have been extremely wealthy. The information given was that the female was an immigrant, leading conclusion she was likely to have been a sex worker or had fallen target to a sexual predator, motivated by a controlled operation, someone seeking a female body as a conquest? She felt curious to learn of who the woman once was, what kind of person had she been? What pieces of the jigsaw puzzle was missing, and what was the real story behind this young woman's death. For Rose that meant performing post mortems and understanding the manner and cause of death, covering all the fields of murder, suicide, accidental, natural or unknown, she would be responsible in providing the imperative details needed as bitemark evidence in criminal court. Something Matthew would often like to remind her the better she did at her job, the less miscarriages of justice there would be in the world. It was his way of putting on the pressure, he would be there in court to bring down the opposition.

The sky had lightened to daytime in a blink of an eye. Rose had begun recording, photographing anything seen as evidence, writing down notes way before the governor arrived.

He always arrived furious, irked. Past tense to the point that it appeared extremely uncomfortable anytime he revealed a smile. She could never get used to how forced it made him look, solemn was his natural look but that was just the way he was, for as long as Rose could remember despite the visual concept, there was something sincere, something very dignified about him. To her she held the upmost respect and admiration for him always.

"Rose," he said in acknowledging her presence.

"Guv."

She stood at his heel instantly as he led the way down the footpath.

"What's the team here? And I'm not interested in the imbeciles"

Rose picked up her pace only to come to an abrupt halt.

"Who the hell is that sitting on the garden sodding bench?" the governor asked

"DCI, Detective CONSTABLE DUNCAN GUV, him and his rookie was first on the scene."

"That is no constable Rose, that is an imbecile." Immediately he demanded that Detective constable Duncan remove his hind end hopefully in time to avoid spoilation of DNA or any relevant evidence that might have come from the very same bench.

The way the governor spoke was as if everything was his, and it was. This was his crime scene and, like Rose, he had no room for mistakes or negligence.

When she had woken the sky had been dark from the early morning hours and it was dark again now, twelve hours from the day had passed. Another grisly day, she could only be grateful for the way she was gliding through each shift with no pregnancy sickness, it would not be long before things would become obvious.

As she left her mood swayed from excitement to dread but,

professional as she was, Rose rolled back her shoulders and reset her brain. There was a hideous project to get crack on with, as well as her life.

Walking to her car she felt as though the trees were whispering to her, but she would only believe in the practicality of everything going on. Rose had suggested the supernatural was for the superstitious and she believed science had an explanation for everything, leaving her more of a sceptic than her other sisters.

Once she had driven off, she selected the call list from the car's hand-free system, she waited in a small queue until finally someone had connected.

"Oh, hello," she said.

"My name's Rose Anderson, I have an evening antenatal check-up, I'm so sorry, I'm on my way but running ten minutes late."

"OK Rose can I have your date of birth please," replied a very soft-spoken receptionist at the clinic.

After being reassured she would still be seen by the nurse she still had rather wished she could go straight home, climb into bed and sleep everything off.

She checked the car's clock, she would have this quick check-up, and then straight to shower and out to Matthew's very important business meal with his business partner, his best friend Ashley Peterson and his wife, Vicky. Rose really never liked any of them but, still, when you were a forensic pathologist a bland canvas expression came as convenient to there being little said between the wives.

She felt at ease walking into the antenatal clinic. She looked around as she slowly waked in, it had not been the ideal way she had planned a first pregnancy. She stared at the other expectant mothers, some had been in late stages, some were proud new mothers holding or rocking their bundles of joy to and fro.

And for herself she felt out of place. Confused, wishing she could write herself out from her own situation. Abortion was now becoming a strong preferred alternative.

It was not long after checking in that she was called. She took a deep breath as she got closer to entering the consult room.

She knocked the mahogany-coloured door adamant she had now made a final decision. Abortion...

Back home everything felt rushed for the rest of its evening, her shower, her hair, getting her dress on, it was just ridiculous, especially when she had a spoilt childish man standing tapping his feet looking at his watch and cursing away every ten mins.

Quickly she grabbed for an expensive Chanel handbag, one Ruby had conveniently left and forgotten about.

"Oh, come on Rose, you look decent enough, just hurry up, I'll be in the car for five minutes."

"And then what? You'll go without me? My pleasure darling," she replied, trying to guard her sensitivity.

"Rose, you're coming and I'm not asking you I'm telling you, now hurry up."

"How about please? And you look nice? Prick." But Matthew was already gone from sight before he could hear her.

As they entered one of London's exclusive dining spots, straight away folding her coat over one arm she rushed off towards the restaurant's rest room it was a way of psyching herself up for a long night of pretentious game planning and boring, political debates.

She was always forced by her husband to attend and accompany him, but it was only on specific evenings, she knew nothing had been anything more than a false stunt, she was just satisfying a male chauvinist's pride and image.

The restaurant's guest room was simply breathtaking, it really was quite glorious, with gold and cream decor, with suave-looking sofas, long wall mounted mirrors behind every cubical, beautiful wash stands and a black glittered marbled floor with spotlights making it picture heaven for any social media attention.

She knew the restaurant and bar well, herself and sisters were VIP themselves and the evenings spent were always superb with Ruby and Lily.

Rose placed a few notes in the tray placed on a beautiful glass table. There had been a supply of perfumes, creams, sprays, anything anyone needed was offered to them at a small cost.

The female toilet assistant sat behind helpful with a calming aura.

The woman was black African with a strong, excited accent, the assistant's smile was beautiful Rose always had told the woman so, she wore all black as part of her uniform and you could tell it dressed her image down and hid the most amazing shape, the most beautiful curves.

The assistant treated the Anderson sisters like they were royalty, of course they each tipped her generously and routinely and she spoke well of her pay.

But the conversations she shared about Haiti in Africa were fascinating to listen to. She spoke of being a queen back home, herself.

The assistant was clearly making her own small honest wage, and most would just dismiss the African women as poor.

But little had they known that the woman was real royalty back in her homeland.

The two women from different walks of life shared a giggle

together and Rose kissed the assistant on her cheek as she left.

Heading back to the table she saw Matthew stand and greet her.

"Darling, Ashley's ordered for you, the same as he did for Nicola, Nicky, this is my wife Rose."

Shocked she was when the woman introduced was not Ashley's wife Vicky, instead a woman stood up revealing a baby bump estimated of around six to seven months. They stared at each other for a while as though they were already familiar, like they'd met before.

"Oh, that's it," Nicola said sitting back down.

"I knew I knew you from somewhere, you were at the Mary Rosewood antenatal clinic this evening, we bumped into each other, you was going in the lift as I was coming out."

Rose posed as still as a statue, speechless and off guard she said nothing.

"What the hell did you just say?" Matthew shouted out to the whole restaurant.

Nicola looked apologetic and embarrassed at the same time as her eager and very personal outburst.

But more to Rose's horror Matthew was grinning from ear to ear, he was ecstatic, like he had come alive, reborn, happy.

Rose felt nauseous, she could have thrown up all over the table right there and then.

A disturbed horrible feeling stirred inside. Was he even the father? What about the abortion she had decided?

She wanted to vanish from sight right there and then.

The thought of being caught out was unbearable for she considered her contemptible behaviour antagonistic.

Every time she opened her eyes after trying to blink all the madness away she had felt like everybody else's eyes on that table were solely on her. She could see the way they were staring at her, observing her figure. Rose had suddenly felt as though she was being judged.

It was as though she was now the one on a witness stand.

Chapter 9

Betty Hughes Anderson
Second Sibling

PRECIOUS TIME

It was true that Georgina had left Glasgow, she had been in London for two days' straight with there not being a single sound or trace from her.

Betty had made an emergency exit at little Ivy's celebration meal to search for her, but she never had managed to locate her whereabouts.

As per usual thankfully no questions had been asked yet by the others. Lily and Ruby had entertained the toddler in Betty's absence, sensitive to their siblings' troubles.

There was always just such strong support, and that was the thing about the Anderson women. When crunch came to crunch they all acted together as a team. It was something that always did seem to shock Betty the way her sisters became supportive and forgiving in nature in a family crisis, for she had not been there once for not one of those girls when it mattered of any importance. The only women Betty gave any time and love to was to her mother and to Georgina Blossom.

Some say the worst thing about cancer is finding out that you have it, all so suddenly life quickly slips like a bar of soap between your hands. The way life then becomes and feels more important but at the same time it feels like it also seems to stop right there and then.

Betty's eyes felt sore, smudged black where mascara had been smeared in several places and tissues seemed to lie everywhere.

For the first time Betty had felt completely lost, confused and numb.

She always thought being a nurse made death easier but that was not true, not when it was your own loved ones. They say nurses make the worst patients because they know and see too much, they see the mistakes made, they see the pain, the journeys, and that when death calls no man or science can bring the patient back.

Terminal, incurable, were the last words twisting around and around in her head. She had to go look for Georgina again, to find her best friend, she had to hold her, catch her. She knew she would be feeling so scared and lost the same way she was.

Betty concentrated hard on where Georgina could have been. She could not help feeling stern and angry with David. To Betty it felt like he was to blame for being the bearer of bad news, she had hoped he had got it all wrong, or that he'd been teasing her again expecting his apology from something meaning no harm, a joke. But she knew it was not a joke, nor was this her husband's fault.

At that moment she could not stand to be around him, she was desperate to hear Georgian's voice. She wanted to save her if only she could.

She stood by one of the windows in her bedroom. It was dark so there was not much to see outside the window she peered out from, but she knew it was facing out into a deep forest, a place where they had wondered off together many times growing up, where they both had played, laughed, cried and explored every part, crack and corner of the forest.

Then without warning it was as if the lights had been switched on.

"I wonder? Is that where you are hiding Georgie?"

She had remembered their sacred place: a thinking bench, hidden, surrounded by a lake. It was a place where they would go when rock bottom strikes no matter when and it certainly had so now, she guessed.

In both of their lives they had lived like the world was their oyster. Life had always been a smooth affair for them, the lake was a place that they had never needed to go since they had been young women.

"Where the hell are my hunter boots, David?" she screeched out to him.

"Darling, you spoke? What did you say?" He looked at her obediently.

"Wellies, my boots David, I can't find any of them, I'll never make it through the forest without them, I need them."

She was frantic and David knew his wife well. He restrained her carefully, just holding her for a few moments, proving that if she would fall then he would catch her.

He was certain his wife was going to need him in a way like no other time before and prepared to become a brand new rock.

"Darling sit down, I'll get your boots and we'll go to the forest together Magda is settling Ivy, so don't you worry. What are we going to the Forest for?" he asked, taking any pair of boots he could reach for from a collection of many.

"I think I know where she is. It's not that late to check." She rushed for his response.

"OK, look put these on, I'll go and grab your coat darling."

In daytime the sun would shine but in the night the rain would pour.

With no hesitation David guided his wife down the stairs and to the front door. As he opened it there, in the pouring rain, drenched and shaking stood Georgina. She looked terrible.

David welcomed her inside to the warmth, being attentive immediately. He was the type of man who learned how to keep a high-maintenance woman happy and, although she was demanding, spoilt and had a raging temper, he was sure his wife was misapprehended most of the time because underneath her thick skin he believed she was just as vulnerable as the rest of the Anderson women could be.

He laid out satin pyjamas for them both with hot tea. It was true that he stayed the devoted husband and proved to be honest and faithful, that good men really did exist.

Georgina and Betty hugged for a long while with no words spoken. There was nothing to be said at that point.

After showering and changing the women met downstairs to talk things through.

"Betty darling," said David. "I've stripped and changed our bed so you and Georgie can tuck up together. I'll sleep in the guest house just so you women have your space and can be yourselves, if you need me for anything just ring me darling."

He kissed her sincerely as he did Georgina and made his way out to their idyllic 1420 guest house.

Georgia had a blank stare that stayed with her but there became a calmness about her.

"I think I went into a bit of shock Betty, I'm so sorry, I know you were worried. I thought David would have mentioned it to you so I knew you would know why I went missing in action."

"Yes, he told me what Doctor Maddy said, look Georgie, I'm still confused, what is it? Is this as bad as it seems?"

She still could not help but hold on to any faith she had. The older she grew the bigger an atheist she became, until now, right now she prayed upon the Lord's name hoping everything would all be OK.

"Yes, it's bad." she ended all false hope in that second.

"I need you to be brave, OK? Can you do that for me?"

She did fight back the tears as she muttered her words, the only lump Georgina could feel was one from the inside of her throat.

"It is stage 4B cervical cancer, metastatic, incurable, it's also spread to my liver and it's aggressive Betty and things are going to change rapidly."

"My God, how long are we talking Georgina?"

"I'll be lucky if I get six months."

They never had shared silence between them like they had that evening.

The feelings were empty, it was a strange isolating time.

The women both sat curled up to each other feeling despondent.

In great bravery they then gave each other a nod of acceptance.

For they knew it was really happening.

"You're the only one I have got to rely on, to see me off good, a proper party Betty."

Georgina had not wanted to settle in a grounded relationship or wanted any children. She was estranged from both her Catholic parents and Lily dwelled on the fact of being an only child and Georgina Blossom decided to live life as the free spirit she was.

Of course, it seemed irresponsible in the current circumstances as Georgina carelessly missed a fair amount of smear tests travelling and getting caught up in work commitments, wanderlusts and short getaways.

It had only been five months where she had become strangely unwell, suffering with rapid weight loss, sickness and bleeding.

There had been no pain until three weeks ago when she was sent in for urgent scans, testing and biopsies. Dr Maddy had been able to find everything and diagnose practically instantly.

"I've been offered chemotherapy, but please understand this has been offered to me in end stage. It's just to ease the pain now really, but I'm a tough old cow Betts, I declined, I want to go out as me with every strand of hair on my scalp. I want you to know it's me you're looking at when you say goodbye."

"George," Betty's body fell to the ground like someone had taken all the oxygen to breathe.

"Oh Betty." Georgina fell down beside her, together they held hands, crying silently, sharing thoughts silently, eyes up looking at the ceiling because sometimes saying nothing was the best and easiest thing to do.

The wind started to howl through one of the windows left open, and through all the doors of the kitchen. They had both fallen asleep by the fireplace downstairs, the draught was coming in strong, stirring and waking Betty first, unaware of the hours that slipped by.

For a moment she thought maybe it had been a bad dream, but the pain reminded her differently.

At first, she did nothing but just stare at Georgina, looking at her asleep for now but she wondered how on earth could she expect her not to wake up at all, one day?

The thought of it made her want to spill her guts out. She hurried to her feet and off to the basin where she emptied her stomach.

Everything just felt so bleak. She needed David, she wanted to him to hold her. She also craved for the stern and strong words of her mother's, but her mother had been sidetracked and had not spoken to her daughters since they had all found out about Paul's dirty affair.

She looked outside to see the guest room lights on. She assumed he was awake; she found her phone to see six missed calls from him and eight missed calls from her mother.

She decided to text David and call her mother. It was early hours six a.m. in the morning and even in such solemn time the sun had greeted all with its shine and glory.

Georgina lay sound asleep still and Betty covered her with a blanket as she crept past her.

She never wanted to go over to see David just yet as she feared she would break to tiny pieces and her world would come crashing down in floods of tears. Georgina begged her to be strong and that is what she was going to be.

Their mother had a subtle approach to everything. But David was sweet and affectionate to the point that she could not resist but give in and crumble and for a while longer she wanted to block out as many emotions as possible and her mother was the very best person to do that with.

"Mother it's me," Betty said standing on the front lawn away from the guest house not to be spotted.

"Betty? Oh hi, I've been waiting for you to call," replied Florence who had sounded extremely flustered and slightly distant.

"Mother I need to talk to you, who is that I can hear in the background? Where are you?"

"Oh, it's just Paul." I'm round here early I know but I came round as soon as I woke up to confront him about you know what."

"So where is Sue? it sounds like you're having a party, why's the music so loud?"

"Sorry darling, it's Paul, he's drunk already I think."

"Mother, please just tell that man to leave. We can all help look after Sue until she gets back on her feet, it always feels like you're protecting him these days."

Betty began crying on the phone talking and telling her mother everything about Georgina's cancer that Florence never needed to justify the accusations about protecting Paul.

Betty leaned on her mother's words and her mother's guidance, her mother agreeing that Georgina deserved to have a beautiful send-off. Nobody would be invited to wear black, only bright vibrant colours to mark the colourful woman she was would be worn on the day.

Florence would assist in making sure she was in the best palliative care there was to have and that she could rely on herself and Betty to live out her last days as she desired.

"You need to keep your shit together darling; she needs you and not your tears. Every woman wants to die the true dignified lady she is, she needs to be at ease with what she faces. She can't do that with you whimpering, feeling sorry for yourself and breaking down every two seconds or just don't bother Betty, you can either support your friend or be a burden. Your choice darling. Look, I really must go. I'll call you later." Her mother hung up without hearing any tearful goodbye. A cold attitude was a sense of survival, to Florence.

It had been Georgina who also reminded Betty that no matter how life ended up, you got to give it your best shot, and what people did with their time and money or how they chose to spend it and with whom was no one else's bloody God-damn business.

It all came down to a choice in the end of who you wanted to be and how you wanted to live, Georgina would say to her.

After all, life really did seem as though it was nothing more than precious time.

Chapter 10

Florence Anderson
The Mother

LITTLE WHITE LIES

A few nights had passed and what Florence hoped would all be forgotten, trying to get the normality back into her daughters' lives was seeming doubtful.

When Lily had shown her the photo of Paul, the need to get away from her daughters that night was a must.

She remembered starting with a straight whisky, something strong she would hope to take the edge of everything. She had felt like an old fool every time the young girl flashed around in her memory.

He was clearly a man that did this type of thing before, she wondered how could she ever had been tempted to cheat on her husband no matter what pathetic reason she had given herself. And as much as she had preferred to ignore certain things going on in her best friend's marriage, Florence's suspicions towards Paul grew stronger, she was going to confront him not only about the deceitful photograph, but the bruising on Sue's body was now an urgent matter.

Florence Anderson never knew the green-eyed monster as well as she knew her now. The immediate jealousy and rage boiled her blood when she saw the young woman with Paul in the picture, with no real interest in who she even was, it had caused some insecurities to how she was feeling in herself being middle aged. She was the type of woman to hold on to her beauty like it was a matter of life and death. It had been rather complex to explain the impetuous urge to confront Paul, it was almost used as an excuse because whether she wanted to admit it or not, she was already drawn in. Her actions were vehement that evening; thinking Paul was laughing at her, just playing her and Sue like toys. It was as though she wanted to punish him for the twisted sexual thoughts she had of him.

It was easy, less painful to pretend no attraction was shared between them, easier to hope her best friend was going to get over her drunken hurdle and that surely it was not her best friend's husband's fists that were the cause of the horrendous bruises?

But denial was a dangerous game, for why would any women want to get involved with a violent, abusive bully?

On every new visit over, Florence started discovering several marks on Sue's body followed by Paul's excuses and fabricated stories.

Behind the closed doors of his wife's manor away from public view he had been cruelly hitting and striking Sue in her paralytic states where she was none the wiser. He used her drinking to cover up the domestic abuse he inflicted upon her.

But what had made her look for any truth in his lies or how she stayed tempted to look the other way? However, now she had no choice, she had to do something.

Before she had arrived over there, she thought back at herself as she stood alone in her kitchen that evening having downed three whiskies. It definitely gave her the pluck of courage she needed.

A convincing performance it was when she poured her heart

out to him explaining Paul had been having an affair, and that leaving in the middle of the night was only for the good purpose of potentially saving the couple's marriage.

The saddest thing about it was that she had believed her own deluded lies. Ben had looked straight into them at that point. She could see he also believed her.

For Ben they had not been showing any problems between them. He was devoted to her, learning of any infidelity would have devastated him.

Ben had stuck by his marital vows and remained faithful. Fooling around is not what good Christian married people did, was his response to Paul's scandalous cheating.

She did not want to tell him about how worried she was about the bruising she had recently found on her until she knew herself what was going on. She brushed off the flirting as a desperate bid to feel young, silly and sexy.

As she left her manor, she discarded the guilt when she kissed him goodbye.

And as she closed the front door stepping out of her manor gates, she knew it was not just a confrontation she wanted, but an explanation as to why Paul had been flirting with her all along. How cliche was it that he was flaunting himself onto a minor?

Florence was mildly inebriated by that time and the previous whiskies were beginning to wear off. It had been extremely late once she arrived at their gates, but she never had to say a word, Paul opened the gates expectantly.

"Want a drink? A martini?" He greeted her with his infamous smile.

"Martini is for playing Paul, and I'm not in the playing mood. Pour me something stronger."

The stare exchanged between them was intense, keen, as

they both looked for answers. It had been the very first time she looked right into his eyes. How could an uncontrollable jealous rage seem to suddenly disappear into thin air as she stood there in his charm?

"Come now, tell me what's wrong with you woman." He pulled at her to come closer towards him.

"Where's Sue?" she said, knowing full well she would be lost in a better place asleep. "I don't want her to hear what a two-timing cheating scumbag you are."

"You gone mad? When did me offering you a drink turn me into that?" He was genuinely baffled.

"Don't Paul, there's no point in lying, the girls, well Lily, found the picture of you and some girl that could be your own daughter. I mean she was practically naked Paul and you looked quite happy about that, how could you? Who is she? And don't think I've not noticed the way you've been flirting with me either?" She never knew what she felt but it was something new and something bad.

"Oh, so that's just me, right? And why are you so bothered, I'm not your husband, I don't need to tell you nothing."

"You're disgusting, I'm leaving, and I'm telling Sue everything in the morning, you pig."

She had been sure she meant every word, but she could not figure out the tiny thing that was stopping her from leaving.

"So, what's everything? You mean me and you?"

It was true he was calm and persuasive. Although it would not have taken much for Florence to have stayed. Florence welcomed his attention at first, the attraction between them felt was wild. She wondered if there was any truth in when you can't have something you want it more? it was the strange sense of something feeling so wrong but so right. Florence knew even then there was no question in how much she really did love her husband, she thought about how much she cherished her friendship with Sue.

Could lust really be so evil, she thought? The temptation of him was devilish she knew, but yet she had no will left to resist him.

"Flo, that girl was no one, she was young but not infant young. Nothing happened, her friends got her twisted and it was a silly girlish stunt, a dare, she threw herself at me and the camera lied, I swear to you, you know I only want you Flo."

She felt that fire burn again inside of her as though someone lit a torch inside of her and her skin felt like flames themselves. Maybe all this was a midlife crisis, menopause, one last hitch, a last attempt of owning youth. Despite her growing doubts about him, it never changed the fact that Paul made her feel young, sexy and sexually desired. It was almost a good enough reason why she felt less guilt and more selfish towards the idea of just having one quick, meaningless bit of harmless fun.

Even so she hesitated enough to slip away from his grip on her arm, but that only left him feeling empowered and challenged.

She knew Sue would still be asleep, but she crept in on her anyway. The smell was putrid, a mixture of bad hygiene, faeces and retch hit her immediately.

She rolled her over to one side, placing a big pillow to prevent her from rolling on her back and choking on her vomit. She was sure she had caught sight of a nasty-looking bruise but ignored it as quickly as she'd seen it.

Sue had become a burden of dead weight. That was the thing about alcohol. It was a completely self-inflicted disease Florence had considered.

The help was all there but only if she had wanted it or thought she needed it, and trying to tell an alcoholic they needed help was plausible. Whenever she did say anything it was only ever to say she was not an alcoholic.

But to Florence it felt like it had become impossible to get any real support as Sue refused every AA meeting, she missed every counselling session offered and all her hospital appointments. Paul had told Florence he had tried everything but would not be prepared to drag her or force her out to the doctors against her will. That there had been nothing he could do and that if she wanted to help, she could just make sure she was clean and fed at least.

Something told her to pull the covers away from her. She was ready to face what she had quickly caught sight of changing her, but it was something now she wanted to look at properly.

The disturbing marks and bruises on the side of her hip and an older-looking bruise on her cheek had flared up her suspicions towards him.

"Oh God Sue, what have you done to yourself?" She had to find a way to intervene without Paul finding an excuse to stop her from taking Sue out of the house. She knew it was time for a serious plan something was not right.

Florence tidied up around her and cracked the window slightly for fresh air before she headed back downstairs. Their manor was completely different inside to hers, just as big but the house was not open-plan. All the rooms were separated by white doors except the most spectacular room of the manor, the kitchen dancehall.

Paul was lounging casually around, the kitchen was built right at the back with a gigantic space, which compensated having a large conservatory. It was where you would always find him. It had a built-in TV projector, an all to appealing sofa, a perfect romantic seating area for two, set with a glass dining table, a pool table filling a spacious curved area, and large double doors opening to their large grounds. The kitchen dining area was his haven, all inherited from Sue and her side of the family. he was an entitled man who showed his wife little gratitude, what was hers was his, he alone was enough, and she was lucky he had not left her by now was his narcissistic outlook of his marriage. And then suddenly her plan became clear; she would trick him into thinking he could trust her, and the only way she could do that to its full potential was to keep flirting with him, making him feel she believed all he was saying.

"Paul, listen to me, I'm really worried about her. What's she done this time? Her whole side is literally black and blue."

"Well, I never touched her, she heard me playing one of her favourite tracks. I never see her up and dance like she was for a long time, so I thought I'd leave her happy moving to the sounds of reggae."

Now as she listened to him none of it seemed right the more excuses, he gave the more ridiculous he sounded.

Florence was lost in an exchange of so many different feelings, attraction, fear, doubt, and she was now prepared to do whatever it took to get her friend safe and out of the manor.

"Was she really dancing? That's a good sign, isn't it? So then what happened?"

"I can't remember, she just stopped and walked out. Next thing I heard her come crashing down the stairs. I'd already turned everything off to follow her up."

"Oh my God that's awful," she thought, screaming the word *monster* in her head.

"I thought she was dead, I was so scared, but she started

moving and she asked me to put her back into bed, so I did. I stayed with her all through the night though, I never left her side." If he was guilty then the man showed either remorse nor passion at all.

"She's getting out of hand now, it's serious Paul, we need to do something. I propose we wait till she plunges the drink down and once she's passed out drunk we just take her into A&E and tell them everything about her addiction. They will at least be able to indicate how severe it is and if we are looking at any liver damage done. If she walks off the ward the next morning without doctor's discharge then at least we tried." Florence burst into tears. She could see that her last attempt to get help was impossible so she would have to go through with her plan, she could feel him yearning for her, their filthy thoughts and perverted nature was unforgivable in that moment between them.

He pulled her into his muscular arms.

"Let's just keep a close eye on her for now. Give her one more chance, she would never trust us any of us again and your friendship would be over, I can tell you that for nothing."

Only Paul knew he was doing everything to protect himself and his image. Any hospitals meant police checks and an adult safeguarding team who would involve themselves in Sue's wellbeing moving forwards he most likely thought. So his plan was very similar to the one in mind to Florence.

The only way he could get her on side was to get her to trust him, and the only way he could do this was by sex.

Just like a man who grieves for his dead wife using sex as a way to supress the grief or avoidance towards his loss, Paul used his cunning charms to seduce her.

He started first with gently kissing her neck and stroking her until he felt her responsive and breathing heavily.

He kissed her deeply, touching and holding onto her with need and both bodies gave into each other. Entangled together, he became strong, dominant, physically charged. He became impulsive, his gentle touch turned into sexual hunger and there the foul play began as her best friend slept, her husband who lay in wait for her return, and her daughters all expecting an explanation on Paul's cheating behaviour. Instead she lay down with the man her daughters despised, a moment of insanity what could potentially destroy so many lives if the truth ever be told.

Florence had one of those personality types where every bad memory was repressed and that only meant now she would go to deep lengths to bury the truth of what they had done.

She had a way of blocking out what she needed to. It was a defence mechanism she possessed from childhood and Paul could read into this immediately, giving her all the reassurance she needed, nothing they were doing was wrong and no one would ever need to know.

They lay sleeping for the rest of the night. There was no room for any thoughts or any one person after the deed, they just slept.

It was not until the next morning after they had woken when she felt she had made a terrible mistake. She was stark naked, she looked at Paul still sleeping stretched out.

She thought of Ben, he would have got up to go to work, she thought, and she knew he would have just thought she spent the evening in Sue's room. She had woken to receive a supportive text message from him as soon as she turned her phone on. There had been missed calls from Betty, too.

Florence woke Paul up that early morning ready to face the consequences, ready to take oath that they would never do what they had done again. But none of them spoke, or looked at each other, it really was as though it never happened. Paul turned on his music loud, dressed in his robe and frying breakfast as though it was just another typical morning.

As drunk as she might have been she remembered every bit and every part of that night with Paul, and whatever drunken plan she had come up with it was over. It was something that would never happen again between them both. When she had attended to Sue that morning it had been carried out with genuine love and integrity. But it had been difficult. She could not bring herself to even look at her.

For once, Sue had surprisingly been awake that morning, confused, spaced out but awake.

She appeared to be mumbling but Florence told her she would be back later and quickly left in guilt.

It had not been long after that one of her daughters had finally got through. She had picked up the phone call to Betty that time she had called her from her front lawn about Georgina's cancer.

Florence had used this phone call to put together her own story of why she never returned home to her husband that night. Betty had questioned why she had been over there so early in the morning.

To Florence she felt there were all different kinds of lies for all different kinds of reasons.

And for Florence Anderson to her the only way to save her family from collapsing was to tell the ones she felt the best at telling.

As a wife and mother, desperate to protect her family, the only way she could do that now was to protect them from the truth.

Because sometimes the truth hurts more than the little white lies do.

WEDNESDAY

Worry is like a rocking chair: it gives you something to do but never gets you anywhere.

– Emma Bombeck

Chapter 11

Ruby Anderson
First Sibling – Wednesday's Child

IT'S JUST A BAD DREAM

There are many people who ask the same questions; like where is it that we go when we sleep? What is the real meaning of our dreams? Could they be signs, lessons or warnings? Or could it even be a spiritual process? A gateway to our truest and deepest feelings from one's unconscious mind?

Ruby had only been able to relay back one previous dream she'd already had so far until one fine, particular day.

The morning was a Wednesday, autumn was passing mildly with its vivid light shining only until midday when the air and mood would then darken, although this was not the sun with any warmth to it. Although that was still not likely to be a cause of the morning sweats, Ruby was suffering from, her body twisted and tangled in sheets soaked to her skin. Her body trembled unconsciously as she was led further and further, deeper and deeper into complete distress, her body flipped out awkwardly and aggressively as though electric pulses were running through her. Floating further and further away from mundane existence, Ruby began to dream.

Everything was red, everything appeared so real, she heard herself screaming. She could see Rose again, crying exactly the same way she had been crying before, exactly the same place in her bedroom, desperately trying to tell her something. The images became clustered with more of the colour red, her body to look at was as though it was looking at a person who could not breathe.

Her mother appeared in the dream, she saw her own car. The same black Mercedes. As she was able to focus onto the car, she could be certain it was definitely her vehicle whereas the reflection of who it was inside was a mystery.

There was the colour red again and more screaming, screaming so terrifying it was enough to bring her out of her nightmare and back into the wakefulness.

Ruby leaped up to feel anything solid. To feel safe, she placed her back firmly against the headboard and gasped for air, confused as to how her loss of breath continued through even though she was now awake.

"What the hell Ruby Anderson." Talking out loud as a third person seemed to ease any anxiety.

Slowly coming back around, more precisely so, she began using a towel to wipe away the sweat from the back of her neck, her chest, all over, she was drenched. Her straightened hair had started to curl from the outside humidity.

She checked for the time it was still early, she must have been sitting up alone scared and awake for at least half of an hour.

At ten past nine Ruby reached for her diary to take down notes of the tremor, the details of the date and the time. It was becoming clear that her fears of being born in sorrow, a Wednesday's child, could all be true. Was she destined to some tragedy, to death even? She began to suspect there was a frightful coincidence being born on the same days that her nightmares occurred. Why Wednesday, she thought?

Still perched up on her bed, she heard her phone suddenly ringing which made her anxiety kick off into its full attack. She breathlessly picked up.

"Lily?" she said in great relief to hear from her.

"Sis, are you OK?"

"Yes, well I think so. What makes you ask that?"

"Oh, I don't really know, can't really explain it, just had this strange feeling for about an hour."

Ruby was going to come clean about her dream and that her worrisome instincts was telling her that something bad was going to happen, but she held back. One anxious brain was more than enough, and she never did really want Lily to worry so she decided to remain Shtum.

"Oh, don't worry about me I'm fine sis I just slept rough that's all?"

"OK, if you're sure, what time are you coming round tonight? Bran is more excited than I am with you both to be acquainted at last. is seven p.m. still, OK?"

"On the dot sis, love you, see you later." Ruby hung up the phone still a little shaken but wide awake. Putting away the traumas, regarded as nonsense, she moved herself towards her bathroom. A long bath was exactly the way she intended to wash the bad omens away…

Her mother was sitting, resting perfectly posed on long curved furniture out on the decking where the sun would hit her directly in any spot, she sat in. even as chilly as the mornings were, there she would sit until the sun would all but disappear.

Ruby was the only one who had not left the manor. She had flown back to her mother's nest permanently after a dating disaster. Never again did she seek a husband, instead there were very many male flings she conquered, there was no child to be responsible for, and a career that could be over in a flash. But she did have Lily, she did have her family.

Ruby at first had wondered if her feeling of failure was more so because of the disappointing nods, the sound of tuts and disappointing comments she was used to receiving from her mother.

When the others were not around Florence was a different woman to the fiery hostess she would become, Florence could also be a rather mysterious woman, at the best of times she would sit looking lost. It was something in the way she would sit gracefully, calmly and still, hidden behind her large hat and shades, revealing no expression of any kind, reading no books, listening to nothing but air and nature, no company, no phone. Just thinking about whatever it was a woman has to think about.

Ruby would not usually disturb her mother in these times but, as none of them had any clue to what and who Paul was cheating on Sue with, she felt it was only right to proceed forwards with the questioning.

"Morning mum, what time did you get back?"

Florence remained silent, obviously stuck in thoughts elsewhere.

"Mum, did you hear me? How did the talk go with Paul, then?"

"Ruby, you really must learn to start and finish the same sentence you begin with. The answer to your first question was eight forty-five a.m. The second answer is pull up a chair and I'll fill you in."

Florence new whatever she had already told Betty it would not be questioned with any other doubt equal to Ruby taking whatever she said based as factuality. Lily and Rose on the other hand were a little more challenging, and she knew whatever discrepancies they had would be discussed until the problem was entirely closed. Lily was the sensitive one, but Rose would be the hardest one to settle for anything but the truth.

As Florence went along with the same script she'd given to Betty earlier on, Ruby seemed alert to an unknown number flashing up on her phone.

"Sorry Mum, let me just take this call, I'll be right back." Again, Florence sat still, calmly with no reply for she knew too well she would not be there on Ruby's return...

There would be at least another hour until the sun would hide until its next return.

Ruby had dashed back up to her bedroom intrigued as to who was on the other end. The only screaming she was paying any real attention to now were screams of delight.

"Yesss yesss yesss Ruby, you did it," she said looking and smiling in to her reflection.

One of the casting directors had made the phone call to inform her she had been picked for the part.

She was ecstatic, jumping around and biting her knuckles in disbelief. She owed it all to Lily, for her sister had taught her well and helped polish her skills as an actress. Regretfully she knew Lily was the real star, and until she knew how she would feel about it, it was an offer on short hold. She would drop the opportunity in a flash if it caused Lily any upset.

Completely forgetting about Sue and Paul she flung out every item in her drawers in search for her favourite dress, the dress that made her feel like she was a lady and not a sexual temptress.

Excitedly pulling it over her shoulders, she could feel the excitement spreading an exhilarating rush of feelings all around her body.

Meeting the love of her sister's life and landing her biggest role yet was turning out to be a spectacular day after all, Wednesday or not, bad dream or not…

When you came from as beautiful a manor as theirs nothing much impressed Ruby, even if she had all the money in the world, her mother's manor was her perfect place to call home.

And as she entered a private car park, with million-pound investment apartments overlooking beautiful lakes, she could not pretend to be thrilled and slightly more elevated on these grounds than her own.

It had always been a tough ride for them both with love. Ruby had given her heart to a boy who stole it and crushed it to a million pieces until she eventually became a robot, leaving no feelings attached to her sexual encounters, and for Lily she learned of rejection each and every time the boy she liked would be head over heels, in love with her Ruby, which she knew was no thought of her sister's, in fact it was Ruby who choose to deliberately dress down and tie her hair back and be completely stand-offish to any of Lily's love interests that came sniffing her way, and Lily loved her dearly for her loyalty and Ruby loved her dearly for her trust.

Meeting Bran was massive, the one who had stolen her best friend, the man that would have to share her or his attempt in any future with her sister would be doomed.

She hoped he would be a genuine soul, not a fraudster in hiding or otherwise come with any bad intent.

She was going to make sure they were going to get on like a house on fire. She just had to make sure about that.

She pressed the code into the security gates Lily had given her. These led her into a private lift and straight up onto the top floor's apartment.

She remembered the feeling as she was heading up, as though she was an A-lister herself. This was how the real celebrities lived, even though it was very peculiar to Ruby how people chose to live on top of one another in glass houses as that just wasn't for her. Yet she was not complaining, she was thrilled with the experience of feeling like a movie star and how surreal it was that Lily was dating one.

The rest of the family were in line to find out over the next few weeks or so before Lily and Bran would leave for Hollywood. It was a very important evening for Lily, Ruby could feel it as she heard the bell to the last stop.

The elegant lift doors opened wide to the little petite frame of Lily, smiling beautifully, her brown skin glowing, her black long curly hair dominating her features, she was picture perfect. Ruby hugged and dragged her arm as always tucking in with Lily leading her way through to the apartment.

"Oh my God, Lils, I feel like this is how Vivian felt the first time in a penthouse with Richard Gere."

"Ah yes, the beautiful Julia Roberts, the classic pretty woman. You're real funny sis."

The apartment was nothing like the space the girls were used to, but it was in London and their mother had mentioned many a time that Ruby's bathroom was bigger than a whole apartment anywhere in London. They'd all be mad to live in a suffocating shoe box, wasted, money as she so called put it.

But looking around, how could she just not fall in love with the fine art displayed on the walls? The prestige taste of high-end modern class. Of course, there was her discovery of the service in a Michigan restaurant in the apartment's ground floor kitchen taking it to the final selling point for Ruby.

"Bran's apartment is so stunning sis, I thought we could

order up whilst we can all hear the sounds of our own voices. It gets so busy downstairs and I know you, you'll be turning your head every time you spot someone."

"Bla bla, well anyway that does sound lovely, and you know I don't get star-struck, I am the star darling."

Ruby clung to her sister, squeezing her, laughing, taking one quick moment in pulling her aside to share how happy and proud of her she was, how much she thought Lily deserved all of anything good and more.

After their sentimental moment waiting impatiently, standing with a bottle of exclusive rare champaign, there stood Bran smiling from cheek to cheek, nervously she stepped forwards to welcome his introduction and sweetly satisfied she became, for the very first time Ruby felt as though she was invisible, she could have been wearing a bikini and still the only beauty visible to his eyes would have been her devoted sisters The feeling was evidently admiring for them both as they soaked up Bran's exhilarating and sublime stories, it was a healthy aura and a room filled with truth and love.

The evening had been a true success, Ruby and Brans connection seemed to be neutral. Bran showed how passionate, how important it was for Ruby to like him, that his only concern was to not disappoint Lily.

They all moved out onto the seating area of the balcony, Bran carefully watching the pair of them become each other's ball of energy and light.

"So, then sis, go on, what do you think of Bran? Go on, you can make his head bigger than it is. He gets stopped in the streets," she girlishly laughed as she glanced Bran's way,

"NO, seriously, he's pretty great isn't he?" she said kissing him as she left the two of them alone to touch base on a more personal level.

Ruby fidgeted, but only to nestle into the leather sofas, she felt safe alone in his company and for that she was already fond of his heedless attitude towards her feminine beauty.

"Yes, Bran has done very well for himself. How did he get you, hey?"

They all agreed in laughter as Lily strolled on through to the bathroom.

"I kind of feel like I already know you Ruby, she does not stop talking about you."

"I can imagine. Yes you seem pretty cool, I can't say the same back though, it took her a long time to spill the beans about you, and I know that's only because she does not want to get hurt, and I'm trusting you're not going to do that Bran, I don't need to tell you how amazing she is."

"No, you certainly don't, but thank you for saying such wonderful things about her, she really is the most important person in my life. Can you keep a secret?" he asked profoundly.

"Well, I guess that would have to be down to the secret. What is it?" she demanded urgently.

"I'm going to ask Lily to marry me. It's only been six months, I know, but I've never felt like someone is so important and who I love so much could exist, why waste another day?"

"YES, YES YES, do it, Bran I'm so happy just so happy, for you both, and about Hollywood." Naturally they both hugged and shared a deep connection through the woman they both loved.

Ruby knew Lily would be so overwhelmed and would deem herself not good enough to accept his proposal, and so when that proposal would come, she was going to make sure she was involved in every part of it, as there was going to be no victims there would be no doubt. This was the man of her sister's dreams and she had completely approved of him.

By the time their show of emotion was over Lily arrived back in the lounge room that was accompanied by a light pine staircase circling the whole lounge. This took you up to a cosy beautiful, picturesque, a romantic scene from a movie, the place of lovemaking and sharing dreams. It would have no space for a lady's boudoir however, but she imagined the mansion that awaited her arrival in Hollywood was going to be something out of a whole entirely different world. It was only London you paid a small fortune for, all quite for nothing.

"So, what did I miss, what were you both squealing about. I heard the pair of you."

"Oh well, I was just telling Bran how you're looking at the new staring actress of the new hit drama series *The conflict*."

"Oh, my good little lord, Ruby that's bloody amazing news, I just knew you would do it. Come here and give me a squeeze, well bloody done sis. How did you keep that from me you little madam, Bran isn't that amazing? You might be having two stars making you look good in Hollywood."

"Well, you never know baby, never say never," he said, quietly shocked and pleased by Ruby's confession being such a good cover-up to his plan of marriage. Showing not a glimpse of anything than good faith as he welcomed the news of Ruby landing the leading role, although he strongly felt the part should have been given to Lily, Bran only admired his fiancé even more the way she oozed her warmth and genuine happiness towards her sisters success.

Turning down another glass of champagne Ruby decided to call it quits on the evening, there had certainly been enough excitement in one day. She was feeling exhausted with the hours and the earlier events, it was all beginning to catch back up with her. All the trauma from her sleep paralysis she experienced earlier when she had woken had stayed with her subconsciously.

In the dark behind the covers she was very, very afraid, afraid of her thoughts, afraid of her fate. But why?

After all, it really could all just have been a bad dream.

Chapter 12

Rose Anderson
The Baby Sibling

NO REGRETS

They say not to look back, only forwards. Yet for Rose Anderson, how could she not look back on the deceitful encounter herself and Eli had with each other?

At first she had wanted a baby at some point. Something she never thought would be possible, she had once felt that her husband would steal the blessing from her and she'd be deprived of being a mother entirely. It was making sense to her now by the way he was always stand-offish and closed any conversations or discussions that would be raised in topics about pregnancy and children, when really, all along he was hiding behind the fear of being infertile.

And now he thought he was a proud father to be and took it as the champion news of his life. She would never forget that smile from him, she had never seen it before, but she had never until now felt so detached from him either.

At first, she had never even wanted to take a pause in her career. She never wanted to do such a thing initially, until she was staring hard at the pregnancy test in clear blue writing: pregnant. For one fairy tale moment Rose had wanted to keep the baby. The thought of Eli's confession that he was in love with her only made her cling onto another picture, another life, she imagined she could be pregnant with Eli's baby. She would be married to the man of her dreams, the one she was truly and always meant to be with, Eli Bardon, who never knew about the pregnancy either. In those thoughts she wanted to be pregnant, but those were the fantasy thoughts. Now she was unsure, unsure about everything and everyone. Seeing how happy Matthew had been when he found out that night at the restaurant made her feel ashamed, guilty of being unfaithful, but that gut feeling that thumped deep inside of her was Roses truth that she did not want Matthew to be the father of her child. She had wanted to keep that fantasy of Eli a little longer, she had wanted it to have been his instead, she was in love with him back the same way he was with her.

And now Matthew knew? And now what if the baby really was his? And what if her husband was not infertile after all, there would be no way on earth he would be a supporting husband who would understand such a thing as an abortion. It was all becoming a bigger mess than she could have imagined. The thought of her husband knowing the truth petrified her, for her husband was the leader, the man with all the money, power and say-so. Sure, she was earning a fair amount herself, but without him her life would become the bare minimum. For Matthew led her to sign a prenuptial agreement that the house and his investments were solely his in marriage or divorce she would not inherit any of his fortunes or properties of which there were so many. She would be facing the journey of starting all over again, alone, pregnant, she feared Eli would discard her for being no more than damaged goods, a women who owned nothing but jewellery, shoes and a sports car. It was more than some, she thought, and she did have an excellent career with a great pension, she was beginning to feel like a failure having to go crawling back to her mother's manor ashamed and divorced with not a penny from any settlement. Her mother would be livid, her life would be doomed and she'd be forever miserable. Florence went ballistic once she learned of the prenuptial, she pretty much told her that she made her bed and that she would always be beneath him. After leaving the antenatal clinic she only remembered feeling dead set on having an abortion arranged, the nurse had made the referrals and recommendations and it would be down to her to turn up.

Leaving the restaurant that night was the only way out of anything She remembered she flew towards the exit, begging Matthew not to follow her and, taking his car keys, she had bolted.

She drove around for a good while before pulling up on her mother's forecourt. Turning to Ruby seemed like the only sensible thing to do; she knew her mother would tell her to stick at being a good wife and deny any truth to any affair, stay married to the man that provided a roof and paid the bills. She could save his and her own money over every year she stayed put, just in case he decided to divorce her one day.

Florence was a relentless woman, but Rose did not think of things in such a ruthless way, however, she was scared, and she was confused. everything really had changed now…

She parked out of sight and, instead of going in through the main front doors when Rose had arrived, she had tried sneaking past Ben and her mother walking out onto the grounds to the back doors of Ruby's, but just as the outside lights turned on as she crossed the hedges, Ben spotted her.

"Why are you sneaking about at this time, Rose? Ruby's not back yet, come and say hi to your mother." He frowned waving her inside.

"Hi, Ben, yes I knew, she's just left Lily's, she asked me to drop something off, I'm not staying long," she said, following him back round to the front.

She caught onto the discussion they both must have been having before her unannounced arrival, tittle tattle about Sue and Paul, she had heard her mother repeat the words everything was a false alarm, she had wondered if that had been about the photo of the girl he was kissing, how was that a false alarm, she wondered? Still, with everything going on in her own world she decided to listen like a fly on the wall rather than be involved. She had felt slightly irritated by the way her mother was defending Paul any time Ben had his suspicions, the way she just brushed past the night they'd all seen him in full rage and assault Sue, but yet her mother stood to deny it was nothing more than drunken stupidity, an accident, and nobody was in fact guilty of having any affairs.

She heard Ruby's car pull up and, with no time to spare, she left Ben to make sense of it all himself.

She called out to her as she saw her sister walking away from her car and there Ruby waited for her to catch up. As tired as she was and as determined she was to receive a better night's sleep, she would always have time for baby Rose.

"Sorry sis, I did not know what else to do but to come here."

"Don't be silly sis, come here whenever you like. You know that. What's happened?"

"He knows sis?"

"Who?"

"Matthew, he knows I'm pregnant, he found out by some woman who saw me at Mary Rose's antenatal clinic."

"Oh."

"Sis, I'm totally screwed. What shall I do now?"

"Does Eli know?" Ruby hurried to reply.

"No, he's been trying to call me since, well you know, and since he told me he loves me, but I've been dodging his calls. I just can't think straight, sis."

"OK OK, wow, this is tough Rose." Ruby gave her sister a huge hug, wiping her tears as she looked at her broken expression. Ruby gave her sister the best and biggest advice a big sister could give and that firstly was to know what she wanted to do for herself. Did she want the baby or didn't she? Ruby insisted she listened to her own intuition, did she still love Matthew or was she now in love with Eli? She would have to make those decisions first, then make a choice to stick by her guns, own up to her deeds, stick to being honest and the rest would just fall into place. No matter what the circumstances she believed God knew what each one could handle, that Rose would always be OK in life, she would make sure of that.

"Before you leave sis, I do think you should tell Eli how you really feel about him too, and whatever decision you do decide to make now, about the abortion, he still deserves to know you are pregnant."

"Yes, you're right, I will. Look thanks for everything sis, you don't know how great you really are. I love you, bye."

She left feeling like she had already made one of the best decisions and that was in talking to Ruby. The next few decisions were going to be the biggest decisions of her life. It was an indecent hour for a lady to be prowling around in the night, but Rose found herself doing exactly that, pacing up and down a neighbourhood like a crazy woman muttering different words. Different tones in her voice went over of the conversation she was going to have with Eli Bardon. She had called him and granted that she sounded desperate, so he wanted to console her and invited her round at any time she needed to turn up, he would be awake for her.

But there she walked up and down, scared of rejection, scared of any outcome. She plucked up the last bit of courage in ringing the doorbell to Eli's beautiful cottage, smaller than the one of Betty's but little, innocent and sweet his home was, it was a place that definitely had a homely feeling to it.

She had remembered the cottage well that evening they had spent together, an evening that was so short but so magical she'd not been able to erase him or the way he had made love to her out of her mind, since. The feeling she felt hearing he loved her, it was not the kind of confession made to get a wicked way, it was meaningful, it was real. It had to be because she was feeling exactly the same. She never loved Matthew, she never even liked him the older she was becoming, and loving Eli felt easy as though something had always been there between them. Their encounter was not planned, they had both bumped into each other after years of graduating from the same university, a time when her mother was willing to arrange her wedding with the first wealthy man in a suit, and Matthew had been exactly that. At that time she thought her mother was right. At one time she even tried to love him, and then one day she woke up realising she was a stranger to the man that walked past her every day, who ignored and belittled her. He had been of a highly insensitive nature up until now, until she could give him what he wanted, what he could produce what he thought he couldn't. But her marriage was suddenly coming to feel too late. She no longer felt the same about him or about her marriage.

The night was freezing, and she could see the clouds of breath that appeared in every breath and mutter.

Eli opened his door and, like two schoolkids, they giggled as they immediately fell into each other's arms, kissing heavily.

"I can't do this Eli; I need to tell you something."

She turned herself away, crying as she tried to hide from him. In whatever way it was addressed Rose expressed her love back and told him the truth about the pregnancy, of it being either his or Matthew's.

The outcome had been one she had only dreamed of. Eli was there and willing, pleading with her to leave Matthew and keep the baby. He would love her and take care of her even if the baby turned out not be his, he would love the baby as though it was his own, because he loved her.

And although there was no hand in marriage Rose was truly pulled into the deeper emotions of believing there was another life she was meant to be living and the old one needed to end.

As she left it remained undecided whether she was going to leave Matthew, if she was going to take Eli up on his offer, or if she was even going to keep the baby and disregard the abortion.

She had kissed him sincerely as she left to go back and face her husband.

Rose body felt tense although her mood levels were calm stepping back inside her marital home. She looked around the three-bedroomed house she'd been living a lie in for too many years.

There was nothing rehearsed this time and, as unsure as everything still was, Rose had been very sure of something that evening, and that was that no matter what it was her life had waiting for her, she was not prepared to live any part of her life looking back at it. For she would only now look forwards, with no regrets.

Chapter 13

Lily Anderson
The Adopted Sibling

GUT INSTINCTS

There had been something nibbling away at her for some weeks now. Something just wasn't sitting right on her chest, and after getting a vague explanation for the cheating and violent incident they had witnessed, Lily was sure Paul was the culprit behind the way Sue was always asleep when they called, why she was never popping round or staying around their mother's anymore.

There had been no point in talking to her mother about anything serious, as any issues she did have would be brushed off and everything and everyone was just dandy.

But ignorance was not bliss for everyone, certainly not for Lily Anderson. After Ruby had decided to turn down the offer of a lift back to the manor or to stay over, she had been thankful for the rest of the evening spent talking with Bran. They had discussed many things, the way she was going to miss Ruby so much when they left for Hollywood, but it had been decided it would be for a couple months max just before Christmas day. She would never wake up without Ruby at Christmas and this year would be no different, she had met a man who was willing and rich enough to travel back and forth whenever she wanted, and if he had been filming she would be a free soul to visit her family as much as she also wanted to. They had spoken about the dark truth about Paul's domestic violence towards Sue, how Lily had planned to take the matter into her own hands. They spoke of Betty's troubles with her best and only friend Georgina blossom's cancer and the way she was always cold and opiniated towards all the sisters, but particularly more so with her, maybe because she had not been real blood related. Bran listened tactfully to the way she expressed her deep concerns of her mother's own issues, ones she was beginning to learn of more and more, always looking the other way and pretending everything was always fine.

It had been decided that Lily would ask her mother to host a dinner party to make an important announcement, an evening with a full house, all of them, Betty, David and Ivy even under the circumstances, Sue and Paul, Ruby, Rose and Matthew unaware of her baby sister's love triangle, her mother and Ben and leaving herself and Bran to complete the party, it was here she would reveal her movie star boyfriend, her move to Hollywood and would take advantage of getting Sue alone and away from Paul. If Sue declined to come then she would make sure her mother would make Paul attend without Sue as it was all just so important, she would naturally want him there as well, to Lily this would be a way to then sneak round to Sue's manor. As soon as Florence would go to pick Paul up she would quickly sneak in before she herself would arrive with Bran at their mother's. Bran would be waiting outside for her and she would confront Sue and find out what was really going on. It was all planned out…

November had arrived with an unwelcomed bite. The morning sun that had come to greet was no longer in sight, instead all but chill and frost was now upon them, and the months ahead would only be dark awakenings and dark evenings cold and bleak. But for her and very soon she would be in Hollywood, in warmer and certainly brighter days.

Lily woke early and impulsive to make the proposal to her mother about having a dinner party for the next day.

She had wanted to leave with Bran the following week as he was called on set for filming a new movie. She was beginning to feel empowered, her life was beginning to make sense, and she was beginning to believe she deserved to be happy. Although Lily struggled to believe she was ever good enough for any man, the orphaned, adopted, damaged child to her she would always be, but her boyfriend had taken her to a place of security she never thought she'd find or go to. She had remembered the way he fussed over her that morning, it seemed she was looking a bit peaky and coming down with something that he asked her to eat a little of the breakfast he had made A little more rest before things started to get complicated, whatever the outcome, Lily was determined to find out the truth to what was going on with Sue, but what Lily had not realised was the way her life was about to change by the meddling she was about to get involved in. After all, their mother had always said, if you search you only find, then the truth stares you in the face; but what you decide to do with that truth lies in the person's hands that found it... It had been a while she had not spent any time with Rose, it was like their paths were always crossing but never meeting these days. She wondered and hoped often that Rose was well and happy, she admired her sister's role in forensic pathology and believed nothing beat a rewarding well-lived career, although she could not pretend not to notice the way there were holes seeping through her baby sister's marriage with cracks on display. She would only pray and hope she would never give up settling for anything more than what she deserved. Although Ruby was her right arm, Rose was never far from thought, and neither was Betty. It just saddened her the way Betty showed a lack of interest and affection towards her and the others. there must have been a reason, but whatever it was it was one only Betty would know of and, the way their mother had always separated and divided them, it was no wonder why she felt she was above everyone, she was moulded that way. As shocked as they all might have been hearing about her new adventures, she only but hoped they would be generally thrilled for her the way Ruby had been, but she was about to find out soon.

Bran had been right, she was feeling slightly light-headed. Maybe it had been all the stress and excitement with everything she had been feeling recently, she decided to ignore the interruptions and get on with the day, anyway.

Lily was the one who never drove, she walked everywhere in the village she'd been raised in and Virginia Waters was indeed a beautiful place she would miss. Yet she knew whenever she would return nothing would ever change and it would always be as though she never left.

She had a chauffeur-driven car on demand driving her back and forth from London to Virginia Waters and, once she ordered the driver to pull up, she arranged a time she would meet him back.

When she had stepped out of the esteemed vehicle, she felt excited to walk a rather long route into the village that particular morning, it was a busier one than normal. She wanted to see the activity, kids playing out, women gathered around in coffee shops gossiping, hair salons full to the brim. To pass the noise from the children playing at the village fates, she had wanted to mark her walk with memory and gratitude that morning.

They say caffeine is the way a woman carries on no matter what the task or the headache she has, and passing a coffee shop she decided to pop in and order herself exactly that.

The coffee shop was always packed as she stood standing in a big line. It was then she had noticed a distinctive looking long beige coat.

She bugged herself to remember where she had seen it, or rather on who. Then yes, she had suddenly remembered, Ruby, the night at a party. Ruby had got far too drunk and there had been a very handsome man who had passed her sister's car keys to her, very believable and kind he had been and trusting those points she never even blinked in receiving them from him. In fact she had been instantly grateful that someone had been keeping an eye on her. She had remembered because she had asked his name, and took his full details down before she ditched the party. When she had run off into the arms of Bran and left the party.

Lily would never have usually considered ever leaving her in that way, but there really had been something very decent about that guy, she just felt it at the pit of her stomach. She always had a way of knowing when something was wrong with Ruby, she always had a sixth sense when it came to her. It was quite an odd thing, they both shared.

The guy in the coat had been standing about third from being served. She watched him obediently, as he reached in for his wallet, she silently whispered, "Turn around turn around so I can see you." Then he dropped something from his pocket that, sure enough, made him head to the floor to pick it up and take a glance back to see his audience.

"Oh, hi it is you, erm Mr Harrington, isn't it?"

"Erm, hey, well it's Mark actually, Mr Harrington is when I'm important." He laughed to himself and pleaded Lily to remind him of who she was.

"So, you don't remember me? That's a real shame."

"Sorry darling, is there something you know, and I don't? Oh wait, it's you, I know you, you're Ruby Anderson's sister, it's Lily, right?"

"That's it, yes that's me, yes that's my sister Ruby." Lily was delighted at his presence. There was a good fit about this guy, good humour, dressed well, quirky just like Ruby was. Surely this was not coincidence? Surely this was the man of her sister's dreams who was now standing in front of her?

They both had sat over a coffee discussing in more detail how he even knew Ruby in the first place. Even before the party he had been admiring her from a distance, he had explained.

Lily discovered very quickly that this man was very fond of her sister, but he had not heard anything back from her. He had definitely written his number down before he had left her bedroom, he mentioned it was another sister who had come bursting in to talk with her that he was too embarrassed to stay.

Lily listened and smiled as she knew Ruby's character very well. She never did call the men she actually liked.

After playing the cupid Lily cunningly managed to set up a blind date for Mark Harrington and her beautiful sister.

She was sure they would make a handsome match. She exchanged telephone numbers giving an introduction on the best way to win her sister over.

Lily bade farewell and set off back to her driver and off to her mother's, she felt satisfied with a feeling of great hope that it was now Ruby's time to find the love of her life.

She'd hoped and assumed it was bound to definitely take the guilt and strain off by leaving for Hollywood.

When she had reached her mother's, Florence had been

sitting alone staring into space as usual. Lily had noticed she was slightly shivering so, picking up a blanket, she walked over and put it across her shoulders.

"Mother, you're shaking, you look cold. Why are you sitting out here in the cold, Mum?"

Florence never answered rather she smiled at her daughter sweetly.

"You're such a good girl Lily, I hope you do know that."

"You tell me often enough mother." She kissed her as she guided her through the warmth inside the house.

"What time are you going over to Sue's? I could follow you over there today and help you out."

"Oh, you'll have better things to do my dear, and anyway I'm managing just fine. Sue's fine darling, she was up and dancing the other day?"

"What? mum, what are you talking about? How is that even possible? She has become totally incapable, you must see it, it's not right, something's wrong I'm telling you Mum, something's definitely wrong."

"Oh Lily, you always were the one taking on the rest of the world, worrying like an old fool. Stop being silly now, everything's fine, don't you be upsetting me, you cause more harm than good making things up. Now don't say another word, I'm going to Sue's soon and she's absolutely fine, I know what I'm doing Lily Ann."

Lily decided to say nothing and simply stick to a good enough plan. She would wait until she got Sue alone, herself.

"Of course! You're right Mother. Anyway, talking of taking on the world I've got some really important news I'd like to share with the whole family tomorrow evening. I need you to be the queen of hostesses and arrange a wonderful dinner party. It's really important everybody is there Mother, everyone including Sue and Paul."

"Argh well, I'm certainly intrigued, you leave it to me darling, of course, and I'll let Sue know when I go over I'm sure she will do her best, you know that."

"Yes, she would do anything for us, I know you know that too."

Lily said goodbye and left her mother to see to Sue. She was not convinced that she would be attending the dinner party, so she was determined to see for herself that Sue was absolutely fine...

Lily said goodbye to the maids as they were leaving. They arrived for work extremely early and left at a reasonable time of the morning, to enjoy the rest of the day before returning at dawn.

Lily thought it would be practical to give a heads up about the dinner party plans as such things would never be completed alone. She went on through to Ruby's room, finding her awake in bed looking agitated, bemused; she was holding a diary, reading things out loud and writing stuff down.

"Hi, beautiful, what you doing?"

Ruby glanced at her confused at first, then pleasantly surprised.

"Oh my God sis, I had such a good time last night, Bran's great, you did really good."

Lily moved over towards her and squashed up beside her sharing the duvet. There they spoke and giggled.

"What you writing anyway? What is that?" she said peeping in at codes and messages and drawings from the inside of her diary.

"If I tell you something, don't freak out." Ruby gave her full eye contact.

"Oh my God, what? why you always scaring me?"

"No, nothing like that, but I've been having these dreams, bad dreams, and you know how I feel about being born on a Wednesday."

"That's just a myth, an old nursey rhyme."

"I think I'm going to die on a Wednesday, or something bad is going to happen at least."

"Sis, please don't, I can't listen to this, and anyway, I would know if you were going to die, I would know if something bad was going to happen to you, I would just feel it at the pit of my stomach. nothing's going to happen to you Ruby, I promise."

They hugged for a while before Lily said she would not leave her, she would not follow Bran back to Hollywood, that she would wait for another time, but Ruby would have no such thing she would know she would be back in a flash anytime she needed her to be and that was enough to let her go and live her dreams.

"So anyway, I've told Mum to host a dinner party for tomorrow, I'm going to tell everyone then about Bran and leaving."

"That's real good sis, I'm really proud of you, can't wait to see Betty's face."

"Sis, Sue's in trouble, I've been having my own premonitions and something's not right over there, Mum's not saying a word. She keeps pretending everything is fine, she's acting really strange as well these days, more than usual."

"Yes, I've noticed, and yes, you're right sis, something's not right. I don't know what's going on, not even about the supposed affair, can't get no sense out of Mum who the girl was."

"Well look, I've been speaking to Bran, and I've come up with a plan, but I'll need your help sis, for when I go away."

"OK, you know you can count on me for anything Lily."

Ruby listened as Lily confessed to sneaking into Sues as they would all be waiting for her at the party. She told of her plan to speak to Sue and check her bruises and state of mind. She expressed that she would also set up a secret camera that she would need Ruby to get hold of without Paul knowing to hand in as evidence to the police if she was proven right.

The plan was sounding strong and something they were both going to take seriously.

The two sisters engaged tightly and felt they would both achieve a great outcome from Lily's plan and they would be closer to helping their dear beloved Sue, to help her return to life, get medical advice and do anything to bring her soul back. They would find a way to get Paul out of her life once and for all, but how they were going to do that, neither yet knew.

"And one last thing sis, this is also important, I need you to meet me at the little French place, the one you love, Friday eight p.m. Be there please."

"You need to tell me a little more if you want me to turn up," she laughed suspiciously.

Lily felt excited at the thought of Ruby meeting Mr Harrington on her blind date. She knew full well she had liked him just from certain things and how quickly offended she was if Lily had tried to bring him up, he was all but forgotten until fate had its say. Now all Ruby had to do was to turn up.

"Well, I can't tell you much, but what I can say is trust me sis, you need to be there, it's just my gut instincts."

And when it came down to Lily Anderson and gut instincts, they were ones that were usually right.

Chapter 14

Betty Hughes Anderson
Middle Sibling

BEHIND THE MASK

The human body can react to death in many ways Either when we face our own or when trying to cope with the emotions of looking at a person you love and knowing that, one day soon, you could wake up without them. For Betty Hughes Anderson her world seemed to feel like it had come crashing down on her like a ton of bricks, a pain that was taking her last breath away. They say there are no guarantees in life and in Buddha terms all we really see is a dead body, not a dead man.

We are sometimes told our loved one's spirit will live on through our souls or we shall meet again. These are the typical, common bereavement theories and euphemisms shared around the world that we have all heard at some point in our lives to avoid offence or discomfort. In life there is death and sometimes all one can do is learn the valuable lessons of life and love, which is exactly what Betty decided to do, trying to come to terms that she was losing her best friend was already life changing. The feeling of emptiness the fear of being alone, without that person. At least, so she had always told herself, and so she believed.

When Georgina had opened up about her cancer with the plans and list of all the things she wanted to do in the time that she had left, things she had truly wanted from life. Betty reflected on where she had gone right and where she may have gone wrong and all the things she would have done differently if she could rewind the time, which she couldn't, she could only be grateful for the friendship she had found with Betty and told her so, as a person who knew her better than anyone had, other than her husband. Georgina took a harsh lesson of her own to help her best friend reflect on all she needed to and all the things that she had to wake up for, each and every morning.

That was the thing, Betty truly did love her husband. She truly did adore her daughter, she knew she did have sisters and what she always thought was a fantastic relationship with their mother. It was only until now Betty really questioned just what was really fantastic about it? She idolised her mother, that was for sure, she was also the only other friend Betty had, or at least she had told herself to believe that.

She was beginning to look back to her early childhood, Georgina had been asking her to backtrack to when she was just a little girl. No more pretending, Georgina wanted to know before her last moments what really was her side of the story.

What really did happen to that once very sweet, loving little girl Betty Anderson…?

If she could step back in time and rewind the clock, what Betty did know is that she and Ruby shared two years between them and there was once a time when it was just herself and her big sister Ruby. She would have only been four when Lily came into the family and she remembered feeling grown up by the time Rose had been born. She had remembered her father as a kind and gentle man, but a man with deep sorrow in his eyes. She remembered always feeling ashamed that her father had been black but she had loved him dearly, it was what she was taught, behind closed doors, they were a normal loving family but to the outside world they would duck and dive and suffer shame, embarrassment and resentment for being different. She was the one that had always looked like the odd one out, more Indian. The other three had always teased her and had been treated differently, being seen more on the white side. Well that's what people would say when their curiosity got the better of them and they would touch the frizzy texture of their sister's tight-curled hair compared to their silky straight manes. They would ask her, "Oh what are you? Where are you from?" Her skin tone had been slightly darker than her sister's so the questions were also different for her.

The redness in her hair was strong and gave her an independant look, iron straight. She had freckles and was tall like her father was and, to be honest, it was always hard to tell what she was mixed with and she had always handled the curiosity about her ethnic looks well enough.

When she looked back she could see just how fascinated she was by them, jealous of how much she thought Ruby and Lily looked so similar to each other and to not be related was surprising and strange.

She had only remembered that one day she was a happy, sweet and loving child to one day seen by the world as a cold, stuck-up and ungrateful bitch. One day she had the coolest big sister in the world and then woke up to find a new sister she had never even asked for, and one that took Ruby away from her. Ruby and Lily became inseparable and Lily had felt pushed out, rejected and intimidated by her new adopted sister. Betty would have been too young to really know the meaning of adopted or the tragic experience Lily would have been a witness to. She would have been too young to understand that Lily needed new parents and those people were to be her own mother and father.

She would have been around nine when baby Rose had been born and this was the time she had remembered her father leaving. It was practically straight after her birth, she would have still been too young to really know why he had left, she had only ever remembered her mother and father loving each other dearly.

Betty had always considered herself being a confused little girl and grew to resent her baby sister for being the reason their father had walked out and did not return back home one day. She thought Rose must have been a naughty baby and drove him to despair. Her mother had never sat any of them down with any explanation as to why their family had broken down, and her days were faced with Ruby and Lily having each other's back. Which was the main reason why she thought their father leaving had affected her the most. Rose had never known him and she only had herself until she had met Georgina.

Neither of them had ever really understood why her mother would never hold her father's or any of the girls' hands outside to the world. Their mother thought it was necessary to pretend racism was part of their normal society, that they had to put up with it with a smile.

They never did see the tears their mother would cry behind her bedroom doors. They never saw the strain from all the abuse, attacks and hatred, they never knew the fear of turning poor. So it had always been a shock to them and psychologically damaging not to have understood when he had gone and the blame went elsewhere.

Betty began to feel angry, rejected and abandoned. She had secretly hated Lily for taking Ruby away from her, she had been placed in every room separated from them and she would spend time sipping tea with her mother instead of playing with them both. Betty had never warmed to Rose on account of the blame she secretly had held towards her and had chosen to show no love or affection towards her. But the girls had always been so beautiful natured it was hard to grow to dislike them watching them in secret, Betty kept her distance which in time caused sadness and pain, she was left out and never included in her sisters fun that she became insecure and isolated. That she could have ever doubted they love her. She had always learned to be thick skinned as she was her mother's precious one, her mother's pet, the one that was the favourite and didn't the others all just know it?

As Rose grew older Lily and Ruby had welcomed their baby sister into their pact. That was when Betty had begun to keep a high guard up and not let anybody into her circle or her space. She swore never to really let anybody know how much she loved them in case they hurt or disappointed or abandoned her again. She had even done the same with her daughter and her husband, she loved them dearly but always forced herself to hold back from really showing them both just how much. It was never that she took David for granted, it was simply that she pushed him away but he never went anywhere. And it was not that she was incapable of being a full time mother to Ivy. She was sure she would cope just fine without Magda but it had been the fear of not being the best mother she could be, she could blame someone else for the trials and errors.

But the conversation Georgina and Betty shared one afternoon was a conversation that put Betty's life into perspective. She was beginning to face facts and take a good long look at herself and who was standing there besides Georgina, all along. She made a promise to Georgina that she would start a counselling process and help retrain her way of thinking, let go of a lonely confusing childhood and concentrate on trying to build a relationship back with all her sisters and put the same love and energy she had given to her bestest friend in the world back into her husband and cherish every day she would have with her delightful daughter...

Betty opened the thick velvet curtains to her bedroom windows. She could see David watering her gerbera daisies her favourite red flower. little Ivy was out there playing innocently with not a care of the world. She looked at her daughter smiling, wandering and hoping she was happy, Magda had been excellent and was also becoming Lily's playful friend. She began to feel guilty, it should have been her outside playing and pushing her on the swings.

Before the news of Georgina it seemed as if Magda was better at doing everything. She would only be proven to be a failure if she had to do everything and every chore herself. Surely she was making the best decisions for her daughter?

Now she felt as though she could not breath. She was in so much pain about Georgina, she found herself trying to avoid her as much as possible just in case she saw her emotionally wrecked. She imagined how selfish it was for her to be crying every minute; her mother was right, she would be no use to her that way, she had to start getting a grip.

David had moved into the guest house whilst Georgina was resting and staying with Betty for a while.

The once happy, thriving cottage was now desolate with a great feeling of sadness.

She tried her hardest to put on a brave face and hide behind the choke and tears of looking at her wonderful friend, knowing that something inside was attacking and destroying her and she was deteriorating fast.

She felt useless, knowing something like that and there not being a single thing she could do to change or help a loved one other than to be strong, brave and supportive, and that's exactly what Betty was determined to be, even if it did mean leaving things exactly as they were already were in her family. David understood and, well, baby Ivy was happy.

Florence had sent out perfect pretty dinner invitations and they were sent with an urgent request that she, David and Ivy all attend.

Intrigued she certainly was. She arranged the dress she would soon change into and prepared a matching outfit for Ivy to stun them all in.

"What do you think of this one Georgie?" she asked, showing her the one that she heard her say she liked many times.

"I'm not going to stay for long. I don't even know what this dinner is all in aid of anyway."

"Don't rush back, Betty. I'll call you if I need you. I've got the district nurse on call and you have made me extremely comfortable, with everything I need, thank you so much. You're a good friend Betty Hughes Anderson."

"I love you Georgie."

"Love you too."

Georgina was extremely strong willed, the lethargy and sickness, the demands of loose bowel movements, the controlled drugs taken for the hurling pain were still not enough to stop her from doing what she still could for herself before she could do no more. Betty had always remembered a saying her mother had said, *sometimes in life you're a woman once and a girl twice*. She had never really known what that had meant until now, seeing all the independance stolen from Georgina, the patterns of sleep, puke and poop whether that comes to a person from old age or ill health, a person was lucky to escape it if they could.

David had made sure Georgina had his number in her top list of important people, just in case. He was very thoughtful that way and he also wanted to show his wife she could leave for a few hours not worrying too much.

Magda had done an amazing job with Ivy. Her dress was neat and tidy ironed and clean, with no stains; she was an expert at knowing when to get her dressed and how to keep her dresses white with no pen or paint stains. Her daughter had loved to draw, she loved to paint more than she did to dance, it had been Betty's idea and she pushed her and forced her to attend ballet every weekend as that was where all the posh mothers were.

A late night was not something Betty had planned as she would be up and driving the little madam for classes first thing in the morning, although that was what was going to make a perfect excuse for leaving early.

The sentimental talk she had earlier on with Georgina had uncovered lots of questions and emotions she never knew she had and she never really new how to feel about any of them, or about anything. She was feeling completely perplexed, all she wanted to do was sleep and wake up with everything back to the way it was, but that was never going to be the case again.

As David drove them round to the enchanting manor of their mother's, Betty took in a deep breath as she stepped out onto the forecourt. It looked spectacular all lit up in the dark evenings.

Ruby was by the large doors greeting everyone through. The maids were staying on to serve drinks and canapes after the three-course meal that was prepared. She could see Paul socially active and foul mouthed as usual, but there was no sign of Sue, Rose was on her way over from doing a night shift and would change out of her work clothes once she was there.

She did look around but she could not get sight of Lily. She wondered where she was as usually she applauded Lily's timekeeping, thinking it was admirable. She was always so prompt so where was she now, she thought?

Her mother and Ben were putting on a romantic display. Betty noticed the way her mother was making a complete fuss and pampering of him; she had found her actions very odd as she entered the manor, and now it was her own show of falseness she would be putting on.

But just at the right time of feeling overwhelmed she quickly caught a glimpse of David giving her a final nod of approval. He held his hand out for her to take; he would lead her the way, for it was her husband who really knew the real Betty, he had always known and loved his wife.

The woman behind the mask.

Chapter 15

Florence Anderson
The Mother

THE DINNER PARTY

Some say true love is a feeling that will only find you once in life or not at all. Of course there are different forms and different scales of love. Florence remembered the feeling with Mr Anderson, it had felt like a powerful magnetic force, like an everlasting chemistry, but the question now was – was love enough? She regretted the fact of letting the ugly racist opinions of the world matter so much to the point of giving up fighting in her marriage to him. But as a person grows they realise that sometimes love is a sacrifice and a choice. She chose to divorce on the grounds of unreasonable behaviour after he walked out and never came back after baby Rose's birth. But she had already given up on him in the days he had come home from trying to earn an honest pound in plastering people's walls. She had already began to neglect him and found him useless with not being able to provide for her or the girls and the only way for a future, she thought, was one without him, things had become such a strain, it was so bad that, once she and Mr Anderson were cut off from their family wealth, there seemed no other choice for them both but to part with each other.

Love as she knew it never did come back in that way and the

man she always tried to forget remained a man she would always remember out of all them.

But then came Ben, and the way she did love her husband was love but of a different kind. It was love with an agenda, she was rescued, it was love that came with kindness. It was security from a man who offered an easy life to a woman he would love, protect and who would provide for her, all the things she had wanted, all the things she divorced her first husband for. Ben had given her all of this, so why did she still feel so alone? She had started to ask herself why did she betray and cheat in her marriage?

Could any marriage stay the same when adultery has been committed? maybe for some, with different circumstances. It seemed to be worse when the women is the cheat.

But Florence was almost certain Ben would see it as an unforgivable act. Maybe if she confessed to what she'd done, he would stay? Maybe he would decide not to give up in their marriage, but why would she want to take the risk of finding out?

She was definitely convinced it was more than likely her marriage would be left damaged. It would be damaged in the way a man can never look at his wife in the same way he once did.

A woman spoiled, unclean.

Ben was not the type of character to lie and cheat himself, he was not the type of man to run off with a younger woman when he would have enough of his old one. He was a quiet man, shy at times, and when he married her he had meant it, to love, protect and give her a good, honest and decent life. But what was decent about it now? although she had done her utmost to shrug off the flashing scenes of Paul frolicking around with her that forbidden night, she could not block it out as easily as she had hoped. Again she questioned why she even considered such a thing in the first place.

She had again woken up like she was more in love with her husband now than she'd ever been before. The thought of doing such a thing or the thought of Paul touching her like that again repulsed her. But maybe it really was just a quick fix, something she just needed to do to remind herself of what she could lose, surely she could still seduce her husband? Surely she could ramp things up herself? Florence quickly assured herself that the once just did not count and nobody not any of them, was ever going to find out…

She had decided not to go for her usual white tight-fitted dress she planned to wear for the evening. She knew Paul liked her in those types of outfits and Ben seemed to like her in anything she wore, so she decided to wear an elegant long flowing green dress. Perfect for a grand dinner party, she thought.

Everybody had arrived except Lily and Bran. Florence was still making a fuss of Ben in the kitchen whilst Paul was soaking up the male testestorone of David and Matthew, in fact Matthew had been desperate to spread his proud news of being a father to be. Although he thought it was best not to make a scene, thinking he knew how private and anxious his little wife could be, at times.

Matthew and Rose had not spoken since the night at the restaurant. Instead Matthew decided to start kissing her on her forehead every time he left the house, he started to whistle in the mornings on his way out of the door and Rose had found his behaviour more annoying and more fake as the days went past. He never gave a toss about her usually and all he would say about the pregnancy was that it was definitely going to be a boy.

Matthew had wanted a son so badly and a boy is what she would have to grant him with it to be worthwhile.

He also decided it was far easier to follow Rose in silence, thinking it was nothing more than hormonal issues, what he expected of pregnant women. He thought she must feel useless, fat and pregnant, so women would moan and throw tantrums and get cravings. It was no big deal to Matthew; he could put up with if having a son would be the outcome.

Paul had completely ignored Florence. In every room she passed him in making excuses for Sue's absence, he spoke of her being far too drunk to get dressed and even know what day it had been, let alone attend a dinner party.

The way he spoke was completely malicious, he found himself proud and amused at the way he poked fun and made nasty jibes at her to the others, unaware of how calculated his character had become. Yet the family were beginning to see exactly who he really was.

The other husbands paid him no attention and each took a disliking to the man. David knew how strongly Betty felt about Paul's rotten vocabulary, and him not being able to talk or have anything to do with baby Ivy. Ruby and Rose had always made their feelings perfectly clear and Lily was on her own mission to prove what she always knew. The whole family had been slightly baffled as to why Paul had even been invited, it was a free night of booze and food he would take full advantage of as he always did.

Both David and Matthew came with champagne for the special mystery occasion.

Betty was sitting quietly amongst the men whilst encouraging Ivy to play in her princess castle, demanding her not to spoil her clean white dress in the process.

Ruby and Rose had spoken amongst themselves, Rose had changed into a casually fine outfit, although the months were now passing, it was still not obvious that she was eighteen weeks pregnant.

The maids had been offering champagne flutes with prawn canapes as they all waited for Lily and her suprise.

Florence and Ben came into the lounge area to join in with the rest of the family, and instantly Paul set his eyes on her. She could feel his glare, it was as if his eyes looked straight through her dress, like he was staring at her stark naked again.

"That's a bit classy for you love, you're too old to be wearing all them young tight-fitted dresses anyway Flo, no offence Ben," he said smugly and sarcastically.

"My husband loves this colour on me, and to be honest Paul the only man's opinion I care about is this one I'm holding hands with. But thank you for your very backhanded compliment."

She could see his anger flare, she had embarrassed and belittled him.

Florence had told him before she had left the morning after her sordid affair that it would never happen again, and he knew there was nothing between them both. He knew there was no love shared between them, but he was not finished with her yet either, he was going to make Florence's life a misery. He had unethical and bad intentions for both Sue and Florence, and if Florence wanted to stay married to her husband and wanted to bring no shame upon her family then she would have to do as he said, or else…

Everyone was beginning to notice the very odd atmosphere in the manor that evening,

And all anybody could really think was why was Paul even there, and where the hell was Lily?

Ruby kept checking her phone to see how things were going for her sister back at Sue's? Paul never drove to the manor as a way of putting on some front of maturity, for he wanted to prove he was responsible by not drink driving, he almost made himself out to be the poor victim of Sue's alcoholism, a cunning martyr complex game a narcissist likes to play. He was showing no signs of asking to leave, so Lily's plan was hopefully going well.

She checked her phone again impatiently.

"Sis, it's not good, but I'm leaving now, I'll be ten minutes. Let mum know" was the text message she had received. It meant that Lily would be arriving literally any minute, all Ruby could really think about was what if Lily had been right about her suspicions and domestic abuse allegations? Sue had done so much for each and every one of the Anderson women and Sue was not present in any of their lives now except for their mothers who only ever insisted she was fine, she had hoped he was not hurting her in secret.

Ruby quietened the room down and informed everyone Lily would be arriving in seconds and, just like that, she heard Bran's chauffeur-driven car had pulled up onto the forecourt.

Ruby rushed to the doors to welcome them inside, blushing at Bran with a passing wink. At least some of the evening's suprises was going to be good news, she thought, following behind the commotion.

With everybody waiting, intrigued, it was not long before the whole house screamed it down, bursts of screeches, giggles, claps and questions and absolute astonishment at the movie star that walked through the old white antique manor.

Betty's expression was priceless, gobsmacked, how on earth did a West End theatre actress end up crossing paths with an American movie star? Lily looked no different to her usual modest self, dressed in a conservative long blue satin skirt with a light blouse and expensive boots. And he matched her equally well, smartly but casually dressed in a shirt with blue trousers.

Bran always said the trick to looking good was to look like you were not trying to.

Florence was beaming from cheek to cheek, and although Ben was being more romantic than ever most recently which caught her attention, her sudden interest in her husband was short lived, a handsome, incredibly rich, famous man was in her home and she had to be attentive to everything he could possibly have wanted, if she had it, she would be sure to have given it. But Bran never wanted anything other than Lily's happiness and acceptance from her most valued person, Ruby, and those two things seemed to be in place just fine. The rest of the family would have to take him or leave him, he had his personal opinions about them all, it was hard not to, especially getting a peek and insight to a family of highly strung, interesting and successful women.

As Lily had done the rounds, meeting and greeting everyone, she left Bran in the capable hands of David whilst she tried to find a private moment and give Ruby a quick briefing.

As she passed through the room, the atmosphere had lifted into a thriving, buzzing vibe of goodwill and good spirits, excitement and shocked tones of voices filled the room from every corner.

She spotted Paul with his arm folded and slightly worse for wear before they had even sat down to eat. She felt an awful feeling walking past him it was ridiculous how unerving he made her feel, it was like she had walked past the devil himself. She felt like she needed to burst into tears, the worry, the fright of leaving Sue alone in that big house with that man. The evening was going to be hard to get through smiling and pretending. She had never felt so confused about what to do, she would never want to involve Rose either, not until she was one hundred per cent sure Paul was hurting Sue. She was confused as to how much trouble she would be in as well as jeopardising Rose's profession. whatever it was that Lily had seen earlier on that evening at Sue's, it was something so dark so twisted, something she'd been praying was not really going on, but without such a thing as evidence she was suddenly feeling trapped. It had felt her duty to stay in the village until she got all the proof and help their beloved Sue needed.

And she now hoped to get everything she needed on tape…

Everyone was seated around the spectacular display, with different glances around the table, and the star-struck side looks and long blank gazes continued for Bran. Everyone except Ivy was besotted by him, she was innocent and still pure, who thought she was the most important and fascinating being in the entire room. Betty was entranced by her daughter that evening, she had paid more time and more attention than usual, there was also something very humble about her. It was as though she could have been genuinely happy for her sister's good fortunes although their competitive nature caused a rift between them for the first time they were both humble, not shedding an ounce of jealousy towards each other, how quickly and strangely things can change when life gives you a reason too…

"Bran darling, is there absolutely anything I can get for you?" Florence was oozing hostess at its best, her eyes glistened like they were looking into blue sapphire diamonds. Blue was the colour of Bran's eyes, Lily had not been sure if the delight came from him being rich, white and famous or simply because he was not black. Although Matthew was mixed raced, he had been dominated mostly by white genes, and he was a high-end lawyer, also rich and looked white so he had been widely accepted. Yet Ruby's and Lily's love interests had usually been of the same type, they preferred their own kind and all shades of black.

And as much as they hated to hear it, and still both trying to prove the world wrong, that all the previous failed relationships they had in most opinions was that their hardship and failure purely came down to a man's skin colour and his wealth. There had been many sceptics that believed this was why they had not managed to settle down.

Surprisingly Lily had never really cared as much,. She had been attracted to Bran instantly, it was an attraction she had never found before and she would have loved him in white or black skin.

"Well thank you all very much for coming, I really did want each and every single one of you here this evening." She looked straight at Paul with his beady eyes looking back.

"Firstly I just want to say the table and the dinner is just spectacular Mother thank you."

The room silenced as she spoke, everyone fascinated to hear all that was coming.

"So as you've all met Bran who I so desperately wanted you all to meet. I also wanted to take the chance in saying goodbye, well just until Christmas at first and then it will be more of a permanent arrangement. Basically guys I'm moving to Hollywood with Bran, I think I could actually get a break out there and Bran's got some excellent contacts who are wanting to meet with me once I'm out there."

Florence dropped her glass, champagne spilled out everywhere, she was speechless.

"Oh, and sorry guys, Ruby I've not had the time to say, I only found out today sis, and you know the kind of day I've had."

"It's OK sis, you can say now, what is it?" Ruby said.

"Well I thought I'd also let you know guys, I've been feeling light headed recently, and not had one of those monthly visits, I'm six weeks pregnant guys."

Ruby clapped her hands, jumped in delight and threw an awkward glance at Rose. Wow both of them pregnant, she could hardly take it it all in.

Florence was downing the alcohol insistently, and Betty said nothing other than sweetly smile. The men raised a glass, Rose had looked like she wanted to bomb the whole room. She had a face of grim and bare whilst Paul sat and said nothing.

It was seconds after Lily's announcement that Bran had decided to drop onto one knee and propose to Lily right there and then, something he had planned out with Ruby. She knew her sister would want the family to be part of such a thing before she left them, and she was right, Lily accepted, feeling as if she were dreaming, like she was floating and at that point she had forgotten about Sue but only for that second. Once all was a little more calm she decided she had not finished with her announcements. What could there have possibly been more of to say, was what she read on the expressions of her family members. And then in a serious tone she spoke.

"On a more important matter, the reason I asked you round here, Paul, was to get the chance to see Sue and speak to her. I want you all to listen loud and clear, Sue's not well guys and she needs all of our help. I don't know what you've been doing Paul, but let me just tell you something: you're sitting at a table with a forensic pathologist who's best friends with the boys in blue, a top lawyer who will not be defending you but trying you in court for domestic abuse." The whole table looked completely horrified to believe such a dreadful thing could really be going on behind closed doors.

"You're a damn fool, I've not touched her." Paul stood up

raging, demanding Florence drive him back to his own manor immediately.

"Well that's hardly the truth now is it, Paul? Have you suddenly just forgotten about your violent incident the other day that we are all hoping was a one-off drunken accident, as mother likes to put it."

The atmosphere had again turned sour. The mood went from uplifting to complete anguish and strong emotions were flying everywhere. Out of the blue Rose stood up, it was unclear if she had been drunk or just nostalgic.

"And I would just like to say I'm eighteen weeks' pregnant. I got two weeks to make up my mind if I'm having an abortion, and I'm leaving Matthew." She turned her chair to face him and said it again, loud and clear.

"I'm leaving you Matthew, and I'm sorry but I don't know who the father is. And I'm in love with someone else."

It was dramatic for sure but Rose had never felt so empowered and she had promised Eli she was definitely going to tell Matthew she was leaving him. And she had decided to pick that cold evening to do so.

Matthew had looked completely dumbfounded, lost for words, stricken by a complete out of body experience.

He just watched Rose run up into her bedroom where Lily and Ruby and this time Betty had followed her behind.

They say there is calm before the storm.

Which had certainly been the case that evening for the Anderson family.

When came the division, shame and humiliation, it had all left a devastating effect on each one of them, leaving them shocked to some extent, wrecking the joint in seconds.

The dinner party had been spoiled, ruined and regretted for

some.

And this was certainly going to be one dinner party they would never ever forget.

(I think vestigially there's a synthetic in me)
(But not like a real one who immediately knows what colour Wednesday is)
– A.S. BYATT

Chapter 16

Ruby Anderson
Firstborn sibling

WEDNESDAY HYSTERIA

At eleven thirty p.m. on Tuesday evening, Ruby had kissed all her sisters goodnight after an explosive night of confessions. She began to recap on all the shocks of the evening, it was not possible to line any of them up for first place, they all put a spanner in the works some way or another. There had been Rose's confession to being pregnant, leaving Matthew and running off to Eli. She was bound to be keeping the baby, no way could she be willing to go through with an abortion now, she would have been kidding herself if she had thought so. Besides time was literally running out on that idea and how on earth could such a cruel alternative even still be an option up until twenty weeks of a woman's pregnancy, she thought? Ruby had been totally mortified Rose had implied at the table she was thinking about it.

There had been Bran down on one knee proposing to Lily who confessed to being six weeks' pregnant, leaving for Hollywood and basically threatened Paul at the dinner table to let him know she was onto him for domestic abuse. For the rest of the family there had been mutters, sarcastic comments, disgust and anguish in all of their tones of voices, in all of their eyes, in all of their actions a time when cerebral cortex was in high force.

You could see their tiny brains working, billions of neurons allowing them to be free with conscious thoughts, movements and sensations. Each person trying to digest and process all and every detail. Florence and her family had looked entirely broken, damaged, but what none of them realised was that the real damage had not even began...

(The dream)

Everything was red, everything appeared so real, she heard herself screaming, she could see Rose, crying in exactly the same way she would always see Rose crying it was the same dream the same tears every Wednesday.

Ruby became stuck in that same dark place, in the same corner of her bedroom. Rose was frantic, desperately trying to tell her something, the images became clustered, with that potent colour red. At this point in the dream the real senses, the real fears were of ones that made her choke, hold a breath for a minute or two. Her mother appeared again, so did her black Mercedes, she was able to focus upon the car, but she still couldn't make out the reflection inside. Who was that inside of the car? As she got pulled deeper into another nightmare she flipped and tossed, looking at her could have almost appeared as though there was convulsions occurring.

There was more of that potent colour red, there was more screaming, a terrifying scream, screams of mercy, screams again so petrifying it was enough to wake her out of sedation and into Wednesday morning.

Ruby had been born on the twenty-fifth December, on Christmas Day with a light fall of snow. She had been born on Wednesday, and every Christmas Day since had been on a different day except this year, this Christmas, her birthday was indeed falling on a Wednesday.

Lily and Ruby were ecstatic about turning forty, Lily's birthday would follow shortly after but there was always an odd feeling it was always something more than just Christmas for Lily. It was almost like it was both of their birth dates, it was an odd feeling they both had grown used to. But this year seemed massive, how on earth did turning forty happen? Ruby wondered how a woman was supposed to act at the age of forty? was she supposed to dress in long dresses only? Was she to cut her long hair, own a huge house, be a mother and a wife? It was hard not to feel failure, it was hard for her not to feel depressed. The pressures of what the human tells itself it needs to be happy, how to survive. But with just a couple of months left before she reached into a new dimension she was now beginning to feel punished, she became obsessed, convinced, paranoid that her nightmares on Wednesdays meant something bad was going to happen and she could only hope Lily was right about it not being true, right that she would feel it in the pit of her stomach if something bad was going to happen to her.

Although she felt like she had not done or accomplished what she thought she was supposed to before turning forty, she wanted the chance to be able to still make things happen. There was still so much waiting for her, she prayed the Lord that morning for her life to remain as it was.

She had spent the rest of the morning recording and writing down parts of the dream she could remember. It always seemed to be exactly the same part over and over again. It was Rose that stuck with her the most, she was trying to tell her something dreadful, but what? And if that was the case then she acknowledged she would have to have been alive.

Either that or she was stark raving mad. The GP had said sleep paralysis was extremely common after explaining she felt things in her bedroom had felt so real and she had been so sure she had been awake, but could not get up or even move. Sheer panic had started to sink in after the research done on sleep paralysis, suggesting and speaking of dark forces and of an unwanted presence.

She had wondered if she should had gone to church more than she currently did and she questioned whether the crazy spells, all the worry and anxiety over Paul and Sue's issues as well as turning forty was unavoidably stressful. She had not even figured herself or her life out yet, and praying that she was not a crazy mad woman, that it could really all just be a bad pattern of reoccurring delusional thoughts she was having. Something she could sort with hypnosis or some kind of cognitive therapy is what came to mind.

This was already beginning to be one mental Wednesday. Ruby was distraught about having yet another nightmare and then she literally felt as though she had woken up to a real one. It was time for the family to face the repercussions and adjust to some changes, all from the dinner party the night before.

She had heard her mother shut the front door an hour after she had woken, her mother would have been making her way round to Sue's, it had felt extremely deceitful of Ruby that she had known her mother was going to be on a secret recording. There was almost a sense of urgency to warn her mother she was being watched, and to wish hard she was going to be shown as a good person. It would be all down to her now to make sure that in seven days exactly, when Lily and Bran would already have landed in Hollywood that she would have to find a way of getting into Sue's and find the hiding place Lily had told her the camera would be. and even if herself and Lily would be in some kind of breach of someone's privacy, if the camera proved right it would be worth it, that was for sure.

Ruby also thought about her confused but pleasant feeling towards Betty, she thought she had seemed different, kind. She never spoke much or of Georgina, it was like they had suddenly reconnected at the dinner party, all with the power of a real smile.

It was the first time any of them as sisters became a team, a unit. If anyone who had realised how much they all needed to stick together it was Betty. It was she who enjoyed feeling part of the camp for the very first time.

Ruby and Lily had decided to keep the secret camera amongst themselves only to avoid getting any of the others in trouble but they had all shared their deepest sorrows, fears, wishes and good fortunes to one another that evening.

A cold day had passed by in the old white manor Things were quiet, with just herself, Mother and Ben, no maids on board, no family. It was certainly not the usual setting, there was some distance, an emptiness, a sadness without any explanation. Ben seemed attentive but Florence had only remained to be shut off, in a completely different world of her own; where did her mother's mind disappear to? Was it normal for a woman to become so lost all of a sudden?

Things were certainly feeling very different and very strange, although Lily was only away until Christmas Eve it was still going to be a daunting experience in having to say goodbye. Lily had come so far, newly engaged, pregnant, in love with a good man and living life to its full. It seemed Rose was taking charge of her own destiny and believed in herself and that love did exist with the right person.

It had almost been funny to think that how one day she could go to bed with a normal dysfunctional family to one day waking up not really knowing who anybody was, or what anybody was capable of doing or being.

She made a couple of calls, doing the rounds on her siblings. They were all coping and doing fine, the last call had been one with Lily. Their conversation had lasted for two hours, they had exhausted themselves with plotting and gossiping, Lily leaving a final demand that Ruby was not to be late to the restaurant and that she was to make sure she turned up as requested.

Lots of thoughts ran wild with her that evening as she lay beneath the covers. Desperate for sleep and peace of mind she tried to take all the positives out of the negatives and her remaining thoughts for the evening as she lay awake restless was of Lily's random request, demanding that she turn up to her favourite French restaurant. She had wondered what on earth could that woman have up her sleeve now? It was a mystery to Ruby but one she would wake up to find out about.

The night seemed short and all Lily Anderson could think about was hoping everything went to plan with Mr Harrington. It seemed only fair to tuck up beside her and stay the night.

"Good morning sis, rise and shine you little beauty."

"What time is it Lily?"

"Time for you to pick a stunning outfit so you don't feel rushed once you get back from the recording studios, are you excited?"

"Excited about what? This filming or tonight at eight p.m.? Oh come on, pleassssse sis, this is so annoying, just tell me what's going on. I can't deal with any more surprises miss, I'm a mother to be." The two women giggled and sighed and expressed their genuine shock at the pregnancy news. But still Ruby was left with no clue or reasoning as to why she was being ordered about on her favourite day of the week Friday.

"Oh this better be good," Ruby had teased.

She had felt nervous in taking on the leading role for the new BBC series. She had felt ecstatic at first and now all she felt was dread. There were so many things that seemed to cramp up all the space inside of her brain that she felt half involved with it now.

Really she just wanted to bail out on the whole thing, pack a suitcase and tell Lily and Bran she was coming to Hollywood, That she was heading straight round there after the TV studio to say farewell as the couples flight was set to fly out at midnight, but she knew she would not be able to have gone with them and besides she had made a sworn promise to be solely responsible in getting her hands on the secret camera planted at Sue's, after a seven day investigation on Paul.

This was a massive mission, if there was nothing caught or shown on the tape then she was to plant it back for another seven days and check again. She had no idea what to expect even, what she might recover, what her eyes would see. That's the thing about life, you think you know someone but really you don't…

Leaving the recording studios later than hoped or planned her goodbyes were now going to be cut short, Lily had been adamant she must be at the restaurant by eight p.m.

Whatever was going on Ruby trusted her sister's judgment and knew it would be important if it was to come between their time in saying goodbye to each other.

As happy as she could be for her it came with an emotional separation detachment immediately, but she was determined to fight it, fight the dependant feeling she had always held towards Lily and be strong in letting her go.

Even in brown skin Ruby felt as though her cheeks should have been as red as strawberries. She had fought back every tear until she released them all behind the wheel of her Mercedes, she hugged Lily so hard at the door and then made a run for it, fleeing into her car and driving a little faster than usual.

She had managed to change into a spare dress in the car as there would have been no time in going back to the manor and the suggestion had been made that she should make an effort. Lily had also asked for her to stay close to Betty, and their mother? Maybe she thought she would need them both more now that she was leaving her behind.

And there Ruby drove en route to a random bizarre arrangement.

The French restaurant was one of her favourite places to which Lily had been dragged along a fair amount of times to. She approached the black marbled reception.

"Hello, I'm Ruby Anderson, I'm booked in for eight p.m."

The receptionist referred to the booking screen to confirm her seating area.

"Argh yes, thank you Ruby, your table has been set in one of our fine outdoor forest domes. A waiter will serve and cater for you, a table for two. Follow me please."

Ruby had now really begun to wonder who exactly it was she was meeting. She arrived a little early, and taken aback on how beautiful the dome was, that had been a new touch to the establishment. She sat down inside, ordered her drink and waited in anticipation.

Looking into the dome was like looking at something out of Cinderella's carriage to the ball. It was like an enchanting crystal, it was clear looking out but misty looking in, there was a large zip centred in the middle of the domes door and once fastened it gave you all the privacy desired.

Although she could see out perfectly fine, at first she could make out two shadows approaching, one looking ever so familiar. Her heart was beating quickly as she heard the sound of the dome's zip being unfastened. She had definitely known his face, it was him? But how on earth could this be?

"Hello lady."

He had always referred to her as this, she had kind of liked that feeling, feeling like a lady like she had felt the last time she was around him. Instantly she became enraged, she found him patronising, and annoyingly perfect.

"Don't lady me Mr Harrington, what are you doing here?"

"I like it when you call me Mark actually."

"I don't care what you like, how did you know I was here?" She was fierce, she knew she was keen on him by the way she was being so hard with him.

"Sssh now, don't get all excited lady, your wonderful sister Lily sent me." After he seated himself inside of the dome, he sat opposite her at first gazing into absolute beauty. But as the night unfolded and the evening of Friday settled, the stars had landed sparkle. It had almost felt like she had known this man for a very long time, more than just the drunken night where nothing happened between them. Mark had admitted that he had always had a crush on her, he had known Matthew, Rose's husband very well. Journalism and being a respected reporter led to many close encounters at conferences, court hearings and party functions the ones she had always been at with Lily and Rose, where he would watch her all night and dance with many men and go home with one. Yet he always thought there was something missing in her life, why she felt the need to pursue one-night stands. He was intrigued by her. She fascinated him.

Sometimes they say if the soul finds its mate and you feed it what it wants, great things can happen.

And it was an evening where a handsome charming man met a beautiful hopeless woman, a magical time when love says hi back. They both ate, sipping slowly into the everlasting remains of their alcoholic beverage, the legal limit to drive had been reached. With no more alcohol the evening captured their real personalities, there were no acts, no false pretence or heightened confidence, just themselves. They talked, they laughed, they opened up to each other, they shared and told selected secrets, she told him about her crazy dreams on Wednesdays, he told her she was crazy, they shared life's ambitions and interests. Until the night had come to its closing point, customers were being encouraged to leave the area. As they left the dome, they were holding hands, there was so much more to talk to be had, there was so much more of a night they both wanted to enjoy and share.

As her hand was in his, walking out to separate cars, she had the warmest feeling in her stomach. She had not thought of Lily once until it had been midnight walking hand in hand with Mr Harrington and what could have felt like the end of the world was now beginning to feel like the start to a brand new beautiful one for herself. she had smiled sweetly and thanked her sister out loud to the dark skies as she watched out to the darkness and imagined her sister's plane taking off on that romantic winter's night.

"You're the best sister in the world Lily," Ruby said out loud with no tears, only smiles. She held his hand tighter and Mr Harrington squeezed back each time. He was going to be there for her.

She had needed that moment, she needed a safe feeling, and it had only been Friday. There would be no sign of the mad woman for another five days.

What would Mr Harrington make of her then? When she would change from beauty into the sweated beast, a distressed wreck?

For when Wednesday would be sure to creep upon her, so would a little bit of Wednesday hysteria.

Chapter 17

Lily Anderson
Adopted Sister

THE PORCELAIN DOLL

The flight had been fairly smooth, eleven hours and two minutes making their arrival to Hollywood in the morning of a warmer setting, and leaving Ruby eight hours ahead back in the UK. That's one of the wonderful things about life, no one knows what is around the corner and, as Lily learned, anything can happen at any given time even when you are least expecting it. Last year she would never have predicted she would be engaged to a movie star, pregnant with a new inviting life in Hollywood any time she wanted it.

She was out of Virginia Waters, well just until Christmas, Ruby's fortieth birthday, Lily was glad the time away was not a long stretch, the homesick issues that had kicked in had become a bigger problem she had bargained for. She had no morning sickness, just a deep gut, hollow, empty feeling and as much as she hated to admit it, it was the feeling of something bad.

She had felt lost in Hollywood, useless, her brain was clamped down with thoughts and visions of Sue which were driving her insane. She questioned whether she should have stayed after hearing of Ruby's nightmare, she had after all told her she would stay with her. Yet now she only sank in deep regret as she wished she really should have just stayed put.

Surely she was selfish, she thought? It was unfair to put all that pressure and responsibility onto Ruby, and what if it all went wrong? Or worse, she got caught?

Lily began to wonder if she had done enough. The instructions to Ruby were self-explanatory but, even so, she went over as much as she possibly could and took care not to miss or leave out any tiny detail what so ever.

The airport seemed huge. Bran had been desperate to get a coffee and an easy bite to eat. Lily had looked around taking in a first impression of everyone and everything exaggerated, over the top. It seemed to be full of extroverted characters, people smiling with white teeth and hiding behind big shades.

Bran had mentioned his good pal's wife was a high profile make-up artist keen and insistent on giving Lily a whole revamp, a new Hollywood look.

She had read Ruby's text message as soon as her phone had come alive. Ruby had thought of her exactly at twelve midnight the same time Lily had thought of her and Mr Harrington. But now all she wanted to do was to go back home, she was feeling guilty for leaving, guilty for the way Bran's expressions had changed from his face all lit up, beaming, grinning from cheek to cheek during the landing to now a face of deep concern, sad and sorry for her. She battled with herself, the talkative side of her brain adamant that leaving was the wrong thing to do, for she knew deep down something bad in fact was going to happen, but what?

Lily backtracked the night of the dinner party, to the scene before arriving at her mother's manor.

Everything had been timed and planned out precisely.

She had remembered the feeling of bare-faced lying to her

mother when Florence had asked her and everybody if they had seen a set of keys? Namely the spare set to Sue and Paul's.

She had denied taking them herself to conduct a plan of action, something that was going to expose Paul for what he really was. Yet it had been useless in trying to speak and confide to her mother, she assumed her mother was going through some psychological breakdown in the last few days in particular. This change would have taken place a few days after the dinner party. The more she came to think about it, her mother had lost all of the spark she had left that made her Florence Anderson and Lily also needed to find that reason out. Her mood in Hollywood was panicked, congested, alarmed.

She slowed her breathing down to help reduce the stress cycle, once her mind became a little more quiet she directed her focus to the disturbing events leading her back to that night at Sue's.

The visons replayed, she found baffling, repulsive and confusing.

Everybody back at her mother's manor had been waiting for her to arrive, aloof to the introduction of Bran. Her time of arrival should have been six thirty p.m. for the pre-announcement drinks.

Ruby's job had been to distract and keep the glasses topped up and everyone entertained. She had completely lost track of time once she had let herself into Sue's. she recalled a weary feeling, as though it was an invasion on a woman she loved like her own mother, a woman who had helped her and had done so much for her and all of them, and yet she was the one feeling like a criminal. She was an imposter, a stranger who was completely lost in the dark. Lily felt extremely uneasy as to how dark everything was once she stepped inside the old manor. She asked out loud why on earth everything had been switched off. There had not been one lamp or night light switched on the whole of the downstairs mansion. It was difficult walking around in darkness, she knew their house well but not in complete blackness and not blind.

They say the brain tricks you when you lurk around in the dark with the lights off. The human visualises things that are not really there.

Lily was scared, the manor was silent, the fitted alarm had been dismantled. As she staggered by the front door she could make out a part that had been forced off the wall.

Using her arms out ahead of her to touch and tap anything she could, she found herself to the first room. The lights would be exactly the same in theirs as it was at her mother's. She felt for the smooth, cold texture of the gold-plated switch and, with a tiny tap, the light appeared on. She looked around. She followed on through the whole of downstairs, the place looked like it had been deserted, it was filthy. The kitchen however was magnificent, a huge attractive space, spotless and welcoming, Paul's pride and joy. She snooped around, collecting bills, letters left opened and unattended. Lily had definitely suspected Paul was using Sue for her money as well. The house was freezing, it was as though nobody lived in the manor, like the kitchen was a separate house. Ruby switched back off the lights, and set the torch on her phone to guide her way upstairs to Sue's bedroom.

She began thinking how this even happened, how this couple ended up in such a toxic mess. The girls had remembered when they actually believed they were ever happy, it looked like Paul doted on her once upon a time, but really when you looked in closely anything Paul ever did was to benefit from it in some way. If he was to buy her flowers, it came with an apology, if he ever bought her an outfit, he had bought himself two, and always on Sue's credit card, and then once the heart-breaking news of not being able to conceive and failed attempts of IVF, brought out a dark, a different, abusive side to Paul, he became a nasty man, cruel.

They say domestic abuse is not always obvious, sometimes it's a gradual thing. At first there may be emotional abuse, verbal mental damage shown by a lack of interest in oneself, life or friends. At first you may notice their low self-esteem, distancing and substance abuse. Lily had noticed all these things before she started noticing bruising and physical contact from Paul towards Sue, a shove there, a nudge here, a violent push and many accidents.

The stairs seemed to go on for ages. She did call out to identify herself to alert Sue of her presence, but it had been no good, the manor was completely silent.

Sue's bedroom would be the furthest one along the second-floor landing, the dimmed spotlights came on as soon as she walked along the hallway. Their manor was creepy, it had a derelict feel to it. Lily took a deep breath as she got closer to the huge bedroom door.

She decided not to knock but to gently open and go ahead inside.

The door had been locked, which she deemed a health hazard and very twisted. Why would Paul lock her inside? And did her mother know he did this, she wondered?

"SHIT," she said, dropping the keys onto the wooden floor.

Picking the keys up she noticed there had been three different types, she fumbled around and tried the other two keys to the bedroom door. On her third attempt the bedroom door opened.

"SUE, it's Lily, can you hear me?" She rushed straight over to the bed where she saw the outline of her body underneath the covers.

There had been no reply from her but she knew she was alive from the troubled breathing sounds, belching and wheezing, it was some sort of hiccups.

"Sue?" by this time Lily was tearful and calling an ambulance seemed like the most rational thing to do and to abandon the whole plot.

She gently removed the duvet from her beaten disorientated body. Her complexion had been somewhat an off-yellow grey, something that she swore with alcohol only happened over a very long period of time. Surely alcohol was not the cause? She had only started really drinking heavily at the start of the current year. Lily was baffled, there was a mixture of blood and vomit staining the covers and sheet. As she turned on the table lamp she noticed fresh bruising, purple blue ones, and green yellow kind of bruises all over her arms and legs, red sores and scratches over her flesh and face. She was wearing a long nighty and Lily could not think what possessed her to look where she did, but something had told her to lift the dress up and in shock horror she discovered bruising between her thighs, stains from seminal fluid in several places and swelling between her buttocks and inner thighs. It was unclear if penetration had been the cause of that but her question started with was Paul having sexual intercourse with her? And could Sue even be in a consensual state of mind for anything of that kind? Surely not. Lily could not comprehend any truth that was staring at her. People say you either have a flight or fight instinct and no one really knows what they would do until the situation they are in.

Sue began to stir, blabbering out and mumbling. Lily held

her hand and sat down beside her.

"It's me Sue. Lily.'

"Lily." Her voice was weak, tired and faint. Lily rushed to the table her mother left with topped-up supplies of water, fruits and biscuits. She held a cup to Sue's mouth encouraging her to just sip, which she did, she was able to sip the water that is what Lily had remembered and clung onto that she was going to be OK. She had decided to continue with her plan even more so as Sue squeezed her hand and moved her lips, trying to tell her something.

"Don't let him catch you here. You must go now."

"What? Tell me Sue, it's OK. Just tell me what's he doing to you."

Lily broke down sobbing, telling Sue exactly what she was going to do: plant a secret camera. She swore to Sue she was going to get Paul, he was going to prison for a very long time if he was hurting and abusing her, and he would never hurt her again.

Sue could not speak much and she seemed to drift in and out of being illusive.

As she fell back asleep she was all cleaned and covers changed, Lily had taken a good look around the whole room, she felt disgusted and angry, what could any police force do with a weak case, she wondered? She guessed Rose would know what to do. She began to wonder whether she should involve her. But then if she was on that side it would have to be done correctly. Of course they would have to investigate, of course they would even arrest him, but what if the police thought he was telling the truth? That she was falling over from being far too drunk? It would be hard to prove without catching him striking or doing disgusting things, she felt she just had to be certain. She looked around thinking of where she could have planted the spying device. Somewhere Paul would never check, but where…?

"Lily?" Sue forced her name out as she lay bedbound, Lily went running to her side.

"A letter, you must know the truth about you. The letter Lily, the letter."

Lily tried to understand what she could have been thinking or implying or talking about, but it had been too difficult to make out if she had been talking about Paul? But Lily had shivered, she had a feeling this letter was for her and about her, but what?

She had tried going over with what she had mentioned but, once again, she had lost her natural state of being, and again she slept.

The evening felt like it was seconds since she had let herself in. The time was moving fast, she checked her watch and text Ruby's phone to keep the family distracted back at their mother's. She had to finish the job here first and find a place for the camera. Then she could make the grand entrance with Bran, but if she did not hurry up then they might all have become suspicious. It was not worth any risk in taking any longer than she needed to in being there, even if Bran was outside in the chauffeur-driven car keeping guard. She wanted no surprises or no interruptions.

She sent a message to Bran's phone to let him know she would not be much longer and she received ten heart emojis in a row.

As she spotted an old vase with artificial flowers inside she at first thought that would have been the perfect discreet place but, just as quickly as she had thought so, she started to make out stirred mumbling words from Sue. She was awake again.

All Lily could make out was Sue's index finger pointing over to what appeared to be a beautiful porcelain doll, and just like that she then caught sight of a beautiful tall porcelain doll on a huge stand. The doll was holding a suitcase and she was wearing a long, red velvet coat.

Lily became entranced by it. Picking her up and studying the beautiful glass doll, she inspected the perfection, as she had been made with a clever real life looking feel to her. On her stand the doll's name was displayed, her name was Freda, and neatly tucked inside the doll's jumper fitted to her was a folded envelope attached by safety pins at the back.

As Lily carefully detached the letter she quickly without hesitation stuffed it into the inside pocket of her jacket. That was obviously the letter Sue had been trying to tell her about. The doll stood elegantly oblivious on a strong white stand and it seemed almost genius that the doll named Freda was holding a secret camera, the device had been discreet enough to record catching clear footage, so she agreed that would be it, the mission was accomplished, the start to catching the villain all lay in the mystery of the tall, beautiful porcelain doll.

Chapter 18

Rose Anderson
The Baby Sibling

A BLESSING IN DISGUISE

You have probably heard of an old saying *stick with the Devil you know?* Some people prefer to stay in the relationships that feel familiar to them, others, like Rose Anderson preferred to take a full leap of faith and jump ship. Some people can either be the making of you or the breaking of you and, sometimes a certain person can bring out the side in you that you never even knew existed.

The day was a Sunday. It was the expected day of rest, and whilst on this day she watched outside her window to a grey dismal sky, wondering what it was that may have caused the clouds to darken with such rage, a frightening clap of thunder startled her as she stood close by. The rain was gushing down fast, she could see objects being lifted into thin air, caught in the midst of spiteful winds. What had made the Lord so angry, she asked herself.

Rose had not been on call for work, her schedule was four weeks on and four weeks off. This was proving to be effective and she liked the flexibility, too.

She had stayed at Eli's cottage the night of the dinner party, going back with Matthew would have been ludicrous. Matthew had been stomping around as she heard him from upstairs with her sisters just after she came clean, they had each advised her to either stay put at the manor or to stay with Eli. Inevitably Rose had chosen the sweetheart option, he would have been waiting for her anyway.

She had remembered Matthew had become unreasonable, approaching her bedroom door as he demanded her out to speak and rightly so. Yet once all the insults came flying her way, with his absurd requests to his fatherly rights to the child if he did prove to be one. She heard his voice in her ears playing his words over, recalling his arrogant choleric anger in her head.

"If it's a girl, whether it's mine or not, I want nothing to do with it, or you. You could both rot in the garbage for all I care and that broke loser of yours is welcome to the pair of you.

"If however it's a boy and that boy's father is me, I'll see you in court. I'll fight you for full custody, I'll prove you're unfit in everything you do, mark my words." Matthew had said, absolutely outraged.

I suppose you could say that's the thing about people – couples, when the average human gets hurt, the most unimaginable, hurtful and unkind things can be said, meant or not. But that's all it ever comes down to in the end is sticks and stones.

Rose had been slightly taken aback by his comments, remaining hopeful that he was not going to be the father of her baby.

Being hopeful and positive were the only useful tools she had left.

Although Matthew had been fuelled by anger, his frustration mainly came from his insecurities of wanting something so much and hoping so much he was going to be a father. He could put to bed his own doubts of being infertile, before the dinner party Matthew had known nothing about Eli. He felt there had been no point in chasing the referral on after the shock surprise of his wife's pregnancy. It has our hun in an awful position now for Matthew truly believed women like Rose never cheated or left their husbands. They were a part of a high society, learning along the way to put up or shut up. Much to his disgust his wife had thrown him into complete turmoil, he was feeling beat, his power felt tested gaining no control in the matter. He had no choice other than to sit back and wait to find out.

It appeared as though Matthew had not really been too fazed, it seemed like it never bothered him too much about Rose actually leaving him. Again he just assumed that she would go crawling back to him anyway. Rose on the other hand continued the belief system that everything happened for a reason.

She informed Matthew that she was going to let herself in and leave the keys behind on her way back out. She was aiming to collect as much of her belongings as possible and would send a car to collect the rest a later time in the month.

Rose thought she knew her husband reasonably well, that she could rest aside in thinking he would want to be present on her arrival. He was not that type, quite suddenly there was just nothing left to say, no more words or awkward smiles to be exchanged, it was over.

She had wondered what on earth everybody was thinking. What were they saying behind her back? What would her mother be thinking about her current situations? Although she thought about the way her mother strangely seemed preoccupied in something else, weirdly she did not seem at all too interested in any of them.

Rose was not going to let a little bit of judgment get in the way of her happiness. She was not fussed what others would say or think, nor any pity some would give, she would reject it all.

She knew most of her own workforce and those of Matthew's superficial world would think nothing more of her being a crazy fool to leave a man like Matthew Hughes.

Rose held her arm over her developing bump. She felt movements and little flutters; the more her hand was still, the more she felt the baby move around inside of her.

She was thinking about her work seeking the right time to announce she would be needing to take maternity leave. She would be entitled to a full year at home with the bundle of joy.

She was planning on finishing the case she was currently working on and aimed at taking on one more, thinking it would always be possible to pass it on if it got too much and she needed to rest.

They say at twenty weeks' pregnant inside the womb of a woman carrying her unborn child the foetus becomes the size of a banana and measurements begin to be weighed from head to heel instead.

Rose had been one hundred per cent sure abortion was just a selfish second of panic, for she was already so attached, as guilty as she did feel, each night she felt the same anguish, hoping her wish would come true, desperately clasping her hands together praying she would give birth to a beautiful baby girl, a daughter, a lifelong friend. She knew she would have to go back to the house that afternoon but, before she did, she focused on her work. She was behind in the official report from her current murder case, with everything taking place in herself and personal family affairs. All she could do was promise to work on it between her time off, she was expected to deliver a masterpiece piled on top of the governor's desk by the next morning on the final demand.

The young female's name had been Anna, maybe she was haunting the downcast Sunday skies.

Rose was sitting in the dining room of Eli's cottage, it was a peaceful room, therapeutic and calming, quiet with only the sounds of the thunderstorm outside.

She opened her laptop and began to edit a downloaded file in need of completion.

Forensic science regulator
FORENSIC PATHOLOGY SPECIALIST GROUP

The Fourth Audit of the work of forensic pathologist's based in the United Kingdom

– 2013 –

7.2.4 Scene of death

7.2.5 The external appearance of the body

7.2.6 Description of the injuries

She had remembered Annas' body being found in a well-kept Edwardian building on a private estate in London. Local residents had experienced no such thing before.

Each neighbour complained that nothing had ever taken place in all the years they had resided on Oak Drive.

The female's body had been cleaned, fresh make-up had been applied, and her fingernails had been painted in candyfloss pink. The body had been posed with a black towel neatly laid over the back of her body, hiding the severity of the woman's injuries.

Anna had been found face down with her head tilted and hand posed in a specific way. One hand was placed under her chin and the other hand was laid out beside her body. the body appeared to be deceased for approximately nine hours. She remembered putting the scene together, putting together different scenarios which outlined how there had been a struggle: a fight had broken out. Anna had tried to fight her attacker off before the perpetrator potentially hit his victim, her, over the head with a champagne bottle. She would have then shortly after been dragged from the front-room floor up to the upstairs bedroom where Rose had initially found the young woman, murdered, lifeless and soul taken.

She would not try to describe the feeling of what it was like to discover the dismaying facts of how a person faces their death. It was a feeling she learned to tackle in group therapy, listening to points and understanding the way seeing, looking and working on murder files can affect the mind. Yet also Rose found her way of accepting death for herself and, in her own life, she would be helping those that had theirs snatched and stolen.

There had been twenty knife wounds inserted into Anna, barely leaving anything left of her but bitty types of flesh and veins ripped and torn around her torso. A urethral prolapse was evident, her body had become at this stage stiff from the range of different chemical changes in the muscle fibres which happens after death occurs.

The report from Rose Anderson was being written in complete respect and duty towards the deceased victim, Polish-born Miss Anna Kaminski.

A good few hours later...

Rose took a slow drive back to the home she once spent many confused and miserable year's living in, of course it was going to be difficult not to naturally miss the three-bedroomed house with its quirky character. However, she never shared the same thoughts about Matthew, really she knew there would be nothing much to miss about him, they had become completely separate and different people as she grew older. Matthew had stayed the same man she married at twenty-three but as Rose matured and grew large wings. One day it looked like she found their purpose and she used them.

She had a brief look around but rushed everything through, grabbing for essentials and keepsakes more than anything else so far.

Rose boxed a varied amount of shoes and bags, outfits and suits, make-up and jewellery. The house was looking ransacked, unintentionally she knocked Matthew's suit jacket from the wardrobe door. Collecting bits of paper that had fallen out she could not help but notice hotel receipts, strip bar bill receipts, condoms and, crumbled deep down inside of his pocket, was a pair of another woman's laced underwear.

There had been no mistaking that Matthew was living his best life anyway.. That man had taken part in plenty of sex scandals, devaluing women inside the sleezy doors of various gentlemen's clubs.

At that moment, alone in her marital home, Rose began thinking how sometimes one might think she is the most unlucky woman in the world to then thinking she's the world's fortunate one. For what Rose had realised that night was that, sometimes, when a door closes a window opens, and some things just have a funny way of working out. Rose was feeling as if bumping into Eli and falling in love again had come at the right time. As she removed her rings, engagement and wedding, she placed them with the house keys onto the glass dressing table and with a smile she felt relieved, free and extremely thankful for Eli Bardon, as he really was in fact a blessing in disguise.

Chapter 19

Betty Anderson
Middle Sibling

GOODBYE GEORGINA BLOSSOM

They say there are five stages to grief, the final transition being acceptance.

But even when we may know the time will come, we can never really be prepared to say goodbye.

Betty had been fairly quiet on the drive back to their cottage, after the family dinner party. Baby Ivy had fallen asleep in the back car seat. David had only spoken of how proud he was of his wife for the effort she had put into bonding with her sisters that evening.

She remembered her hand had been touching his lap the whole journey home.

She was also keen on telling Georgina all about the scandals and shocks of the Andersons' family dramas.

The eagerness and excitement to tell Georgina her wish had come true, that herself and Ruby shared a magical smile repairing any old wounds they once had.

To share with her that David and Bran immediately embraced a bromance hitting it off together. That Betty and Lily had hugged and laughed at the irony and, after all their years of bickering and hard feelings, the two women had connected beautifully, there had been special moments of that evening as well as life-changing circumstances.

The evening had ended with an invitation to Rose's bedroom. After her public display of shock confessions she had then asked her sisters to her room and, for the first time, the invitation was to include Betty. It was a delightful feeling she had remembered as they had all cried, spoken, listened, laughed and hugged, each making a sworn promise they would all stand by one another. From now on they would all have each other's backs...

Approaching the cottage, Ivy was flung over David's back walking into their front garden. Georgina was staying in their downstairs bedroom which showed her bedroom light was switched off, the front room lights however were still on.

The hour was just after midnight with it not being known if Georgina would be asleep or not. She had only hoped she had not tried to stay up in wait for her return home, or had fallen asleep in the front room cold.

She kissed Ivy as David carried her straight upstairs to lie her down. Betty walked on through to the kitchen to put the kettle on, she did not feel her friend's presence in that room but she quietly called her name out anyway.

"Are you in here Georgie?" She stepped into the front room for a clearer view. Georgina's wheelchair had not been in sight so she guessed she was likely to be sleeping.

Georgina was always in her chair now, her mobility had worsened suddenly with her health. She had taken a nasty strain catching little Ivy's cold, hospitalisation became imperative but it was always declined by Georgina as sometimes a resting place in a warm, familiar home with memories and love is sometimes all a person needs to make their peace spiritually and mentally when ready to pass on.

Her body had weakened and she appeared painfully thin in the last few days.

Betty creaked open Georgina's bedroom door, it had been dark inside so she left the door slightly ajar for the light to shine in from the hallway. She was silent in walking over to where she lay. When a person is asleep their eyes may still twitch underneath their eyelids, their breathing is reduced but visible.

Seen from Betty's angle, it looked as though all Georgina was doing was sleeping, she switched on the bedside table lamp with it not being long before understanding the reason why her best friend did not stir in the light, while she felt her cold with no beat from her heart.

In reality Georgina had died in her sleep. In the subconscious mind however, Georgina's death was temporary, after a long rest she would of course wake up was the way her brain had tricked her into believing.

Although it was a strange feeling for Betty, she was not scared, she showed no emotion, numb to any real instinct.

As the minutes passed it became more real, Georgina was no longer there but she pulled the second cover over her anyway, she stroked the thin strands of her hair away from her face.

Although she knew she would never see Georgina's eyes open again, although she knew she would no longer hear her voice. All of those important details she found difficult to accept at that point, there had been importance in the time she would now spend in saying goodbye.

"You just rest now Georgie, my angel."

She switched back off the bedside lamp and laid down next to her beloved friend. It was hard to accept she had not been there holding her hand when it had counted the most, but for Georgina she had been a private lady and her ending was the opposite to feeling alone. She had felt safe, at peace and ready.

Sometimes all a person needs is just one person to have loved and to have been loved by, to experience the purpose of life.

She thought about a saying Georgina used often in her final days, she would say:

"Everything will be OK in the end. If it's not OK, it's simply not the end."

And strangely there was something quite beautiful in those words that Betty would cherish.

And it did seem looking at her that was exactly the case, wherever she was, wherever Georgina now was, it looked somewhere heavenly. She had a subtle smile, she was a sleeping shell.

Betty welcomed that all her friend's pain, her fight with cancer had ended, that now everything for Georgiana would be forever OK.

For the ones we leave behind, life must go on as they say, another breath we must take, and time is our biggest friend for soon again one day we will have a reason to smile, a reason to laugh and a reason to live again once we retrain and learn how to.

We might want to go to the same place our loved ones have gone to at first, we may feel a part of ourselves equally died with them. We might even feel we want to be alone from everyone and everything, but for Betty Anderson it seemed she was fortunate to have a doting husband that would remind her of all the basic things of self-care that she was about to forget. His wife would grieve in the love of his aiding arms.

David had approached his wife lying on the bed with

empathy and respect to Georgina, he felt that it had probably been deliberate to have chosen a moment when the whole family had been away from the home on her passing.

For David he would now take the carer's role. He was well aware his wife was now lying next to a deceased body, the on-call doctor would need to be called. This was an expected end of stage death, the doctor would provide a medical certificate, he thought about how to register the death, and the very next thing to do would be to arrange for the body to be collected and taken to a funeral home.

David thought it would be wise to give Betty one of her sleeping pills and let her sleep. He lifted her away from Georgina's body and into the master's room where little Ivy was sound asleep. David thought it would be better to surround her with love when she woke, as she was likely to grieve once the shock lifted.

There would be no family members to contact on Georgina's behalf and David held a short breath going back into the bedroom. He felt cold, and saddened; in life he was certain you should always feel like you have been loved on earth. And his best friend's wife had exactly that, she had been a wonderful friend to her, he thought, who was loyal and cherished her to her very end.

That was enough for his own closure, that is what tool he would use for bereavement handling. Life was set to be different now, but sometimes when a person changes it's because the circumstances of life have changed them.

The funeral had followed twelve days later, it was beautifully arranged and Georgina had stayed on top of her life insurance which covered enough details. It was put together also with the love and generosity of Betty and David. Betty knew her send-off would have done her proud.

Although it was just themselves with the rest of the Anderson women present, with the exception of Lily being in Hollywood. The service had been perfect and one Georgina had wished and spoken off.

Ruby and Rose stuck by Betty in the church running to her aid every time she choked on her words as she spoke to describe what kind of person Georgina had really been. The church echoed the funeral director's instructions to follow one of the hymns as they all stood to rise.

"Sis! What the hell is Mother playing at? She's not said or done anything so far, where are her flowers?" Ruby said in frustration, noticing their mother's distancing and weirdness."

"Oh, I'm glad you said that, I thought it was just me. I'm not sure sis, she seems to be in a completely different head space recently, and she has not hugged or reached out to Betty once all this with Georgina," replied Rose. She was suspicious and more worried than usual about her mother's odd behaviour.

"I'm going to see if she will tell me anything later, I'm just going to come straight out with it. I think something's wrong, and she should tell us."

Ruby had decided enough was enough.

"Yes good idea sis, I'm literally up to my neck in work but we can talk about it again soon, and leave me a message if you find out anything important."

"Oh my God, you don't think Mother is sick do you? And that's what's wrong with her, being at a funeral as-well? Ruby glared at Rose as she said it in shock and horror.

"Don't say such a thing Ruby, Mother does not do sick, and we would be the first to know if she was, we would."

The two sisters hushed their talking as uplifting music filled the church walls. One by one they were asked to say their final words, with choosing to see Georgina one last time before the curtains closed.

Florence was first up, with no eye contact to any of the family she silently whispered some words to Georgina, her expression was stern and frozen. When she did walk back down the aisle she never sat back in her seat, instead Florence had left the church entirely.

Betty had been the last one up. David was nearby just in case she would need him.

She stood pale with no feeling of existence but just a floating energy.

Betty never took her eyes off Georgina, to her she saw the way she did look different now. She could tell it was still her but she never looked like she was sleeping anymore, or was about to wake up any minute.

Betty stood and analysed the work of the artist who had done her make up, it had been done to just take away the blue in her lips, a powder to give a hint of natural skin colouring to her cheeks. Yet Georgina's skin tone had now changed as well.

It seemed a long while before David led his wife away, but as he did it was a peaceful feeling up there. She had never got to say goodbye until now, the first goodbye had not been real in acceptance but, as Betty smiled and cried in the last few seconds spent with her, she finally felt her peace. She kissed the top of her forehead for the very last time, her words were soft and clear.

"Goodbye Georgina Blossom."

Chapter 20

Florence Anderson
The Mother

RED FLAGS

It has been said that what we are exposed to in child development can follow us through later on in life. According to Sigmund Freud, the Id, Ego and Superego are all unique in ways that have a powerful influence on an individual. An imbalance of the Superego is likely and often caused by early childhood traumas.

Florence assumed she had seen a fair bit of life in her time. She had a full book of memories and the most compelling life stories, it was not all pretty when she reminisced on past and present events, and even coming from a disruptive toxic background, Florence Anderson came to a pragmatic reality, that in her fifty-seven years of living she had not yet experienced anything as corrupt, ugly and as dark as what she was experiencing now. The question was, what the hell was she going to do about it...?

She had become a woman of sheer exhaustion. She felt panicked and on edge in the last few days, Lily had flown off to Hollywood and her daughters' lives were rapidly changing. Nevertheless there had been a dreadful amount of time that was passing with no other choice but to isolate herself from her daughters and hide away from her husband. She and Ben had recently gone from a sudden burst of romantic impulsive interactions to complete utter avoidance in each other.

After walking out of the church at Georgina's cremation, she had barely consoled Betty or shown moral support from her part. Ben was becoming confused by her actions; it was only a matter of time before a confrontation was bound to arise between the pair of them.

Florence had found herself bitten hard, karma was a bitch indeed, she was now dominated by a ruthless cruel blackmail. Paul's words had been final, have sex with him again or the whole family would find out about their sordid affair, although there had been no video footage there was certainly enough vocal evidence he recorded on his phone to suggest adultery had been committed. She was banged to rights, what does a woman do? Desperate to keep a squeaky clean image, to keep her family strong, protect them even? Or does a woman hold her hands up confessing to every filthy accusation, on her knees, she prays to God for forgiveness. Everything that was occurring was all having a detrimental effect on her, things were picking at her brain, she could not concentrate on anything but his disgusting, horrendous sexual commands.

The sleazy deed was set to take place later on in her evening plans, she would make her routine night visit to Sue, whilst he would be waiting for her in the kitchen. The man had even gone to the lengths of choosing the lingerie and dress she was to wear paid and bought for on Sue's credit card, the receipts were left in the bag printed in black and white with Sues Amex details on each one.

Florence sat numb on the stool of her dressing table, facing towards her bed. She had everything displayed and set out.

The lingerie had been mauve lace with a matching bra and

suspender belt, the dress had been velvet crushed red, sultry and tempting. He was sending out his perverted message, loud and clear.

She walked towards the teasing laundry and threw it across the edge of the bed just in time before the door flew open. There Ben stood before her, watching her intensively.

"What are you doing?" he said, looking around the room with a frosty gaze.

"Nothing, just about to strip the bed and do a wash. Is there any darks you want done?"

"No," he said leaving her back alone in their master's room.

Florence sighed loudly. A few unwanted teardrops followed by a deep, sick painful knot in her gut, then Florence adjusted herself sternly, she had made her bed and now she would lie it in. She was not prepared to lose her husband, send her daughters into complete dismay, look into the poorly eyes of her best friend, she should feel ashamed of herself, for it was in her own eyes the worst betrayal a woman could ever fear from her friend.

Whatever it would take, Florence was definitely not going to jeopardize a thing. No way on earth was Paul going to expose their rotten truth, not a chance in hell…

There were hailstones forecast throughout the whole day, it was going to be miserable, wet. Florence had heard talks of there being a white Christmas to come, the village would take a dangerous drop in temperature with punishing wind storms to cause havoc in the famous lakes of Virginia Waters. The weather had come to feel like her life, the unknown, the unpredictable.

But whatever the case would be, Florence was certain it would be her last sexual encounter. Paul was going to get his way for one more night, one last time, if she could not figure how to get out of this mess, or she would pray for the Lord to strike her down at instance. Remembering to strip the bed as she had said she would. A slight knock on her bedroom door took her off guard.

"Hi Mother, can I come in?" Ruby boldly entered without any welcome.

"Hmmm, you always was the daring one." Florence carried on with any distraction necessary, merely avoiding solid eye contact with her daughter, for the girls would always sense when she had been crying. They would see the way her skin would react in blotchy patches across her eyes and nose.

"Have you been crying Mum? Just tell me, I know something's wrong." Ruby sounded defeated in her voice.

"Mother, are you sick?"

"What on earth are you muttering on about, sick? I'll tell you what I'm sick of Ruby Anderson, I'm sick of your questioning, nosy no good doings thank you." She piled in the dark washing from Ben's side of the bed. She always knew to check, despite what he would say.

"Now Ruby, is that it? And no, I'm not sick darling, I'm busy."

"OK mother if you say so, you know we all love you, and you know where I am if you need me."

"Right then, is that it? I really must get on." No time for heartfelt moments or pity, she thought.

Florence grew up in suppression, the act of stopping herself from thinking or from feeling something, suppression of her laughter, her cries, her guilt, it was all an act of keeping something happening from feeling real.

Ruby kissed the top of her mother's forehead before she left, disappointed with not receiving any details or hints of what was really going on... There would be nothing to report back to her sisters.

Florence carried the laundry basket downstairs. She passed Ben seated on the couch. She would have to create a whole new persona, if Ruby had started questioning then that means every one of them were likely getting suspicious, too.

"What time are you leaving to sort Sue out? And what the hell's going on over there? I've not seen her for weeks now, Florence, and Paul's like a stranger." Ben folded his newspaper and crossed his arms, watching her fuss around.

"Sue's fine, she's got a little bit of a bug but she's getting stronger actually, she's not been drinking, I've not caught her with any for the fifth day in a row."

"This is sounding a little bonkers now, Flo. The girls are all worried too, I'm following you round there this evening."

She felt her heart thump. That was not Paul's plan, she thought, using a calming approach she stopped herself in all action.

"Ben darling, look, you're worried, I get it, but she won't appreciate you poking your nose in. Just leave it for tonight, I'm going to call a doctor out anyway, just to do all her observations at least."

"Whatever you say, she's your best mate." Frustrated with all the constant excuses and repetitive denial, Ben wanted nothing more to do with the topic.

Florence showered, warmed a little of the lamb stew in the pot but, with very few mouths to feed, she satisfied her own appetite before heading off to Sue's manor.

It was a chilling thought of how someone like Paul, who was once so charming, could change to such drastic measures. Now he was a beast, no mistaking, a good for nothing, dead piece of weight, a leech to empathy, kindness and money. He had meddled his way in, clearly wrecking Sue's life in the process of wrecking her own life. This man had to be stopped whatever his final plans were. Florence knew he had to be stopped.

How on earth was she supposed kiss her husband goodbye and leave the manor dressed in something that looked like she dug up from her past? She had destroyed every inappropriate dress she once owned as a hostess, she would have to get changed round at Sue's, she hoped the ordeal would be over as quickly as possible.

Packing a little bag, it was time for Florence to leave. Ben had disappeared, but she found him to say goodbye before she left. He was always talking with his brother on the phone these days. He looked up to his brother, admired his graft, fortune and his brother's humble wife.

Florence felt uncomfortable as she left, guilt-ridden to the core. At the beginning it came with thrill, it was as though turning a blind eye to Sue's health and well-being was selfish, as callous it may have been, it seemed a stunt of denial would make her feel better about her unrighteous decision to sleep with her husband. now all Florence's concern was for how to save her family, and call a doctor out for Sue and get to the bottom of what was making her so sick, Florence visioned the bruising and lesions she had last noticed and now all the excuses and fabricated versions from Paul sickened her. The truth was staring at her in the face, her friend needed help and medical input before any questioning of domestic abuse could start, because even though Sue was not drunk on the last couple of visits, her mental state still appeared that way.

Florence was going to blackmail Paul back. If he would not allow Sue to be visited by a doctor then she would call the police to check on her instead. She was a prisoner locked in, the poor woman had seen no daylight for at least two months now enough was enough. Even if she was going to lose everything she was not prepared to let her dearest friend suffer anymore. Florence was appalled by herself, how could she have ignored what was staring hard at her?

Paul had not asked for the keys back. He had found the carer's role from Florence convenient, as the weeks passed he left everything for Florence to do, caring, feeding, washing, dressing and cleaning.

In the master's bedroom where Sue slept, weak and feeble, Florence was unaware she was being watched. The secret camera had been recording, Ruby was due to investigate from the next day on Lilys instructions.

Florence went over to Sue. She was always asleep most of the time now. She looked over to the bedside table and wondered how on earth a bottle of red wine had got there, Paul and herself had discussed that they would discard any alcohol, not supply it to her.

"Sue, can you hear me? It's time to wake up now."

Florence stroked her head, and gently nudged at her to wake. Sue stirred and mumbled, dribbling as she did so, it looked like she had been sick whilst she was sleeping. Florence propped her up on large pillows to see if she could get some recognition.

"Sue, can you hear me? do you know who I am?"

"Flo is it you?" Sue could make out Florence's voice, she could barely keep her eyes open but she reached her hand out to her.

Florence cried, and held on tightly to her fragile, lifeless grip.

"I'm going to call for help Sue, I'm calling a doctor, you're not well." She was in a crippled state. Looking at her it seemed it was more neuro complications Florence was baffled.

She was confident enough to assume Sue would make

another night. She would be careful in her approach at first to defuse Paul's temper, he had shown his indignant side to any mention of Sue's bruising.

Having cleaned and sorted out everything that needed to be done with Sue, Florence looked into Sue's mirrored wardrobe. She stood staring at herself, he would be waiting for her downstairs. As she undressed, she made her way to the bathroom to slip into the underwear and into the dress. She walked back to the mirror and stared at her reflexion some more, she was reminded of the hostessing and escorting days as she stood all dolled up. Her appearance had somewhat changed a little along with her figure, she was more full and rounded in age, her complexion was slightly paler and skin not as tight as it once was, she thought.

Standing still for a few more seconds, she caught a glimpse of the porcelain doll. She had never noticed it before now, but she only noticed how beautiful and angelic looking the doll had been. Never had she imagined she was on secret camera, for the question would now be why? And who on earth was Florence Anderson secretly dressed up in a promiscuous outfit? And why was she crying?

Florence took in a deep breath, turning towards Sue, imagining every trick in the book to get out of sex with a man. It was a terrible blackmailed arrangement, she questioned how things had got this bad, how it all ended up like this? Were the signs all already there? In the early days he was in fact a handsome charming man, there had been a few alarm bells now that she really thought about it; at the beginning he was infatuated by Sue, attentive, a big promiser but why and how does a man change so drastically? The devaluing, the leeching, the lies, the sense of entitlement, the selfishness, anybody would surely have seen that these things were always there to see. Do we only see what we want to? Or should we all try how to learn, to recognise life's red flags?

WEDNESDAYS
   Wednesday is nothing but misunderstood
   Halfway through and what will one do?
   Wish for Friday? Wish the days away? When we all wake up
to the gloom of Wednesday.
   – R.L. McKENZIE

Chapter 21

Ruby Anderson
First Born Sibling
Wednesday's Child

IN DEEP

The morning had been Wednesday the second week of December but every day had felt the same over the last few weeks. Ruby had been inseparable from Mr Harrington, and so far so good there was no sign of her reoccurring, haunting nightmare, the Wednesday beast as it had been known to Ruby Anderson.

When she woke, it was the first morning she felt perfect and exactly where she needed to be. She had spent several nights now with Mark, there had been an immediate closeness, something just clicked between the pair of them, they were indeed a couple that blended magnificently well together.

She could not deny feeling suffocated; a feeling not by him but by his small cramped apartment. Every single thing had been in one large space with the bathroom right next to a bedroom, inside was just enough room for a double bed, a small built-in kitchen opened through to a rectangle-shaped lounge area for both dining and relaxing. Although it was a small little place, it was modern, clean and upmarket. Mark had been the first man she had grown feelings for, with a growing curiosity about him every day.

Already in the last month her feelings had warmed to him immensely, quite quickly some would say. So much so that this time materialism just never seemed to be an important detail to her, everything she was looking at and feeling was precisely enough, he had no children, responsible for himself only and before he had become involved with her, he was living a single life as a reporter in his bachelor pad. A few women, not many, and Mr Harrington had a different kind of money, with his finances neatly tucked away, his funds were not shown externally but he kept himself smart, he lived comfortably, whilst reasonably well. Still, she dwelled on the thoughts of Mark being better off with her in the manor, eventually. Her world was filled with so much more space it would be like their own manor, or at least they would have their own part of it.

Rose, Betty and Lily had all left home so that helped and their mother was invisible like splinters of glass, transparent to all visible light, lost elsewhere.

But then she thought of Ben. He was never around, always out of sight working on his construction site every hour God sent. It was unclear whether he had been throwing himself into his project in greater depths because of their mother's erratic and distant behaviour of late. Ruby had thought that it was most likely, but she could only guess, everything was becoming so strange, shocking details leading to so many questions, but still she had no answers.

Things had already changed so much in the family. Now amongst the midst of it all, Ruby was stuck in a place called brand new love: just like Lily, it had come along unexpectedly and even if at that moment Ruby Anderson did not quite already know, her life was about to become a very different one, for better or for worse…

As she lay next to Mark still in bed, it would be the third TV pre-recording she was about to be late for, when she received the call that day confirming she had been given the leading role for the new BBC drama. It had literally felt to her like a dream come true, but now she felt she was actually living a real one, right where she was. Mark was delightful, a breath of fresh air, a true distraction to all things on earth, the whole thing with Lily leaving had already left some open wounds and Ruby felt as though life was horrible without her.

Ruby's thoughts with the whole big actress thing seemed to become less appealing and more of a strain. She could not be certain she even still wanted the part. How many excuses could a woman have for turning up late on set? Ruby's heart palpitated, the thought of the looks, the judgment from the directors. She did not underestimate how heartless the filming directors could be and how likely it would be that she'd be sacked. She sank further down into the covers, Mark was sleeping still with his arm laid heavily on the side of her hip, she wanted to stay put, to be so careful not to wake him or ruin a perfectly good moment. She lay awake silently, thoughts dark and daunting, she started imitating Lily's authoritative tone in her head, the specific detail of the mission, the secret camera. When the hour struck nine p.m. she would sneak round to Sue's manor with the keys Lily had given her, the same keys their mother was still hunting around the manor looking for in complete suspense. the palpitations came back, they were like a fluttering nuisance of anxiety.

As she moved in closer to him his alarm from his phone sounded off on his bedside table. It only took one bleep and Mark was up as though he was never asleep in the first place, upbeat and widely aware he would be awakening always with a smile, happy natured no matter the hour of any morning.

"Rubes, you got to get up babes." he rolled over to her discovering she was already awake. Each stared at the another for a short while before they had kissed good morning.

"Forgive me Lord, no I can't do this to you, babes you'll be late in."

"But I'm already late, and now I'm cosy, I'm stuck, I'm not moving." |She pulled the quilt over her head turning her back on him, reluctant to move or leave her position in the bed.

"What's wrong ladybug? This job is massive for you, you want this, you do? I know you do." He spoke with the feeling of guilt, he had wondered if he was distracting her. Would she resent him for letting her walk away from her dreams just to be cosy in bed? He wasn't asking or even wanting such a thing but he needed her to know he only wanted the very best for her, to support whatever she wanted.

"I think you should just go in Rubes, and then later, this evening, when you come back, I'll have a lovely dinner made. We can review your situation and figure out what you really want to do with this leading role. Getting fired will do no good for your future as an actress, you know that don't you?" He scooped her underneath his large arms, stroking her hair as she lay with him.

"Yeah, I guess so, I mean dinner sounds lovely." She kissed him.

"Although I've got this thing I need to do for Lily tonight, so later the better darling." Ruby was thinking about packing a few things from the manor just as she was spending most of her days and nights at Mark's. Her mother had not batted an eyelid and she doubted very much she would be missed.

Ruby began to think of Lily. She would be back in a few weeks but the time which had already passed felt like years. She missed her incredibly, expecting and waiting for her skype phone call UK time eleven fifteen p.m. that evening. They would watch and play the recordings from Sue's bedroom. She felt a little twang of nerves again and corrected herself by leaping out of bed with a ready-to-do attitude.

"I love you Mark."

"I love you Ruby, I always have, I always will."

Just when she had given up on men, in love, just when she thought she would turn forty left on a shelf to wither away like a once beautiful flower. It had all suddenly changed. Her one-night stands were over, her paths had crossed with fate, it had been him all along, her status was about to go C-B class, Lily was happy, engaged, and if it were not for the Wednesday beast, if the nightmares did not exist she would have believed she was actually lucky for once. For Ruby Anderson was only convinced she would live out a curse or horrible death, that maybe a child of woe does not choose sorrow, instead the sorrow chooses the child…

After leaving Mark Harrington's apartment, Ruby had already decided she was calling it quits. A resignation email was sent directly to the casting manager, and even accepting the fact she was about to take a massive blow, denting her career, nevertheless, she was beginning to feel her own sense of change, growth, her life was waiting for her and she was beginning to think about taking a whole new direction, perhaps a wedding planner, an interior designer. She always did have that creative side, maybe it was just not for the screen anymore?

It was easy for Ruby to feel excited. She was a sanguine personality type, she would get lost in dreams and ideas she was determined: set on having it all by the big four zero.

To Ruby that meant having a reason to smile, and a beautiful smile she most certainly had.

If there was one thing she was beginning to learn it was that when you cry, you cry alone, and when you smile, the world smiles back.

He was the reason she had an involuntary smile every day, why she felt like she had been floating in thin air, he was the one who made love feel so real. Mr Mark Harrington.

December was, so far as predicted, dark and grim from every corner.

She drove back to her mother's manor, she craved a decent conversation with her mother, it seemed like the family had divided before her eyes, but strangely she had stayed connected to Betty ever since their last family dinner party, a closeness more than ever before. Betty had even been in touch with Lily constantly whilst she was in Hollywood. This was not a reason for Ruby to complain, she felt it just proved nobody knows what's waiting around the corner. Life was in fact just full of surprises. Peeping through to the back garden Ruby found Florence in her usual spot outside sitting in her garden chair, expressionless, isolated and astray, it seemed, more and more.

Ruby felt flustered quickly. It was hard to take, hard to see her mother this way, she felt useless, shut out like the rest of them. Betty fortunately was in the magical arms of her husband, confused by the silent treatment she was also receiving from their mother; after all, they had always known, each one of them that Betty was the apple of their mother's eye, the highest of all castles. Yet just lately there had been nothing from the woman, completely and utterly nothing, no reaction to any of them.

Ruby was worried and scared. She thought maybe it was also their mother that now needed looking after as well as Sue. What on earth was going on? She would have to confide in Ben and get some kind of explanation, he must have noticed her odd behaviour as well, she assumed.

She led her mother into the warmth with Ben nowhere to be seen.

"Ben is always working on his new development plan, it's all he does now."

Trying to get any reaction and not wanting to offend her mother, she made her a cup of tea. She watched her as she fell asleep in her armchair, wondering what had happened to her mother's hyper energy? Where was her mother's head space? It was a mystery to all of them.

She was feeling sleep-starved herself, exhausted by doing nothing but dealing with the stresses and confusing circumstances, with everything going on it was tiring in itself.

Still there was much to do. She went on upstairs to her bedroom, watching the time as she packed a few things and accessories. The next stop was at Sue's manor; Lily had told her Paul routinely went out for an hour's jog at nine p.m., something he did without fail. That would be her time to sneak in, check on Sue and get the hell out of there with the secret camera without Paul knowing or suspecting a thing...

A little while after...

It had been ten twenty p.m. when she had got back to Mark's apartment. She had not taken long at Sue's, she had panicked as she found the porcelain doll, forcing the stitching open from the doll's fabric, hoping she had left the doll as neat and as perfectly unnoticed as she had already been. If nothing was on the tape, it would have to be planted back, same place, same way.

Mark had taken the hint that later plans would be more suitable so he did his best to accommodate her needs best as possible. The table was laid out superbly with fine decor, and a plate arranged with an appetising meal. Although the sight of him and the evening's plans looked splendid Ruby could not get the image of Sue out of her head. It was haunting her every thought, the way she had looked in that bed, Ruby felt just awful, that confusing moment struck her violently, with the question was Sue unwell? With what? Or was she dying? She could not really speak to her much, she had never seen Sue like that before in all her years. Sue was the magnet that held the family together.

At the manor she had not needed to do much with Sue. Her mother had been round earlier on in the evening to attend to her, but Ruby could only imagine Sue really was living in a house of horrors.

She remembered the feeling walking in. The manor had been freezing cold, dark, and her bedroom door had been locked just as Lily had warned her.

She had listened well to what shape the key needed to be if it was to open the door.

What was Paul doing to her that would be the cause of all those nasty-looking lesions? She thought about the way her skin colouring looked totally off. Ruby was too flustered, nervous and intimidated by the whole scene. She decided not to check her body, avoiding seeing the bruises if she had looked.

She had kept Mark in the loop, he was unaware of the situation both about the camera or the family crisis.

And so far it proved to be tricky, it was going to be impossible for her to get the real privacy she would need in watching the tape with Lily. She imagined her sister would be furious that another night would be dragged out of not knowing. She became more anxious for the phone call she would soon have to take from her.

Mark had noticed her distant presence and appreciative she

was. When eating she made every effort to enjoy the dinner he had made for her.

Not long seated at the dining table she hands-down confessed to resigning from the role, sharing her plans for a whole new direction.

Mark was an approachable man, groomed, handsome and sharp with deep brown skin and deep brown eyes. Ruby felt she could just be who she was around him, no pretending, just exactly herself. It was the most peaceful feeling she had yet experienced.

Time that evening yet again had not been on her side. She had to cut the evening off short to take the call from Lily, her call would come in around eleven fifteen p.m. It would be a private call which Mark granted her space with no questions asked she disappeared out of sight to his bedroom and gently closed the door as she could see Lily connecting. She loved seeing her face but with their plan slightly changing she hoped Lily would not be to cross with her, she looked into the large screen of her phone.

"SISSSSS, goodness you look fantastic Lily."

"Do you think? It's called the Hollywood look."

"Have you had your teeth done?"

"Don't get me started, I was practically forced into it Ruby. Seriously how do they look?"

"Seriously? You and your teeth look out of this world." Ruby gave a slight cough, a giveaway she needed to clear something off her chest.

"OK, look don't be angry Lily, but I'm not at home, I've been staying round at Mark's so I'm here, in his bedroom, look." She flipped the phone around to show off his very neat, modern teeny tiny room.

"He's outside waiting for me. The place is too small for secrets sis, he sleeps in until late so we'll watch it first thing in the morning."

Lily had felt disappointed but half excited her sister's romance was fully developed. But even so both the women were wracked with worry, guilt and uncertainty about the well-being of Sue.

"In the morning it is then. How was she? Did she recognise you when you went round there?"

"She was asleep, I never stayed long, it was horrible Lily, I never knew she was that bad until I saw her." Lily eyes filled up and Ruby was already sniffling.

"Are you sure we're doing the right thing Lily? Maybe I should just give this straight to Rose, she's trained in this sort of stuff. She would know exactly what to do right now, because I don't? And OK, Mother knows a bit of nursing but she's no doctor, Sue should be in hospital I think, and something's wrong with Mother, she's definitely not well either, she's not right sis."

"Ruby? Listen to me, something's wrong, I just sense it. I should not have left, I'm coming home as soon as I can book a flight."

"Oh my God, I knew it, it's s me isn't it Lily? I'm going to die, have you sensed it too?"

"Ruby listen to me, don't do anything with that tape, I'll try to call you early in England time, you're not that far ahead, but if you don't hear from me, Bran's put me on a flight home OK?"

"OK."

"And sis?"

"Yes," Ruby cried into the screen.

"Nothing's going to happen to you, look at me, I don't know what this is, but it's something very bad Ruby. Keep an eye on everyone until I get home, and I'm so happy for you about Mr Harrington, I bloody knew it.

"But your nightmares sis, I'm feeling them too…"

It really must have been a good couple of hours that had passed by. Yet he had not heard a peep from Ruby, who had been in an intense thirty-minute conversation that put her to sleep just before midnight.

Mark felt curious. He crept the bedroom door open, she had no longer been on the phone to her sister, Ruby instead was suffering with excessive body sweats, she was flipping and tossing, he could see that she was asleep, but asleep in some kind of hellish nightmare, her cries were of unbearable pain.

And so it was, Ruby Anderson again on a Wednesday just after the hour struck midnight was faced with her Wednesday beast.

But what Mr Harrington made of it only he knew right there and then watching her soul distressed.

Whatever it was that made her body twist she was in deep, deep in a nightmare, deep in emotions, deep in love and about to get deep into a domestic abuse investigation.

At the manor she had not needed to do much with Sue, her mother had been round earlier on in the evening to attend to her, but Ruby could only imagine she really was living in a house of horrors.

She remembered the feeling walking in. The manor had been freezing cold, dark, and her bedroom door had been locked just as Lily had warned her.

She had listened well to the description of the shape the right key would be to open the door.

What was Paul doing to her that would be the cause of all those nasty-looking lesions? She thought about the way her skin tone looked totally off.

Ruby was to flustered, nervous and intimidated by the whole

scene she decided not to check her body to avoid seeing the bruises if she had looked.

Even in the safe place Ruby was in, innocently fallen asleep on the bed of the man she loved, but even so Ruby tossed around in her nightmare, there she laid bare, possessed by the Wednesday beast, she could feel she was in deep with something frightening, in deep with death for sure, but whose?

Chapter 22

Lily Anderson
The Adopted Sister

TELEPATHY

Lily was already reaching twenty weeks' pregnant, although she was not presented with any safety issues upon boarding a flight home she could not help but feel superstitious. She was certain it was now she was in the most precious, delicate stage of the pregnancy but, nervous as she was, there would be nothing, absolutely nothing that was about to stop her from getting back home. It seemed destiny was dancing with fate with each and every one of the Anderson women. For Lily, she was not only about to unravel the truth for Sue, but rather yet, some of her own home truths were waiting for her, too...

Sometimes what we don't know can't hurt us but what we do know could change everything forever.

This was certainly about to be the case for Lily Anderson anyway.

She was not there and able to catch an immediate flight back, it would take another five days until she was back home in Virginia Waters, which she granted as rotten luck for a formidable storm was making a nuisance in Hollywood, causing several flight delays and cancellations. It was the worst timing as some sixth sense told her that Ruby would be in dire need. She had told Ruby nothing was going to happen to her, but could she be so sure? The frightful feeling was something they were both experiencing, Ruby was in immense pain every time she would have her nightmare, but why? And each time it channelled through to Lily, whatever pain it was that Ruby was feeling, Lily knew she was in trouble. She would need her and she was going to be there for her, when she did.

As if unleashing the truth about the domestic violence she was convinced Paul was inflicting upon Sue was not bad enough, she had told Ruby not to do anything with the secret camera until she was back. The confusion with it all, the stress was totally unbearable.

As if the sounds of Betty's tears of grief, her anguish towards the sudden abandonment from their mother was not bad enough, now there was Ruby giving a strong impression that something horrible, something wrong was also going on with their mother. Life was a disaster.

It seemed Rose had taken a back seat in everything, not fully aware of how serious anything was at their end. Lily had only hoped she was happy with Eli and, figuring out her own mess of her own life, she knew her baby sister was also distracted by finishing a case at work, and it always seemed that being the baby sibling it was only right they all wanted to protect her. Any stress would be passed on to Rose's growing baby, And just like that, she could not help but feel a little guilty as she thought about her own baby, caught up in a womb of stirred emotions. Out of everything going on the thought of something happening to Ruby was the most unsettling fear she could ever face.

Lily had always been like her with the superstitions, a belief in witches, spirits and fate.

So it was of no shock that to her it was obvious something

bad was going to happen, on a day of Wednesday, she was almost certain, she had to be back before Wednesday came around again, even if it meant Bran sacrificing the premier to his new movie. He had already said if there was any more nonsense with the airlines, he would drop everything and get them both back on a private plane, instead.

As unfair and as unkind as life could be at times it also had its high points and Bran was one of them. She felt like he truly worshipped the ground she walked on, she was so grateful for him, together with Ruby who had also found the love of her life identical to the one of her own love story and, for that, she was pleased in predicting rightly so. Both men were successful, handsome and extremely kind, her gut instincts had been correct so she only hoped her gut instincts that Ruby was in trouble were phoney, false with no truth in it at all other than it all being a pattern of nothing other than disruptive bad dreams. Yet deep down she was afraid there was a reason she could not be too excited about her sister's new love adventure as that thing called intuition said it may possibly be cut short. But *why*? is what she needed to know…

It had turned out that the next flight would arrive in Gatwick in the early hours of Monday the 6th December. Her family was being watched over in her absence, Betty was keeping a close eye on Ruby and Ruby was keeping a close eye on their mother, with herself and Rose looking out for themselves.

Everything was on hold with the plan until she got back. Lily was aiming to resolve everything herself. She would hand the videotape straight into the police instead of watching it. She thought there was bound to be all the evidence on there to put Paul behind bars. She would confront Ben, where she knew he was likely to be either working on his building plans or relaxing inside the huge estate of his brother's. She was going to get some answers about their mother's health and actions? Once home she was not prepared to let Ruby out of her sight, not until that deep, critical senses of pain, those frightful instincts of foul play, came to an end.

It was decided that Bran would be travelling back as originally planned. The night before Christmas Eve, Lily felt slightly uneasy with the fact Christmas Day, Ruby's birthday, her big fortieth was in fact falling on a Wednesday. She had always discarded any old wives tales that said a child born on Wednesday is a child full of woe, but there that unwanted feeling came upon her once more, an enemy was digging deep in her gut.

Bran was becoming more excited by the minute with their baby growing inside of her, they had both agreed they would let the sex be a surprise, the good old-fashioned saying, we don't mind just as long as the baby's healthy seemed more important than any need to know.

They both lay and hugged through most of their last night together before she flew home. It would only be five hours' sleep she would get before waking to travel back, she had a little lump in her throat for having to leave him behind, a little lump in travelling alone. She put her hands on his chest, stroking him reassuringly.

"I'm sorry about all this darling, I can't really explain anything without sounding nuts, but I know you trust me when I say this is important."

"You don't need to justify or explain anything to me Lily, I want to come back with you, that's what's more important to me."

"Don't you dare say such a thing, baby, the premier is big time. I'll be fine I promise, and your be back before you can miss me."

"Hardly true or comforting, but thanks," he said kissing her.

"I'll miss you too baby." She climbed on top of him, kissing him with an inviting libido.

She had made love to him twice that night. To her it was a beautiful feeling of sacred safety. a feeling of true love.

Arriving back to Virginia Waters, the boarding time had been fairly accurate, she was flying home in private first-class service, Lily was prepped and somewhat steady. At ease on the plane she adjusted the luxurious leather seats for a stretched-out ready for sleep position. It had not been particularly busy with no disturbance of the peace and quiet, at least the flight was going to be a pleasant one. At least one could hope anyway.

A little restless she was, she was not quite ready to fall asleep. Instead she got out her notebook with a few magazines, going over stuff in her mind, possible outcomes, possible tragedies. It was only at that given point Lily turned all the attention onto the letter Sue had given her. She had thought about Sue, the way she had vaguely managed at that time, telling her only to read it if something happened to her. Lily began to think what if it already had? No one could let her know in the air that she suggested she read the letter to herself there and then; after all, they had not got to watch the recording so maybe the letter had clues to what was really going on?

Flicking through the different magazines and books she had packed in as hand luggage she was definitely sure she had placed the letter in one of them. She definitely put it in one when she was packing for home. Just then as she was about to get annoyed hunting for the thing, she came across it in the last book she picked up to check. There it was, enveloped and sealed. She gently unsealed the envelope and pulled out the cream paper, the note to her was written on decorative scented floral paper:

Dear Lily,

If you are reading this then chances are I have died.

I wanted you to have this letter so my last thing I did on earth was to tell you the truth.

I know your already scared reading this, now don't cry, be strong.

Lily Anderson, out of all of you, you are the one I truly cherish. I want you to know how delightful you really are and a true daughter you have always been towards me. I love you as though you were my own.

Now listen, you must know the truth on who you really are.

I don't think your mother was ever going to find a way to tell you, so I have beaten her to it and left without feeling I betrayed her trust. But you must know.

When your mother got pregnant, it was really tough back then. White women with black men was no joke, it was a different world then Lily, more racist than you would believe. We wanted to protect you kids, but your mother and father turned poor overnight, they were out on their ears, nowhere to live. Lily, you are not adopted, you were given away to friends of ours that were to give you back once your mother and father became housed. The truth is Lily, you and Ruby are identical twins, with a slight difference here and there. As time went on, your father never wanted to take you back, but me and your mother kept you close by all the time, we thought it would just be best to keep you and Lily connected in some way, so we planned with your then pretend adopted mother to take you to the same elite drama school as Ruby that we both paid the fees for.

When that house burned down, when they died in that fire, we were just absolutely horrified, sick to our stomachs Lily, we were truly thankful to the good Lord you had survived, precious child.

Your mother took you back, your father had already walked out on you all. You were never adopted, you were and are an Anderson, precious Lily Anderson. You must forgive your mother, she just wanted to protect you all. Your mother comes from a place of ignorance, hiding secrets and telling lies, it will catch up with her one day I'm sure, but look after her for me. She has a heart of gold underneath.

PS I think Paul is—

Just as Lily was about to read on, the ink appeared to have run out on the paper making it virtually impossible to make out what Sue was about to say, or what she was going to say about Paul. The only thing that came to Lilys mind was – I think Paul is trying to kill me.

As she sat upright in complete, utter shock and disbelief, at least some part was finally beginning to add up. No wonder Ruby and she had both been so similar to look at, why they were so deeply connected. No wonder why, after all this time experiencing unusual coincidences, it had been no such thing as that, all along. All this precious time, it had always been the simple unexplainable magic of twin connection, twin pain, twin telepathy.

Chapter 23

Rose Anderson
Baby Sibling

DOORSTEP

I don't know if selfish would have been the best word used to describe Rose. Although her actions seemed to lack a little consideration towards her family members of late, she seemed to be chiefly concerned with her own life, oblivious to the real dangers that lay ahead.

As with all the Anderson women, life was yet to take some unexpectant turns and Rose would be no exception, protected or not, clueless or not,

Rose Anderson was about to get the biggest shock of her life yet…

Her personal affairs at home were trapped together with the diabolical emotional black hole she had found herself in, as she was releasing all sorts of anger, expressions of emotions from confusion to stupidity to self-blame,. Then she would flip every situation refusing any logic out of her way.

Rose had taken no blame in the break-up of her marriage to Matthew. Rather she had branded it false and selfish, not wasting any time in jumping ship she grasped tightly with both hands onto true love in which she knew she had now found. She suggested she have a grown, adult conversation with Matthew, pleading with him to file for a divorce as quickly as possible.

She was prepared to be as civil as he had wanted, about both Eli and the baby, until the paternity test would prove otherwise. He demanded to know every step and detail of her pregnancy, including finding out the sex of the baby due on her upcoming twenty-week scan.

Rose had a meeting scheduled later that evening with some of her colleagues as well as her managers to inform them she was a woman with child.

She had left the option open to take on one more case, but only if it was to be a crucial one.

The scan appointment was booked into an early morning slot. Matthew would be working until late evening, making her feel lucky to be accompanied and supported by Eli only, not by both of the keen, hopeful fathers to be. "May the best man win," her midwife had the nerve to say.

Her stomach was beginning to look oddly shaped. Disguised she still was underneath clothing, but to the naked eye it was obvious she was pregnant, her bump was growing quickly by each day. She had felt the baby flutter and kick many times, to finally know what she was carrying inside of her she felt extremely elated with the idea of her prayers being answered, a baby girl, a precious daughter to be born.

Devastation was bound to kick in had it been the doting son Matthew had wanted, instead.

But, optimistic and positive, she would keep up the attitude of all things possible just like Ruby had told her.

She was looking forward to seeing how her baby was growing, how her baby was doing. She had started to go over several names, strolling through different baby girl names, obsessed with searching everything girl child. She recalled the ones that had been resting in her memory.

"So what do you think of the name Alice? Or even better Ayana? It means 'beautiful flower'. It'll be like mother like daughter.?"

"Clever! And beautiful babes, I like Ayana, just makes flower sense."

He laughed alongside her. She was thrilled in his agreement and admiration of the name picked and now final, if a baby girl was to be born.

Eli had become a magnet, her best friend, and agony aunt, whereas this would usually have been Ruby. Yet her sister had been replaced by someone who she felt really got her, really understood her. It had felt a little while since she had seen her sisters, so much seemed to be going on she decided to disconnect, detachment was always a get-out ticket she would use to get out of dealing with any of her family matters. And anyway this time it was different, she thought. Everyone else had just seemed so preoccupied lately, what with Ruby never being at the manor, shacked up in some tiny apartment with some reporter?

What with Betty grieving the loss of her best friend, Lily living her best life in Hollywood, who saw that one coming, she questioned? A movie star brother-in-law welcomed into the family circle, and then of course there was her mother? Sue? Paul? Some weird triangulation was apparent to Rose, a manipulation tactic was obvious to her. Their mother was being a scapegoat to whatever lies and deceit Paul was guilty of on them both, but Rose could only question in self-regard as to why did she even have to let it be her problem? Why did she even have to be involved with all their mess as well as her own? They had all told Sue to leave him years ago. For now all she could do was concentrate on the conversations she was to engage in with her ex-partner, possibly the father of her baby, to only then later engage in another conversation announcing her pregnancy and request for maternity leave.

All in a day's grime Rose was set and ready for her day ahead.

"Make sure you call me straight away if that idiot gives you any hassle Rose, I'm not kidding, just call me OK?"

"OK macho man, besides, I'm going with a calm approach, practical thinking, I mean the guy's a lawyer, I'm not going to win any argument, so I just don't want one, babes. I long for the day that man is just a memory to me and even if I'm stuck with him for eighteen years, as they say in parenting talk. As long as he unties me from our miserable legal bond to be married, I'll be half happy with that. I want nothing from the man, I just want you Eli Bardon."

She ran her hands over his head, his hair had grown out into a short afro long enough to be plaited. When they had first met his hair had been cut low into a fade which took years off his grizzled face, with his hair grown, it portrayed maturity, a grown side to him, matched with a thick coated beard. Rose was deeply attracted to Eli from the minute she had set her eyes on him. His skin colour was darker than Matthew's was, Matthew had been on the fair side with green eyes so her mother had never associated him as a black man as such, But with Eli she would have no choice in the matter, although she was in no rush to make them both aquatinted any time soon.

She thought it was funny how two of her mother's daughter's partners were white men and the other two of her daughter's partners were black men. Not that it had really even mattered but, then again, how could it not have mattered when ever since their own father had run out on them? It was almost like the brainwashing had left them to believe that all black men suddenly all became the same – cowards? – and what now with Paul turning out to be exactly what every wife would dread, a good for nothing, nasty piece of shit of a husband, Jamaican-born just like their father had been, was only going to cause more psychological doubt in many minds. Yet for Rose and Ruby not a single person in the world could have convinced them other than that they would be better off with any other gentleman such as the ones they had fallen in love with. They would surely take down anyone that stood in there way, ridicule any pretentious judgment, even though some people were well intended, others showed great concerns, as though loving a black man would have made her life more difficult.

Yet Rose could not speak of such a life like that, not really, she had always been seen as fortunate to have been with Matthew. He was rich, successful in a white-predominated world, and it was only until she became older did she painfully realise her own skin colour had not been to her own husband's taste. Matthew was never shy on letting on to what women he was truly attracted to, the ones he liked, his type, his preference were the ones of natural blondes, blue-eyed women or better yet green eyes like his own. But in time with no bitterness held, Rose would always come back to that wonderful thought that, no matter who you were or what colour you were, there was someone for everyone, including herself.

She could only now simply wish for Matthew to find happiness with one of his very many mistresses, after all, we all deserve to be happy don't we…?

The day was never light for long in the month of December. Darkness found its wicked way upon them quickly. Looking out the apartment window she gave a shudder of doubt, the thought of just doing nothing, changing into pyjamas and watching movies in bed with Eli seemed the better one in mind.

But Rose's plans were solid plans. Once made, they would not be broken, no matter what; you could always count on Rose Anderson to be a reliable source of character.

Being entirely honest, she had felt rather strange pulling up onto the home she had once known. Already it seemed as though she was like some kind of a stranger, an unwanted visitor is how she felt just as Matthew had opened the door not long after she knocked.

Inside there was a blonde woman in a tight-fitted skirt suit sitting on one of the kitchen barstools. She was possibly one of his interns, disapprovingly she assumed.

"Don't worry about her, just business. Go on inside the lounge." Matthew had disregarded the woman talking to Rose in his usual arrogance and gaslighting nature.

The woman he dismissed looked around the same year's as herself. Rose noticed the redness in her cheeks, she could see the shock in her eyes when she was referred to as just business.

He had a stern, cold glare in his eyes, to her it was the look of audacity.

He had failed to believe she could actually walk out the door and leave him. She could the shock behind his dazzling, callous eyes.

"So I hope you've come here to apologise, I don't mind if you were just having some hormonal tantrum, Rose. I was used to your bullshit even when you weren't pregnant, it's just how you are. I get it."

"Apologise?" She almost choked as she laughed at him.

"Are you fucking kidding me? Sorry you made my life miserable more like, sorry you ignored the living daylights out of me, playing with your little toys, like the one in the kitchen? I'm not stupid Matthew."

They both bickered, traded blame, exchanging faults with each other until Rose made herself aware of the time. She hurried things up of why she was even there in the first place.

"Look Matthew, no, I've not come here to apologise, rather instead, I wanted to kindly ask for a divorce. If you could divorce me on the grounds of whatever you like, I mean, I wouldn't blame you, I'm sure the judge would grant you a very happy divorce, considering."

Matthew remained silent for a while longer. He looked so angry, bruising an ego even more damaged than it was before.

It was a very odd situation for Matthew to encounter, on one hand he only prayed he was the father to her baby, he would be prepared to take her back in a shot and ooze to the world an image of perfection. Yet on the other hand there was an insecure man who really only needed the idea of her, the idea of marriage, a safe base, a man who was petrified of weakness, who could never live or match up to his father's expectations of what a son should be like that he managed to sabotage any decent thing he possessed in his life.

Matthew had kept his high expectations of women, used double standards, seeking loyalty and obedience from a woman. Yet the hypocrisy of his own unfaithful acts became mentally and emotionally draining for Rose to bear. She felt bitter for the years spent guessing, the suspicions, with never the courage to prove it herself.

Until a woman's had enough then she's had enough and Rose certainly felt her marriage to Matthew had crashed and burned.

"I do love you, you know," he said abruptly

As Rose heard his voice, his words went around in her head,

they went in one ear and out the next, as she thought it strange what some men even recognised, or considered as love.

Could a man like Matthew even really know what love was? she doubted very much and no longer even cared.

"I have the scan in the morning, the one to find out the sex." She looked at him, seeing the hope and excitement suddenly appear, like someone had brought him back to life again. The whole situation was really quite sad.

"I'll call you as soon as I find out."

"OK," he said.

Turning to face the door as she was heading out she spoke in a calming manner.

"Please find the quickest way to end our Marriage, Matthew."

"Don't dictate anything to me, you bitch. But yeah, I'll sort something."

And just like that she walked out without looking back, clear on every reason why she had left him and feeling satisfied at those very thoughts she continued her drive on to the secure grounds of where she studied forensic science.

The offices were located at the end of a steep, narrow corridor leading onto hubs and small buildings.

She had been a little ahead of time, keeping a low head purposely trying hard not to be noticed by her fellow colleagues. She would only become the latest bit of gossip if the news got spread about. She waited out in the lobby watching and rehearsing the speech, dreading the disappointed looks she expected to be given because she was one of their best. The worst thing about it for Rose was finding out who was going to be her replacement. Whoever it was Rose had known they had better not get too comfortable. She would be back ready to fight them back to their corner, that was for sure.

"Come in Roo," spoke a cockney accent through the doors to where they would all be waiting.

"Oh thanks." She had felt nervous at that point, totally forgetting everything she had put together, she just came straight out, talking before she could hear herself think.

"I'm five months pregnant guys, it's a shock yes, end of the world? No, it's not a big deal honestly, I need twelve months' maternity leave and I'll have it sorted in childcare before it can say *Mother*. Please don't judge me."

"What the fuck Rose, that's just crap timing ain't it mate? We were really counting on you for the rest of the year, awards, appraisals, promotions that are set to start, now bloody what? OK, well yeah I'll put in for your leave request, I take it we at least got you until the very last moments, Rose."

"Oh my God, of course, I'm not going anywhere until I can't be of any good, like about to give birth literally."

As Rose did when she was a bag of nerves she babbled her way through, giving too much detail when she was suddenly saved by the sound of someone's pager. She felt relieved but also appreciated the request when she was asked if she wanted to get her hands on a crime scene that had just come through, a suspected murder case? The person who had offloaded the case to Rose was newly qualified, needed supervision and by all means not confident, pleasantly relieved, she accepted the work, which was equally satisfying for both women.

"OK Rose, well there's a detective on site already been radioed in, a pal of mine. I'll see that you can ride along with him."

"That's super, thanks boss."

She sent a quick texted message to Eli, only God knew what

time she would be getting back to him now.

"OK! I'm ready to go," Ruby said, jumping into the unmarked police car. After all, it was just one more case, just like she had said she would take. Eli would not mind, she felt sure of that.

With no questions asked Rose got involved in general chit-chat. The radio was crackling with coded information as they were talking and driving, she had not been so curious as to ask any details or questions about the suspected murder, she was just feeling lucky and grateful she was still seen as one of the best, the top girl.

"This will be a nasty one, love. You ready to see the grotesque cruelty of our world?"

"Listen! I've seen it all, nothing shocks me anymore, that's the saddest thing about it."

It was taking the left turn and then the sharp left when Rose started to fluster in a slight discomforting panic. It was one of those sickening moments when you sensed danger.

"Erm sorry, I never did as. Where are we going? Where's the location?"

"Clifton Manor."

Rose shrieked in disbelief. At the same time she heard the radio crackling as an officer related the details at the scene. A female was pronounced dead.

Sierra, Uniform, Echo.

Rose demanded the car to be stopped, to pull over where she could be sick instantly.

She was muted like that time before, in her frazzled head, she repeated the address, Clifton Manor. She knew that place, a place she knew as home,

She began to make sense of the alphanumeric letters the officer had radioed in. Sierra, Uniform, Echo spelt out the name

SUE.

Using the sickness as some excuse, a freak of pregnant nature, she was frantic but determined not to be kicked off the case. The victim was going to be Sue, she knew it was, Sue had been murdered, and she was on her way to the manor, the home she had been a part of with her mother and sisters, she was about to witness the murder of a loved one they had all loved and been a part of one another's lives.

Just when she had really thought she had seen it all in a day's work, she discovered what a normal day for a pathologist was. Beginning to look like, there were some days where she learned to be so emotionally resilient she became numb at any disturbing sight, the twisted excitement that eventually would kick in when you're about to discover the realism of the gory, horrifying truths of different victims. Some that would usually take others years to climb up the ladder to get to those opportunities.

It was true Rose had indeed seen enough to give her that widened knowledge. She had the advantage of being slightly ahead of other police officers in her ranking, however; Rose Anderson was about to get one of her nastiest shocks as she continued the journey to the crime scene.

The car was reaching closer, turning down onto familiar grounds to a random spontaneous crime investigation.

It was a very peculiar feeling as she was driving into the dark, forest-hidden manor of Sue and Paul's.

She had goosepimples prickling under her skin like no other time before, she had been stricken with primitive fears.

Nothing could have prepared Rose Anderson for death like this one. Nothing could have prepared her for this murder, murder on her own doorstep.

Chapter 24

Florence Anderson
The Mother

BLOODSTAINS

Florence Anderson had always been a bit forgetful. Most of the time she had put the sole blame on herself for the way she handled responsibilities, for the way she would just simply block out anything damaging or hurtful. She even believed if you blocked out too much memory your brain would eventually stop working one day, something her daughters had told her was rubbish and that her views were dated, old-fashioned myths that came with no scientific proof to how a person becomes forgetful, other than the possible causes of old age, or through ill health, or through accidents, that the sisters knew of or had paid any attention to. It would be nobody's thought for such a thing.

Although Florence's brain was still working, it was working in a different kind of way.

A way where Betty had noticed after some personal studies, she was showing signs of delusions, visual hallucinations and short-term memory loss, her mood and confusing spells varied significantly from one minute of the day to the next.

The disorder deemed to come on rapidly and suddenly.

There would be moments of glorified memories her mother fluctuated back and forth with. Often in a trance she would remember the past love of her life with Mr Anderson, at times it would seem Florence was suffering from prosopagnosia. where that part of her brain would usually be responsible for recognising faces, rather now, shockingly, that part for Florence had become damaged. She did however still thankfully recognise each and all of her daughters, she knew exactly who Ben was, but the confusion lay twisted and deep and about to turn into some real life disturbing moments for Florence.

Florence Anderson would on some days see Mr Anderson in Paul's face. Paul would all of a sudden become him, sometimes in those moments she was right back married to him. From the outside looking in anybody would have thought she was in lust or had some infatuated crush on her best friend's husband, but with hallucinations, and being somewhere in her past, Florence grew an unhealthy bond with Paul. Attracted to him as she was at one stage, he had always reminded her of Mr Anderson and in some moments Florence started to think Paul was him at times. Those were the cruel moments when Paul would take full advantage of her vulnerability, targeting her with sexual filth and blackmail. On some occasions Florence would recognise Paul as the good old dear friend, but then there were other few times his face would appear as a demon. She would suddenly quickly remember she knew he was a bad man, that he had done something to her. It had all become extremely petrifying and a confusing time.

But despite everything her duty towards Sue had become familiar, routine visits to her withering best friend, but if only Florence had been aware that every time she unlocked the bedroom door, why it had been locked in the first place? Every time she went into Sue's potent-smelling bedroom she would cry in utter shock like it was always the first time. She would stand in disbelief at how unwell Sue would look.

Florence became forgetful of every conversation they ever shared together, right up until Sue became vague and lifeless.

The two women had plotted, planned and shared everything that had really been going on with the both of them.

How very sad it was though that, as soon Florence would leave her, she would leave Sue's home forgetting about every last detail of the horrendous acts of evil that were actually happening in that dark and eerie manor. And who was to say, who knew if it could have made all the difference to a victim's life? If only Florence Anderson, had just remembered to call the police.

The short-term memory disorder was about to have its advantages and disadvantages to what really happened on that dark, forbidden cold night when Florence Anderson went back to the manor for the very last time…

Back to the night of the manor: when Florence Anderson had been in a state faffing around in her master's bedroom hiding the outfit she was to change into at Sue's, at that point of time her mind was existing in reality. Paul was the demon once more, a wreck she was, alone in her room, confused by how things had got to where they had got, crying silently so as to not to disturb her husband who could not really have guessed anything different was going on other than menopause and a best friend crisis. For him that explained her aggression, her weirdness and detachment towards him, he had long decided to just leave her to it.

Nobody could have really predicted the gruesome ordeal behind the closed doors of Sue and Paul's manor, not even Ben.

The journey over to the property was always a short one. Once she arrived that evening, her state of mind was current, she was going to do be doing her usual bit in attending and aiding to

Sue. She had read over and over a text message from Paul demanding her not to forget a dress he specifically wanted her to wear for him. She had reluctantly sneaked it into her handbag ready to change into once at Sue's.

It was quite sad in the way that such manipulation was being used.

Paul had been reminding her frequently of their unfaithful act, he had told her she was a lying bitch anytime she had denied it when she adamantly only spoke of it being a moment of pure madness.

Somewhere during that night her mind got lost in fantasy, almost as though that night with Paul had really been a romantic night of her past with Mr Anderson. But she had already forgotten the incident.

This brought out an incredible rage from Paul. Not sure if Florence had been trying to play the crazy card, he would be sure to tell every member of the family about their one-night stand, he would tell them all that Florence was the one turning a blind eye on poor old dying Sue, convincing everyone he genuinely took her word for granted that, each time she left his manor, she would tell him Sue was absolutely fine and how he believed her like a fool.

Paul had recorded Florence on his phone several times as she would say the same words walking out.

"Bye then, see you again tomorrow, Sue's fine, I've locked the door."

It was something she would always remind him she had done so.

And in no remorse, in no shame, Paul felt certain he had the upper hand, but little did he know he was yet to face some nasty repercussions of his own.

Sometimes one could say thank goodness for secrets, for there was now a secret camera that was also recording him. His every move inside the poor defenceless woman's bedroom would soon become vital evidence with life-changing effects.

Florence remembered feeling hot, as if her temperature had spiked once she had arrived at the manor.

It had not been easy trying to shake things off, to just read and carry on.

Florence would often speak out loud to herself it became her own way of remembering to carry out general chores.

At nine p.m. the manor had been freezing cold, the only heat coming in was from the kitchen. The other rooms in the rest of the manor had been turned down to zero in all of the rooms including Sue's.

It was a spiteful, deliberately intended to cause suffering to the poor helpless woman which had just been one of the disturbing acts that had been going on.

Every time Florence would stand at the bedroom door then a slight trigger would unsettle her. She would question why was the bedroom door locked? Unlocking it would land her in the same confusion as the first time she did so. For the details had been shared but always forgotten.

That nasty Paul had been locking Sue in every day for a very long time, with no other visitors other than Sue, taking full control of her finances. Using next-of-kin benefits in accessing information from her GP notes, he portrayed a convincing disposition in attempts to persuade another character, he craftily sought confidential advice, even stooping so low to leaving paper notes marked with male domestic victim abuse emergency hotlines on her bedroom dressing table.

Paul was premeditating a plot to kill his wife in cold blood, making false claims about her excessive drinking. Her violent behaviour which was now a threat to him and to herself. Everything about her mental health and position would be recorded on medical files as he knew they would be, which was all part of his plan. When listened to by others he pleaded with them to believe him when he said she had become a liability.

It was true that Paul's thoughts were ones of him really believing he had his situation all under control, well that's what he had certainly thought.

That evening he would wait and hope for Florence to become suddenly confused or back to somewhere in the past, he had caught onto this unusual behaviour immediately. He then began to notice how quickly she came to forget he had thrown Sue across the glass dining table. He had been shocked to see how she had quickly forgotten everything.

He was very aware of the times she had accidently called him Mr Anderson.

At first Paul thought she was just playing childish games.

Most of the time he would only assume she wanted it as much as he had, but she was acting too proud to admit it happened.

But soon it became clear to him Florence was not really in any position to know where or what was going on, especially when it usually got to a certain time in the evening which he then deviously arranged for her to come back to look after Sue whenever her mental health was in question. Paul did not think or know anything about memory loss, nor did he care, he could only see a malicious, sick way to take advantage of her when she was in a fragile state of mind, where he would mock her, he would tease her and make her go hysterical, he would cheat her mind by convincing her he was Mr Anderson by singing the songs he knew she had once loved dancing with him. He called out certain pet names he knew Mr Anderson had named her, names that would suddenly make her dive into Paul's wicked arms.

But it had been a blessing in disguise that the man had no patience.

Throughout the last few times Florence had come over Paul could not understand why he was struggling to get Florence to recognise her past husband. This delayed his perverted greedy plan.

For when Florence had been in what Paul had thought was crazy land, these were the easiest times for him. He would grab Florence, sexually molest her, play mind tricks with her. His greed eventually led him to wanting to take things further, plotting to have sex with her consensually or not, one way or another he would plan to have his wicked way again.

Only Paul's plan had not been going the way he was hoping it would go. Instead he became agitated by the fact he could not recently get her to recognise his face as Mr Anderson, not able to bring him back to the forefront of her mind. It infuriated him, he became so frustrated he used bullying tactics to blackmail her when she was in her natural state instead.

Florence had got so use to Pauls convincing nature, his fabricated stories of Sue being drunk who was constantly trying to throw herself down the stairs so that by locking her in was for her own safety, that Florence took that piece of information as sacred, that tiny detail became imperative that the bedroom door must be locked, just there were equal amounts of times she had no explanation or memory to why she consistently continued to lock that bedroom door until the very end.

For whatever unexplained reason, Florence's mind that

particular night had stayed emotionally intact with her whereabouts. She knew Paul had been trying to kill Sue at that point, she looked at the same red wine bottle she always looked at, wondering why on earth would Paul be giving Sue alcohol, why was it just lying on top of her chest? But on that evening Florence may have had many questions to ask but the horrifying truth was right under her nose. Paul had been poisoning Sue mixing arsenic with red wine, tricking her at first, deliberately and cunningly intoxicating her, before encouraging or forcing her to drink the poison. At some point Sue would have been unaware of what was happening to her until she knew, until she felt the inside gut feeling he was trying to kill her. Sue eventually gave up trying to free herself in the times she did have any of her strength left, the fist fights that came her way when she would try to escape in the beginning of it all, the way he would boot her from the top of the stairs to their bottom, then collect her battered body, carrying her back to the bed where he would then violently rape her before locking the bedroom door until the next day he would return to repeat his evil plan. A plan to get paid out from her full life insurance, staging her murder as a drunken accidental tragedy, he would state Sue died from choking on her own drunken vomit, which he had all known they had all seen her do in her good old days, the days before her body was no longer responsive. It was too late for anything to have been done now, he had succeeded in his sick twisted plan, for that evening when Florence had attended to her, Sue was already cold dead. She had died alone, in no state of her own either, she would have been nothing other than a dead poisoned lost soul. Florence could feel she hated the man she knew was waiting for her downstairs in the kitchen. At that point she knew deep down in herself, she was not the same woman anymore, she knew there must be something so terribly wrong with her, she knew that could be the only valid reason to why she never did do anything about what was happening to her dear friend, but for some strange reason Florence continued to stay alert that evening, she thought long and hard talking out loud to Sue as though she was still alive. "I'm going to kill him, Sue."

Florence had already confessed previously and unintentionally to Sue in one of her emotional outbursts that she had slept with Paul, but she thought it was Mr Anderson. She had sobbed to Sue confessing that she would see him sometimes in Paul's face. it was the only time she remembered or ever spoke of the incident in the times when they had both spoken.

At that time Sue knew Florence herself was not well. She never blamed her or even cared, she desperately wanted to escape her abuser. She also felt useless she could not help Florence either, all she could do whilst she was strong enough was to speak out, cursing her, telling her to piss off and not come back reminding Florence to keep her away from Paul, to not come back to the manor, but each time Florence would go back, as if for the first time all over again.

How heartbroken Sue would have become in her darkest hours, how petrified she must have felt inside, alone in pain slowly learning the truth and holding onto every last bit of hope. Her life that lay in the hands of her dearest friend were not lying in the hands of a sane woman, the only peace Florence could take from her ill health was the understanding that she could not get the help her dearest friend had also begged her for. It was not long before Sue gave up all hope entirely, in the later stages nobody would have known if she had drunk all the poison herself that sad, mistaken night, as the empty bottle of deadly poison lay tilted on top of her still, naked body that evening.

Florence could feel something was going to happen, she was certain she would kill him herself.

As she completed her usual tasks, ignoring Sue's dead body, she had looked for her bag to change outfits.

As her eyes scanned the room it was something simple like a black top hat sitting on the armchair that she spotted and, just like that, Florence's mood had begun to change from current to the state of being deluded. Now she was a young woman again excited by the feeling of the clear memories of her beloved Mr Anderson, of course the dress she had changed into as she looked back at her reflection in the mirror at herself was because the man who she believed was really waiting for her downstairs was of Mr Anderson, the love of her life, instead.

How the brain can play tricks on the mind, as it so clearly did for Florence.

She had walked slowly down the stairs, asking herself as she went down if she had definitely locked the bedroom door, just in case something should happen to Sue. With no memory to just witnessing her cherished friend's death, Florence got further downstairs heading in the direction of the kitchen to where Paul was waiting for her.

She found herself enter the kitchen area. It had been noisy with music beating in her eardrums, however this time it was not the familiar sounds of reggae he once charmed her with in making her feel safe, excited, back to living her past. No, this time it was fast, hard and heavy-sounding music, it agitated Florence so much she triggered almost immediately, staring at Paul as though he was now an impostor, what had he done with her husband? This time she was staring at the face of the Devil.

Paul was drunk, his version of a red-blooded male was intense with his beady eyes glassy and bloodshot in the dimmed lights he continued to watch Florence as though she was a toy he so wanted to desperately play with.

He observed her feeling unsure of what kind of mood she may have been in.

Nor did he care. He leaped over to her with entitlement, Florence's reaction was to jump back and run towards the utility part of the kitchen, to where all the knives were stacked in a wooden holder for all different shapes, blades and sizes. Without hesitation or any real thought she grabbed a green-coloured knife, with no acknowledgment as to how sharp it may have been or to why when Paul had suddenly rushed in after her. When he stood standing inches away from her sounding furious, demanding her to turn around and face him as it was just supposed to be another ordinary night in his eyes, but as Florence got lost in those chilling moments. She looked into his eyes, she believed she saw a few faces for the few seconds she stared at him, his eyes first turned to Mr Anderson's, they then turned into a stranger she did not recognise, and then she realised she was looking into the eyes of pain. There Paul stood gasping for air, bleeding horrendously, within a blink of an eye, Florence had stabbed Paul twice, once in the chest and once in the thigh. It was his thigh at that point that looked as though it was causing the blood to uncontrollably spill out from him. There was so much blood, it looked like she had hacked at him to death. Suddenly she slipped into the wet blood-soaked marble floors pushing herself back on the red-stained ground, she still wanted to be far away from him as she possibly could.

"Florence, what have you done man?" He used the side of the table for support in sliding towards her.

"Come here you fucking bitch." Crippled, with vessels punctured for sure, the pints of blood Paul was losing led her to believe he would have to try and find a way to stop the bleeding. It looked like the main problem was coming from the top part of his leg before he would be able to do anything or even stand a chance of survival, she had hoped so anyway.

Florence picked herself up from the floor, still holding the knife. When she looked at the knife she had used as weapon was when she dropped it from her trembling hands.

The knife had fallen slightly behind the back of the fridge. For some odd reason she ran back up towards Sue's bedroom, she was distressed and confused at this point, she had fumbled around with the set of keys to the locked door and, like always, she cursed away that it was even locked in the first place. Desperate to get in she panicked as she heard Paul's heavy breathing, in miraculous strength or plain shock he was coming up the stairs and, just at the right time, she had finally done it, she had unlocked the bedroom door, now she was inside Sues bedroom Florence became shocked and horrified to identify the deceased body as Sue, she instantly felt death in that moment, she froze.

She felt like a statue as palpitations beat so hard and so fast in the room that she was now in with a dead friend and a violent man.

Paul managed to make it into the bedroom, she could see he was badly injured, he was weaker, in dark skin his tone appeared ashen.

Florence took a leap of faith. She ran past him in such force he stumbled to the floor, and the strange but fortunate thing was that tiny little detail of hers, the one that was imbedded in her brain, it would be for Sue's own good, to protect her, prevent Sue from having any more accidents. Florence proceeded to lock the bedroom door, walking away calmly.

Paul was begging and pleading, yelling, crying and screaming at her not to do it, not to leave him locked in bleeding to death. For Paul, he was now living his own nightmare come true as he lay bleeding in the same room in which he had abused, tortured and poisoned to death the woman he was supposed to love cherish and protect. How very sad it is that so much can change in a person and how much pain one can suffer behind closed doors. Well he was certainly the one suffering now.

Florence could never have expected or could have known that on that cold winter's night in December she would kill a man, stab him twice, once her long-lived neighbour, her best friend's husband, nor had she known on that very same night would in fact be the last time she would get to visit or ever lock Sue's bedroom door, ever again.

In lots of ways it could have seemed Florence's neurological disease could have been seen as a cruel condition with overwhelming stages to follow. Yet at that moment, that evening, quite blissfully, Florence continued with her short-term memory, losing memory of anything current, blocking out things one should never block out. Yet for Florence, the door she had locked was now forgotten, she was back to a life where she felt everything was just fine again, she was fine, Sue was fine, and everybody she loved was fine. Everybody she did recognise, she knew, she loved them deeply.

She never quite remembered why she was alone once she was back at her manor that evening, or where Ben had been, but she was sure he was busy working. She had remembered hearing her daughter's voice as she put the kettle on, then walking to her bedroom to change.

The hallway lights had been dimmed, so the manor was not left in complete darkness, just enough light for anyone to see.

For that evening it had been Ruby who had caught sight of her mother just as she was coming out of the bathroom.

Ruby quickly corrected herself, she blinked twice, shook her head, thinking her mother was never usually out that late anymore, but Ruby rejected her intrusive thoughts as being no more than her usual outrageous nonsense, because just for a second of doubt, literally in that second, the crazy thought that had come rushing to Ruby's mind was.

"Mother, what is that you're covered in?"

"Mother are those bloodstains???"

Wednesday's child is a child of woe,
    A mind of sadness learns life's solace so
    But even in her lonely tears
    She wakes, she seeks life's better years
    And all that broke her
    She will learn to mend
    She will see another day
    She will love again.
    By Rebecca McKenzie
    (Wednesday's Child)

Chapter 25

Ruby Anderson
Firstborn Sibling

WHEN LIFE HAPPENS

When the baby sister Rose Anderson arrived at a family friend's manor, she discovered the murders, one being a beloved family friend. It was however a somewhat different evening going on for Ruby Anderson. For Ruby, on that dark evening in Sue's last dying moments, she had nothing better to do other than to soak up the love of her boyfriend. That's the thing about life, people will live different ones, sometimes disturbing things will go on behind closed doors, lives we could not bear to speak of or wish on anyone, not even for our worst enemies.

It was precisely two days until the birthday of Ruby Anderson. Forty years of age seemed it had caught up quickly, now as each person can only try to look ahead, look forward to new chapters, beginnings or endings. Even she could never have known, she could never have seen such cruelty ahead, such an eerie path, such pain, as life was about to happen so viciously indeed for Miss Ruby Anderson.

On Monday afternoon the day before Christmas Eve she lay in between his thick, muscular shaped, deep brown arms, making circling patterns around his chest. It was like she had no fear whenever she was with him, life with him seemed so easy, so into place, he was the love of her life, her comforter, for the first time she heard herself asking how possible was it that both her and Lily became so lucky in love when they had both never found it before Mark Harrington and Bran Glassier came into their lives? It was so pathetic now she thought about it, to have wasted all those times she did obsessing about her failed attempts of love, all the judgment she took, the frowned expressions, outraged reactions towards her promiscuous adventures she'd once had. Most women locked up their husbands spotting any sight of Ruby Anderson, but right at that moment on that cold morning, she saw herself as a taken lady, her heart belonged to one man only, Mr Harrington. In her moment of lying next to him in bed she had been given the feeling of meeting all those high expectations of the way a woman was supposed to feel when she was turning older, turning forty, the safe, excited, living-in-real life happiness kind of feeling, in other words Ruby could not help but feel even despite all the strange and diabolical goings on, she was living a happy after ending, if there could be such a thing…?

"As lovely as this is, doing nothing beside you in bed Mark, I got to go, Betty will be here any minute, I just can't wait to see Lily, I feel like I could burst," she said excitedly clapping her hands.

"I wonder if she looks any different yet? She's reaching twenty-three weeks' pregnant now, Rose is twenty weeks', but she looks no different really."

"Yeah I know, but what I don't know is why Lily is coming back a day early and without Bran? Are they OK with each other?"

"Yeah, everything's fine babes, just some family stuff we all need to sort out. We're kind of worried about Mum and we all need a plan of action, and anyway, like you said, she's only back a day early. It was too risky coming home Christmas Eve, anyway, God forbid she missed my birthday or something. We have this special connection thing on my birthday, it's always more than just Christmas for us, it's like in a way that it's both our birthdays. I know it sounds ridiculous, screwed up, but that's me and Lily." She made an expression of helplessness, unaware of the truth awaiting her.

Throwing on one of his oversized shirts, she headed off into the bathroom.

This Monday's morning had been pitch-black and frosty. She had woken to a thick white atmosphere with a sheet of snow covering the country grounds of Virginia Waters, and a beautiful sight it was. Festivity filled the streets, glistening trees all lit up with each window flashing with lights that were shining from practically every bungalow, cottage and house there was on Mark's private road, it seemed on lavender Drive – Virginia Waters, the whole village was awake with her at five a.m. morning time.

It really was her favourite time of the year, so she stopped to appreciate it all. She could not help but notice how lovely the Christmas tree had looked standing in his tiny apartment. She drifted slightly to a mind of greed and want, slightly fazed by the feeling like she was missing all the real magic back at the manor. Yet more importantly she did feel pleased she would be spending their first romantic Christmas together from Christmas Eve until the end of January she thought, with a smug smile fixed upon her face.

The manor was the most enchanting winter wonderland experience any family could only dream of having. Virginia Waters was one of those ideally pretty places, it was a polite, friendly little village where they had all lived, everybody tuned into positivity and good will on every calendar occasion, but particularly more at Christmas the whole town would just come alive.

Presents were all done and dusted sitting under the tree of each home of the Anderson women. Florence had done hers by September before any of her drastic personality changes had started, fortunately everyone's gifts had been ready to give out, sealed and wrapped in fine crafted Christmas wrapping paper, the ones with shiny bows were for the special gifts.

And Christmas was set to go ahead. The family would be gathered together in the big old manor, bringing with them new partners, new chapters, changes, misfortunes and still to be known a few heartbreaks and tragedy.

But whatever Christmas would plan out for the Anderson family, it was certainly going to be a very different one than any before.

Freezing water came gushing out of the shower pipes. It always took several minutes for the water to heat up, something that grinded on her so much she knew at that point she would pursue a crafty plan that would lead to herself and Mark permanently moving into her mother's manor. Well, eventually, she thought, after all, in the present days they spent every night together either in the manor or at his apartment, it was just she was convinced his place was far too small for a woman such as herself to live comfortably in. She imagined moving into a larger space she felt doing such a thing could benefit them financially as people paid a fortune to rent. Even if it had been a shoebox like Mark's apartment, they could save any profit made for a deposit of their own. She had it all nicely figured out.

As she felt the water turn to a warm heat she stepped entirely under the pouring water. Rubys guilt began to taunt her slightly, regretful of her bold actions of turning down the leading role in the series she was to star in, knowing her bank account would have been settled generously. Now she did not even know when she would see her next pay cheque let alone earn a small fortune like she could have done.

But there was something about Mark that made her feel perfect with or without money.

She dressed appropriately for the airport, she wore a warm matching loungewear set, thick long Ugg boots, the final bit of gear to face the deep December winter's morning was a wind-proof, furred down to the ankles-long coat.

Mark had been satisfied with her sensible and practical choice, no heels, no clutch bag. With a nod of satisfaction he stood for a moment just standing, staring at her hard, capturing that very moment of her, her beautiful face covered up by a furry hood, a thick scarf, her body, her doll-like figure hidden behind more fur. He had never seen anything so precious, so wanted and so desired as he saw her that morning before she left, right there, right then he had known Ruby was the one.

It was on that cold December's day he had told her he would never hurt her, how much he would always love her.

It was a day she felt like the most loved, most lucky woman alive.

"Oh, by the way ladybug, I might have to pop out tomorrow evening." He looked masterful as he smiled at her.

"And yes I know it will be Christmas Eve, but I got to sort something extremely important out. Don't worry, it's a surprise for your birthday, so don't be asking no paranoid questions, you got nothing to worry about my darling, OK?"

"OK," she said red-faced, excited and intrigued as to what surprise it could be.

"I trust you to make good choices." She kissed him sensuously, arousing him. It had just been the idea of her that sent him spinning.

"I can't believe I'm going to be forty? I mean, what does that even mean? Am I supposed to feel different? Act older? It's kind of weird it's on a Wednesday, the first Wednesday since I was born, strange really. It feels like a spiritual test is about to be cast upon me?" Her eyes squinted into space as she thought about the next chapter of her life ahead.

"Where do you get your silly nonsense from? I just don't know," he said, shaking his head.

Betty had left the engine running for a while before Ruby made her appearance, entering Bettys four-by-four jeep that got her through all weathers, paid and bought for from David, Betty had always said as greedy and selfish it was to have a large car, at least the large machines for vehicles had a better and firm grip on the road than any sports car could have.

They were set to get to Lily on time as expected with little to no disruptions, the motorway was looking clear and deserted with all lanes open for use.

The journey consisted of Betty learning more about Ruby's nightmares, whilst Ruby learned of Betty's intense worry that their mother was suffering from dementia. The girls had spoken of possible outcomes, solutions if any, their entire family, worse case scenarios and positive outcomes.

Life almost seemed like a sliding door, it was time all four sisters to meet on the same page starting with the possible dementia issue. Lily was next to find out, and baby Rose would be informed as soon as they got home.

Ruby felt her throat go tight. As usual this was always her big give away something was wrong, she would choke on her words before they came out.

"Betty," Ruby said, to get her sisters full attention. "Lily did tell me to keep quiet until we see her but…" Ruby went quiet, she hesitated, but not enough to hold back on getting things of her chest.

"I think Mum and Sue are in trouble, that's why Lily is also coming home, not just because of our premonitions and weird sense of danger. It's Mum sis, we also found a secret video camera, but we did not watch it, it's back round at Sue's place, we were trying to see what was going on over there, God, things are a real mess Betty."

"Also," Ruby added, "I saw Mother in the hallway, as I was coming out of the main bathroom. That shower is stronger than the one of mine, that evening I just felt like a long hard shower before Mark turned up," She coughed again. "But I'm sure I saw Mother with bloodstains all over her, I'm just sure of it."

There was complete silence as Betty switched off the radio from the car. She drove with force and speed for a few seconds before becoming rational again.

"OK, let's not worry, we're all going to make sure we find out what the hell is going on with our family once and for all," Betty replied ominously.

At that point in time, Ruby, Betty nor Lily had known such harrowing, such terrifying ordeals had been going on underneath their own noses. The Anderson sisters were still very yet to learn of the murders on their own doorstep, of Sue's torture, of her tragic, calculated death.

They were yet to hear of the miserable suffering death Paul himself had faced. Rose was the only sister who had known what happened at Sue and Paul's manor. It was a horrid burden to carry for poor baby Rose and with all three of her sisters unreachable.

By the next morning they would be nowhere in sight.

It just so happened that Rose had just missed them as they left for the airport and Ruby had missed all Rose's desperate phone calls from the night before to the missed calls at five thirty a.m. that morning as she was entering Betty's car. With their iPhones resting deeply into the bottom of both of their bags, they never heard her calling, they never knew a thing.

Betty had parked in one of the airport's car parks, expensive as it was, but to them it was worth every penny. It was already packed and busy with travellers coming and going to and from wherever. Ruby and Betty they were off to the pick-up point, a carefully picked out meeting location where Lily would expect them to be waiting for her.

They had both been far too distracted to pay any real attention to the missed calls and urgent texting from Rose and it seemed like the end part of where they needed to be to meet Lily was miles away from their car, but still, they laughed away foolishly messing about, putting all troubles and stresses behind them. Just for a few seconds they forgot themselves and were back to being carefree, young women.

Lily spotted them, dragging the wheels of her suitcase, beaming, racing down towards them, rushing her way past as if she was dying to come out with the most incredible news. Which of course was exactly that, with the letter still gripped tightly into her hand, and tears rolling down her cheeks, Lily burst out with a voice frantic, tears distorting her words.

"We are twins Ruby, we are twins." She forced the letter to be read. Betty took the piece of paper and read out loud exactly the message Lily had read on the plane to herself from Sue, her dying confession about the truth of their identity and their mother's lies to protect her fear of rejection from her daughter's.

All three sisters were inconsolable for a good while. Betty became completely fascinated, delighted that they could finally make sense of their weird, telepathic connections and, as for Ruby, well she was practically beside herself. A feeling of true sense of belonging, an overdue sigh of relief it was to finally know that it really had been both of their birthdays, after all those years they celebrated, they were never crazy after all.

And how grateful they were to Sue for the truth, to be turning the big four zero together, her twin. The truth was out in full effect at last.

Although Lily landed in Gatwick early enough, the hours they spent in the airport, talking, crying, screaming, using every emotion possible with all that was going on in their lives, as they each discussed plans for their mother's well-being, the morning quickly flew by to the afternoon. They found a table to eat, spoke some more, then sat still like veg digesting all they ate.

Enjoying the atmosphere, winding their energy levels down, they all dreaded the lengthy walk back to the car park.

They all agreed they must leave before dark as the sky would now only get darker by the hour.

The drive leaving the airport was not the smooth one they'd hoped for. Experiencing a tyre burst a few miles down, the sisters managed to safely pull into a lodge. It was already almost pitch black with no clue as to where they had ended up, so they decided to just rough it out for the night, Christmas Eve would be the next day and would be the day they would get home for sure.

Ruby could only think of how much she was already missing Mark. It was a stage where one night without him seemed impossible but still, she thought, at least she would have him for the rest of her life.

By the time the girls had all finished speaking with their

partners about their mini disaster, together with the outrageous, bewildering twin news, the women were excited and exhausted. The day really had turned to night quickly, with it now feeling late. It was suggested, Rose would have left a voicemail had it been that urgent, that they would all call her first thing in the morning, so she would not be worried about, them and try to rescue them by finding and picking them up in a lodge in London. As soon as morning came with light they would get help changing the tyre from the kind reception porters and head back home.

As for Rose, the fact her sisters were all together, lost, broken down somewhere in London made the training for the job easier, that you should never deliver bad news on the phone and certainly not by voicemail. After all, she knew all too well you can never predict what a person's reactions would be to crime and murder. For their own safety, Rose would wait for them to come home but, until then, she was making sure she was finding, stashing and keeping any vital evidence tracing her mother to the murder scene away from the police investigation. The manor had been roped up and sealed off all that evening with open drop-ins from officials and officers guarding the area.

Rose had seen everything on that video camera. She was the only person who had seen everything and she was going to make sure it stayed that way, she was going to make sure her mother was on protected grounds.

Back at the lodge the room they managed to book into was a double room with a double and single bed inside, Lily and Ruby shared willingly, and Betty had expected nothing less than her own space, disgusted with it being a single bed. After a few sighs, grunts and groans, Betty started falling asleep along with her two sisters.

They had discussed their own life journeys, they each put more pieces of the family puzzles together, each solving and piecing together more sense of who they were.

Before they had fallen asleep, Ruby had stared up to the ceiling, recalling everything that happened so far, to what was becoming another end to another year. There had been Georgina's funeral, Rose's affair, and pregnant too which man? She then opened up another image in her mind, she recalled the night she saw Paul violently throw Sue across the kitchen table, again she shifted her thoughts to receiving the delightful news of being offered the part to lead as an actress, Ruby then visioned the perfect men who had entered their lives, Lily's engagement, and her baby news also.

She squeezed in another brain-frazzling thought, about them being real life twins, with her mind active just like a yo-yo on a bit of string she lay quietly, her first set of thoughts were good and positive ones were shortly followed by the bad thoughts and negative rumination. She dwelled on their mother's health, and it was Betty's words that fiddled around the most before she did fall sound asleep.

"Life," Betty had said. "What's it all about anyway?" no one in the room could answer…

Morning had arrived sharply, with another bite of cold chill to the air.

"Morning girls, merry Christmas Eve. Did you sleep well? Twins? Wow." Betty said, already up, reading the time as nine thirty a.m. she pulled her jumper back on with her jeans.

Ruby's selective hearing issue was a deliberate attempt to ignore her on this occasion, she would hear of no such thing about having to get up feeling awfully drained.

"Well, I never wanted to say anything," spoke a timid voice from Lily,

"I thought it might've been indigestion but sis, I've been getting these cramps all evening. Oh my God, do you think something's wrong? I shouldn't be getting these pains, not now almost twenty-three weeks surely?"

Betty became still in her actions, her face hardened and her tone became monotone, detached. She became Nurse Betty, telling Lily to stay put, to lie back down on the bed.

Ruby woke up from an instant feeling of panic.

Already guessing there was something going on with the baby, Ruby called for an ambulance as she could hear in the background Betty asking if there was any bleeding, and from one to ten what was her pain score…?

"You don't have any bleeding, nor do you have a temperature sis, I'm sure everything is fine, but were just get you looked at to be on the safe side OK?" Betty was calm.

"OK," Lily sobbed, afraid to move, to breathe. She began to wonder if her own sixth sense was of what she feared the most, she just could not lose the baby. Lily cried for Bran, but Ruby was already on the case, he would be catching the next flight in.

Between all three of the sisters they had decided, once the tyre had been changed, that Ruby would head on back to the manor to watch their mother, and to check that baby Rose was OK. Since Betty was amazing at keeping things calm and in order it made sense that she stayed with Lily, following her to the nearest hospital. The good thing was that Betty gave reassurance to being in London, she knew it was the best place for her to be seen and the other good thing that crossed her mind is how close they had finally all become. Betty felt her part, her place as a sister, more than ever before.

Betty was sensitive in parting Ruby away from Lily, once the paramedics arrived up to the room Lily was encouraged to sit in the wheelchair to go down to the ambulance. They held hands all the way down and, in the vehicle, Ruby whispered, "Sis, don't you feel it? Don't be scared, you and the baby are going to be fine, I just know it."

Earlier on the phone, Betty had given the medical team all the information of all Rose's symptoms she'd been getting. It seemed the helpful operators were flooded with emergencies but they felt assured there was no immediate risks for the mother and baby, with Betty's experience and monitoring Lily, carrying out all necessary checks, reporting in and recording any time Lily was getting a pain, All was in control the pains seemed irregular and mild, Lily's pains could have been the Braxton hicks or even indigestion problems, she really did not want to assume the worse or over generalise, she was no midwife but always knew how to put on the brave face that came in the role of a nurse.

The ambulance had taken two hours to arrive, the journey to the hospital would take another fifty minutes. Lily squeezed her hand as she was put onto the ramp into the vehicle.

"I hope you're right Rubes, I need you to be right on this one." Unable to turn around to see her, she did have that calming feeling Ruby whispered of, she was calm as the double doors of the ambulance closed, Betty and Lily were on the way to A&E.

BACK AT THE MANOR.

The drive seemed quicker on the way back home than the one there to the airport. Ruby was grateful she managed to get back safe and sound.

It was another day where the hours were disappearing into sight, life was sure moving fast.

Taking the right turn to her mother's manor, she was home at last. She felt like she needed Mark so badly in the flesh it was beyond real.

She pulled up onto the gravel forecourt, staring at the large manor grounds.

Mark had been there waiting for her, open arms ready to greet her. Ruby had asked him to stay at the manor once she knew she could not get back, to keep an eye their mother.

"Hello, you," he said, seeing the frown of all her worries.

"Let's be positive, I've spoken to Betty, we should be hearing something soon, no news is good news as they say. I'm sure she's even been checked over by a nurse, all fine so far darling."

"Oh Mark, I've missed you, it's been awful, life just seems to be so brutal lately," she cried, holding onto him feeling slightly lost, but safe in his arms she was again.

"Look, your mum seems a bit off, she's asleep now. I'd probably let her carry on sleeping before waking her up, but I've been peeping in on her." He kissed her.

"Also your sister Rose is coming to see you at ten p.m. after she finishes up at work. I think somethings happened? I don't know, she won't tell me what's wrong either, it's something though, she just won't tell me.

"Darling, whatever it is, be brave and I'm here for you through absolutely anything, OK?"

"OK." She was always OK after she would ever speak with him or when she listened to him, and so she walked in through the large doors, paying no real attention to the detail that Betty's husband had spent in making sure everything was as it usually was for them all for Christmas in Ben's absence.

She climbed the long steep stairs leading to her bedroom,

waiting in anticipation, waiting for time to fast forward to the next bit of Anderson drama.

She took a long soak in her en-suite bathroom, she gathered together her thoughts. It was a peculiar feeling she was feeling that evening, it never felt like it was going to be her birthday, well hers and Lilys fortieth birthdays, it never felt like Christmas Eve that late afternoon, it felt eerie, something was still wrong, she just knew. She dreaded falling asleep wondering if at midnight the Wednesday beast would make his final call?

It was not long before Ruby was distracted with Mark's face showing a baffled-looking swamped expression, news had come in from the hospital.

"Ruby," Mark said, "your twin is in early preterm Labour. Now don't panic, the consultants in London have said more babies are being born as early on as this and surviving more and more. She is with the best of the best Ruby, there's even talks of her being born on Christmas Day darling, they are going to do everything possible for her." Mark was crying beyond belief, overwhelmed, so much seemed to be happening and he just wanted Ruby and her family to all be fine.

Ruby never found the words to say anything. Although she knew something was definitely not right with the baby, she never thought it would be labour, as scary as everything was and seemed, something settling and peaceful filled her lungs, her heart felt in place. That feeling was a feeling that Lily and the baby were going to be fine, just like she had said.

It was as though darkness was always hiding around the dark corners of the manor. Ruby and Mark had fallen asleep and woken up in blackness, Rose was banging loudly on the doors outside.

The time was ten p.m. Rose was rattled and Ruby was ready

for whatever news it was that her baby sister had been dying to tell her.

Rose was already crying at the front door as she came in, hugging her like it was the first time she had ever seen her. Needing her like the baby sister she once was.

"Rose, get straight to the point, remember your job, you are cold and detached. You can tell me anything sis, you know you can so just do it, tell me, what's so urgent?

Did Mark tell you about Lily? Now that's urgent?"

"Ruby shut up and just listen to me. There's been a murder? it was not an accident, it was cold blooded murder. Sue's dead sis." Rose had no feeling as she said it, she gave Ruby no eye contact, as she relived the graphic and awful image, remembering the shiver down her spine as she stood looking over at Sue's beaten, poisoned, dead body on the bed.

Rose stood robotic, like all the forensic team did, they all stood a certain way when bad news was being delivered.

"Listen Ruby, Mother's in trouble as well. Don't you dare say a word to Mark, I've got a secret camera recording showing some bad disturbing things about Mum, sis. I did not even recognise her on that tape, she stabbed Paul, she locked him up and left him to bleed to death. Now, the thing is Ruby, when I was there, they never knew how closely connected I was to her, I managed to hold my shit together and examine her body, I uncovered the horrific injuries, beatings and torture Paul had obviously been inflicting on Sue. Once the lab tests were done it was concluded, Paul was her killer, they closed the investigation immediately after that, they're not looking for any other suspects in the case. This can all go away if you keep your mouth shut, Ruby.

Now, no one on the force or in my own team knew about

Mother being there at the time of Sue's or Paul's death, no one but you and I know or can know about this video, do you hear me?"

"Yes, I hear you," Ruby cried.

"We will lose her, she will go to prison for a very long time, even in self-defence Ruby."

"Diminished responsibility," Ruby burst out and said,

"What?" Rose glared at her.

"Betty, she thinks Mum has dementia, maybe she can get off with it if she's not well."

"Ruby, just don't say a word to anyone. I'm going to find out what I can, but either way I'm not taking any risk. Even if Mum is not well nobody never needs to find out. He deserved it, he was a horrible bad person Ruby, and Mother is not paying the price of justice."

"Look Rose, me and Lily both know about the secret camera, that was Lily's idea, we plotted to set Paul up, find out what he had been doing, but we never watched it. I ended up stuffing it back inside that porcelain doll, that's where you found the camera, isn't it? Thank holy Christ it was you that found it, sis."

Ruby felt shattered, she wanted to pinch herself to see if she was still in the existence of the now, or if the Wednesday beast had already started. Was she dreaming? Was she acting out the role in a movie? Some kind of thriller, she imagined, but the pain that hit her insides once again, the loss of Sue was unthinkable, so tragic, unquestionably surreal. Life seemed like it was spinning out of control.

"Oh, poor Mother, does she even know? Has she even remembered that night?" Ruby asked.

"I was with mother when the police came round to inform her about it, she was Sue's next of kin.

At first I thought she was just a bloody good actress, she broke down. Then she attacked the police officers like she had lost her mind. Then all of sudden, she never remembered a thing, it was crazy. Ben's still away, he knows nothing either, it's got to stay that way. Now we just need to find out if Betty is right and see if she really is losing her mind, kind of makes sense now why she just changed so dramatically, I guess. The police were fishing and asking the last time Mother would have seen Sue, but she was so distressed, they called it a day and left."

"I actually can't believe any of this, I think I'm in shock. That's why she was covered in blood that night, I found her covered in bloodstains sis, I never even knew what the poor cow just been through, she just went to bed sis, I never even said a word to her." Ruby felt terrible for what her mother had been through in no fit mental state of mind.

"Of course we will protect her, no matter what, poor dear old mother, poor dear Sue, may her dear soul rest forever now in peace." Ruby clasped her hands into praying hands, keeping her faith strong throughout, she was never going to give up in life no matter how tough it got.

"Merry Christmas Eve to us," said Rose mournfully.

"It's clear this really is going to be one of the worst, saddest, strangest Christmases yet," Ruby muttered back.

"Eli is on his way over, I'm staying with you tonight, I know you got Mark, but I just want us all to stay close, to all be together, we got a brand new baby arriving, delicate and arriving too soon, but we got faith." That time Rose clasped her hands together hoping for a miracle, she wondered how something so tiny and undeveloped could survive the world she would be born prematurely into.

"Anyway I need to rest myself now sis, the strain of

everything can't be good for my own pregnancy, I've been through enough already I think, I don't want nothing else happening."

"Of course, you go and rest now Rose. I love you sis."

There was no way Mark was going to leave her on that night of Christmas Eve, not now. He was devastated, mortified to hear about Sue's manor, Sue's death, Paul's karma, he would be there for her that evening as she needed him to be, he could always sneak off before she woke in the morning ready for her big fortieth birthday surprise, because to him he just needed her to know how very loved she was. Nothing was going to stop him from giving her a warmer memory of Christmas at forty. He climbed into bed, falling asleep immediately beside her.

As she began to fall so deeply into a sleep, the hallway clock struck twelve midnight. She stirred but it was not strong enough to pull her back awake, it could not stop her from falling into the nightmare, that feeling of distress and pain, the images of red, nasty little images, images of death? The nasty little nightmare continued, things were far from over.

Just before midnight struck, before the Wednesday beast arrived, before she had fallen asleep the night before her birthday on Christmas Eve, Ruby Anderson was curious to what Wednesday the 25th December would bring her. With every tragedy, every bizarre, barbaric thing occurring, she found herself thinking about what Betty had said at the lodge.

"Life? What's it all about? What even is a happy ending anyway? When life happens?

Chapter 26

Lily Anderson
Adopted Sibling

EVE

She remembered an old saying Betty would say often amongst the Anderson anxiety household:

"Worrying makes a woman old so what's the point of worrying?" Putting it like that Lily could only wish it could have been that easy. The baby was arriving unexpectedly and dangerously early, she thought back to what Ruby had said entering the ambulance. "Can't you feel it? You and the baby are going to be fine."

But right then it was only dread Lily could feel. She could only pray Ruby was right, her baby had to survive, her baby had to live.

Lily Anderson wanted very much for it all to be over with quickly, holding onto faith and the miracle it would take for survival.

The hospital had been a private one. It had been a rough hour away from Gatwick Airport in normal driving. Bran would be flying in on his private jet from Hollywood, Lily knew it would be easy enough for him to flag a black cab to the hospital's location.

Travelling a day earlier than arranged, had meant missing

the last crucial bit of filming in emergency circumstances and Bran was not as hopeful as the text messages, emails and voicemails he had received, most of the family had commented, Ruby being first to say everything was going to be just fine, just because she had a feeling. Yet Bran could only feel himself and his fiancé were about to experience the worst outcome possible. To him, heartbreak was inevitable, but once by Lily's side he would be a man of hope, a man of love and support, nothing less than what she would need him to be.

The hospital had already been informed of his status and that he would not be expected to arrive just gone midnight and, of course, granted special dispensation.

The contractions were slow and mild, by the time Lily had been finally admitted to her own birthing room, the time had been approaching five p.m. on Christmas Eve. The evening had been moving slow, the hours dragged uncomfortably for Lily, the predictions were that by the way things were moving the baby would be born the next morning on Christmas Day.

The clinicians had spoken of weak cervical tissues which had contributed to having a premature birth. Despite the medical facts, Lily had chosen to believe her baby was coming early because that was God's plan, weak tissues or not, she had felt her baby had her own plan. As Lily looked around at the hospital surroundings she reached for Betty's hand; only then did she feel the feeling of Ruby's whisper, that she and the baby were going to be just fine, like she had told her.

With things seeming to go as they normally would have in early slow labour, Lily had still very much known that even in a fine ending this was going to be far from a normal birth.

Her thoughts had very much been scattered. One minute they were of herself and Ruby, thinking how her mother robbed her so, of birthdays she could never get back, she thought of how on Christmas Day evening the special moment Ruby was born, she had followed six minutes after as the second-born twin. She had thought about the false identity she'd been living all her life. That and the tortured memory of two people she could only remember being told were her two parents who had tragically burned to death, to finally finding out the real truth. After all those years she thought she was an orphaned child adopted in sympathy. Yet everything they had felt had been real, which led her to think if Ruby was right about Lily's baby that was going to be OK then she felt perturbed, for who wasn't? She bugged herself about Ruby's nightmares and both of their gut feeling, the disturbing sharp edge at the pit of their stomachs that something bad was going to happen.

The private hospital supplied a patient welcome pack, swab sticks for infection testing, a hibiscrub, toothbrush and some other very much-needed items. Neither of them had been able to change clothes since the morning of the airport, Ruby had packed and put Lily's suitcase right at the bottom of the car's boot. At that point it had been too time consuming to pull it back out once the ambulance arrived, as by then the real panic had kicked in between all three of them that there had been little thought given about her luxuries.

Lily had welcomed the nightgown the nurses had encouraged her to change into. She was feeling at ease in the room, it was warm, therapeutic and had a large leather-seated chair for the guest.

Once Lily was settled, Betty had decided to walk the hospital grounds for snacks and any hot drinks, she was expecting David to pick her up at eight p.m., but he knew she would not think about leaving Lily's side until Bran arrived. Proactive as he always was, he had booked a room at the Hilton Hotel not far from the hospital he was persistent on still arriving at eight p.m. to give his wife some moral support.

"Well that was a waste of time, what a bloody joke that was," Betty said, bursting back into the room bringing in with her two cups of hot tea, and a sponge cake. She frowned at Lily, trying to figure out if she had got any more cramps as that was what they still they seemed too currently be.

"So you've missed the last served meal, but here's a cake at least. The kitchen hostess did say she could bring you in a sandwich if you want?"

"Sis, I'm not hungry, how you think I could eat is beyond me. But pass the cake,"

But she laughed as she reached out for the sweet craving.

Another cramp had rattled her, the contractions were still slow but becoming deeper. The midwife was due in to check her dilation levels on the next visit, she had wondered if she should press the buzzer to make sure she was not forgotten but, within seconds of doubt, a well-rounded lady with a stern look, serious but warm came in introducing herself properly to both Betty and Lily.

"Hello, my name is Pearl, how are you feeling Lily? Let's have a little look at your cervix shall we?" the midwife said examining her as she spoke softly in a Caribbean accent.

"OK all done, only four centimetres m so far, I'll be back in to check in a couple of hours. If you need me before then, or you feel you need some pain relief, just press your buzzer."

Lily took an immediate liking to the woman. She gave nothing away, no assumption, as though she too were hopeful that new life was also possible no matter what odds were against her.

The midwife washed her hands at the basin, turning back

around to give Lily some details.

"You would have been in the first stage for quite some time, you're at the start of your labour now Lily, your cervix has softened. She's still hours away, and your contractions are still irregular, but she could be arriving by Christmas morning."

Before Pearl was almost out the door Lily stopped her in her movement.

"Thank you, Pearl." Lily felt the need to thank her, she already felt dependant on her every word, and liked the warmth in her eyes. Between them all Lily knew they would make a good team.

The door closed behind leaving Lily and Betty, leaving them to bond further and opening up on little discussions where time had no place for, until that early evening on Christmas Eve.

"Betty, thank you so much for being here, I can't bear the thought of you being away from little Ivy though, just leave as soon as David arrives, I'll be fine."

"Don't be so ridiculous, I'll be staying put until Bran arrives, so don't worry."

She had moved the large armchair closer to Lily's bed, they spoke a couple of hours away until Lily's contractions had deepened in pain. Oxygen was in place and given on her first visit from Pearl, soon being used as and when Lily felt she needed it.

After taking a little more Lily relaxed. Soon she felt completely spaced out, with Betty falling asleep in the chair beside her.

It was Betty's phone's ringtone, the vibration which had startled her, that woke her up. Embarrassed she had fallen asleep without knowing so, she peeped her head round to checking in on Lily who was awake but calm, guiltily she apologised to her.

"I can't believe I fell asleep, I'm so sorry, are you OK? Did

I miss anything?"

"No, no, you needed to rest sis, and yeah, I'm fine."

Lily was exhausted, although by now she was concerned about the change to the pain levels, pain that could possibly last the whole entire night.

"As long as the pain stays at this level, I'll be fine," Lily said.

"OK, well David is downstairs in the carpark. I'll quickly nip down to him, I'll be back soon, but call me and buzz Pearl if you need absolutely anything Lily, OK?"

"Yes, go go, give David my love."

Being alone felt like an empowering moment, she reflected and once playing over all the events in her head she felt overwhelmed, she hoped her mother had been OK, Ruby had managed to send in a message to say she seemed OK when she had gotten back to the manor.

Thinking of how quickly the year had passed, how much had happened, all that had changed.

Lily's experiences so far could not compare to the one she was yet to have. In fact, Lily's life was about to change forever...

Betty had found David parked up, engine of but lights on. He definitely had been that type of man who was thoughtful, kind and the kind of husband a woman dreamed of having.

With him he had two bags, one for Betty and one for Lily, a change of wear and some female necessities, he thought, would not go a miss.

Together with a Burger King, he offered the tempting cheeseburger to his wife.

"Darling, I've missed you, you must be starving, get this down you."

David waved the paper bag around, and not shy Betty grabbed for it. The smell played on her empty stomach, she kissed him once fully inside the passenger seat, quite happily she rammed the burger into her mouth, selecting a few chips that slid in with it.

"How's Ivy? Fast asleep waiting for Santa?" she asked.

She thought of how innocent, how pure her four-year-olds world was, no worries in the world other than what presents she would be tearing open under the tree as soon as her little eyes would reopen.

"Yes Magda ended up reading the same story three times over until she finally fell asleep," David said, as he smiled at his wife's question.

As he said it in such admiration for their nanny, it was then Betty changed her mind about letting her go. Sometimes you just never knew when you needed the help, and besides, Betty thought to herself, as long as Magda was appreciated and treated well, if money was not an issue then surely keeping a private nanny just meant she was more fortunate than some who had no choice but to manage without?

"I better get back up to Lily, she hasn't text me but it's time to get back to her."

The couple could not bear to discuss any grim details of what chances the little baby would have, instead David gave her a silent look that wished her all the luck her sister may need.

Arriving back onto the suite she could see frequent gas and air was being used to control the pain levels for Lily, the hours had slipped by and Bran had landed at Gatwick Airport eleven ten p.m. Lily guessed it would be midnight before she was likely to see his endearing face.

In any time she could, she would rest with her eyes closed between the contractions. But freakishly, almost suddenly, exactly at the hand of midnight, her eyes opened wide.

Something was wrong? Something was wrong with Ruby, she could feel that familiar petrifying edge at the pit of her stomach again, the twisted knotted feeling they both complained of a sixth sense that something bad was going to happen, but what and to who?

It was midnight with no show of Bran. Although she had checked a message to say he was ten minutes away, she worried about Ruby, but she would be asleep so at least she also knew she was not in any danger. It must have been the midnight beast she knew of far too well. She went back to the evening when she had never seen Ruby looking so scared, speaking about her visions of death.

Lily was experiencing the side effects from the Entonox, feeling more light-headed than expected she felt reluctant to take more. Somehow it felt important she was focused, that she would be ready to hold her baby.

Alone she had woken, as Betty had popped out to use the guest toilets on the lower ground., Lily could hear the sounds of the busy nurses' station out the front. She thought of how quickly Christmas Eve would pass them by and like a switch had been turned on, like the brain had found infinity, Lily suddenly got it: she wrapped her arms around her stomach and spoke to her unborn child.

"Hello my little angel, I don't know why you're coming so early but I'm looking forward to meeting you." Her cheeks soaked wet as she cried, as then she realized exactly what her newborn baby would be named.

She pressed her buzzer hard for her midwife Pearl, the baby was coming, the pain was horrendous, all so frightening, she was still alone.

But with Betty and Bran stepping off the elevator together,

arriving in minutes with Pearl, Lily was going to have them all by her side in minutes.

She closed her eyes, breathing and speaking in pain she again spoke to her unborn child.

"You are going to make it my precious one, you are going to live. Your name is going to be EVE, in Hebrew this means to live and you will, sweet child, you will."

In that beautiful special moment, bearing the pain and as she felt the urge to push, the sound of footsteps came entering into the room. This had been it, the time was here, and so she whispered the name out loud again in clarity.

"EVE, my baby Eve."

Chapter 27

Rose Anderson
Baby Sibling

THE BONFIRE

In good there is wicked, in wicked there is good. (R.L. McKenzie)

Sometimes when a woman needs to clear her mind she needs space and the right time to do so.

Rose Anderson had always been known as the tyke, the baby, she was deemed reliable, practical and passionate, but it seemed even Rose had her own insecurities. Her question was: when a mother bears more than one child, of course she loves each one differently, not the same, for every child born is unique in its own special way. But does one child steal its mother's heart more than another? It was anyone's guess. Betty always was associated as the favourite, for Rose she was known for being the one who made their mother's eyes glaze in disappointment, being married to a rich top lawyer would have suited their mother an awful lot more had she married him with all financial gain. The wealth was entirely his and their mother had hated every bit of it, in false pretence she would make a fuss of him, just the way he felt entitled to act superior, just the way he liked them all to treat him with Rose at his side serving his every beck and call.

She gave a shudder at the very thought of Matthew and her

previous marriage to him.

As she stood alone that quiet morning of Christmas Eve, she was about to set her mood to something more of a front. Poker-faced, she would have to put on a brave display to her work colleagues, sucking up the passing comments, the sick truths and speculations about the murders of Sue and Paul, it was extremely hard to bear. It was difficult to concentrate on anything other than the bad.

That very early morning she had just felt completely hopeless, thinking of Christmas being ruined already. All she could do was to wait desperately for Ruby to return back to the manor, wishing Lily and her baby all the luck in the world. If she had been given the chance to burst into tears, spilling all she knew, all that she had discovered, spilling the beans to all three of her sisters is exactly what she would have done. That with all three of her sisters, the burdens she was carrying were each demolishing her every last bit of sanity, more irritable she'd become, more nervous at the thought of their mother's guilty murderous hands, she needed to make sure their mother was going to be safe, even if that meant becoming a person she never thought it was possible to become.

It had been freezing, she had remembered the spiteful chilblains in her fingers, her ears had been screaming in agony as she stood frozen with the sheer panic of everything she now faced. The paternity test results had also come back, identifying the blood father as well as the sex at the scan she arranged and attended, too.

She had been in a complete daze receiving the news, she had wanted to be in her own head, finding out was something that she felt she needed do alone, just herself first before Eli and Matthew.

The particular lake she had visited that morning of Christmas

Eve was famous for its ornamental cascade waterfall. Although indeed it was a beautiful sight she had felt rather alone, scared, and to be honest, Rose Anderson had every reason to feel afraid that Christmas.

It's a funny thing life, how one day you can wake up as normal as you think normal is, to then wake up being nothing more than a villain, in the eyes of the law she too was guilty. Yet in her own eyes surely she was just doing what any daughter would do, protect a mother from a monster, from a man that she would not allow to win, not even in his death? Paul was the only guilty verdict, now she just needed to do what was best, to do the right thing for everyone.

It had been half an hour before midnight on Christmas Eve when she had left Ruby aghast with all the details. At least for herself she had got rid of one burden, now she just needed to ditch the other one, because quite frankly who the father was going to be never seemed important news in tragedy.

When she was finally able to make her way home back to Eli, to spend the last few minutes of the hour before the countdown was over. The 25th December was soon to arrive with astonishing versions of events, changes, dread and horror, although, all came with a sigh of relief that she had at least found the only void there ever was in her life, a kind thoughtful man who loved her.

Shocked was one way to describe how Eli had felt when he was informed of that terrible night. Concerned also, taking in the gory details of the deaths of her close family friends, Eli did not need to know any more truth than that.

Rose felt as though she was in some kind of race, desperate to at least spend the rest of the evening with no drama, walk into a warm cottage, she could toast the hour in with a non-alcoholic beverage, find the right time to reveal both sex and father of her unborn child. Surely there was a right time a right place for most things, and what was left of Christmas Eve evening the time had felt right for Rose Anderson to give the news that was going to change both of their lives forever.

What was life like before Eli Bardon? That was a hard picture for Rose to envision. Sometimes a person can walk into your life, complete you in such a way you can't remember a different life other than the wonderful one that now exists.

To Rose, it was all one of life's big lessons, that all life really was, was one big gamble, that a man could easily waste the best years of a woman's life if she allowed him to.

If a woman wasn't happy, then she should do the leaving or be prepared to get left behind. Pretty scary stuff it seemed, especially for women like themselves who were taught they should not grow old alone or grow old lonely, but actually how quickly for Rose that she learned loneliness came from a place within. She would much prefer to be alone than unhappy, trapped and miserable with the wrong man, that can be one of the loneliest places on the planet.

A woman blinks and then she's old.

Even though Matthew had not been necessarily evil or even violent towards her, staying with him would have resulted in a long, slow painful death and she was not prepared or willing to go out like Sue or face any torture if she could help it. Life was too short to be abused.

The baby kicked inside hard as she stepped out of the car. Her womb had become a trampoline, but a safe place it still was, unlike her sister's agony, she begged to the stars that Lily's baby just had to make it. Everybody was on edge waiting for the news, and the waiting game was never any fun.

Warm air met her crisp temperature as she opened the door to the little cottage. The lights had been dimmed, the smell of spiced apple filled the rooms, there was Christmas music playing faintly in the background with a charming man waiting for her, waiting to share any moments he could on their first Christmas together.

Christmas Eve was almost over, but Christmas itself was only just the beginning, the beginning of change.

"You must be absolutely wrecked, darling. How was work today? And how did the chat go with Ruby? Did you clear things off your chest?" Eli was already fussing by her side, taking her coat into his arms, he followed her through.

"Kind of. I'm just glad to be home with you, what's the time?"

The hour was five minutes after midnight on Wednesday 25th December, and on that evening Rose had not been aware of the Wednesday beast that was occurring in Ruby's bed as she slept, nor was she aware of the horror that was to follow.

"Merry Christmas darling, here you are. I poured you a glass of fizzy orange." He smiled, he looked so innocent, so proud of her anyway.

"Well yes, cheers, cheers to us." Maybe it had been the pregnancy hormones but Rose became tearful, overwhelmed, tears flooding down as usual.

"Rose darling, whatever is the matter?" Bewildered he took the glass of sparkling pop out of her hands and held her tightly.

"Eli," her throat tickled as she coughed to clear away any unwanted speech stutters.

"I am having a baby boy, he is yours Eli, you're going to be a father." Her eyes searched widely in his for clues to whether it was something he definitely had wanted.

"Merry blooming Christmas, I can't believe it, I'm in shock, I think this is the happiest moment in my whole entire life.

"Rose Anderson you have made me the happiest man in Virginia Waters."

Although there were many tears still streaming from her eyes, her heart stopped for a second. In utter disbelief, she looked at him as he took her breath away, and how could she be so lucky to have her prayers answered she thought? Matthew would not father any child of hers. She was free. She could now be happy at last.

Well sure, it seemed as though this was already going to be one Christmas they would remember. It had been a cherished perfect moment, a sweet filled memory of what magic Christmas could also bring other than dark twists, if only life could always be so kind.

"Look darling, I texted Matthew earlier, after work, en route to Ruby. I told him the results were back. I never said in the message what they were, I thought it would be more tasteful to do in person."

She reached for her phone, proving she had been bombarded with desperate messages from him demanding for her to just tell him no matter how late, she was to ring him, or she could just cut the crap and go round, face to face despite the hour.

"I know it's late, but do you mind if I just nip over there? I just got to get this off my chest tonight, I don't want to wake up to this shit in the morning, I want to get over to mother's for Christmas dinner, with Mother and the rest of the family and with any luck Lily and the new baby sound and safe. It's all going to be OK, isn't it?"

Eli consoled her, supplying her back with all the positivity in the world. His life had changed in the most extraordinary magnificent way beyond belief.

"You go do what you got to do, just call me when you're there, I hate you being out this late," she agreed, turning towards the staircase, hiding her shame. For Rose had already had the conversation with Matthew, a devastated man he was about to become but she dismissed the feeling thinking he was no longer her problem anymore.

In fact Rose had other plans for the evening, there was another destination she was intending to get to, in a discreet manner she slipped her rucksack into her car and promised Eli she would not take too long, but asked for his patience under the circumstances. Promising herself as she left, those would be the last lies she was going to tell him, but that was the thing about lies, once you start telling one you start telling a couple more and then before long you're a compulsive liar, and that's not who she was, or who she wanted to be, although she could not even recognise the woman she even was herself anymore.

She drove fast, she drove further and further into wooded areas. The sky was dark and murky, there was always a particular area that set off fireworks and a crowd that danced around burning flames all up until, after New Year's Eve. She was dressed all in black herself, in a hurry but in a settled state of mind, it was very clear for Rose, there was no other way forwards, she had to destroy all the evidence. It was either that or let her mother rot away in prison or be permanently sectioned.

The judge shows no mercy on love, and she also knew that just because she loved and wanted to protect her mother, in the eyes of the law she was wrong, guilty for the crime she was about to commit, and just how very possible it was to be on the wrong side of the law, how very quickly something like that could change a person's good character and what were the lengths one would go to protect the ones we love.

There were already sounds of carefree youths disturbing the peace nearby her chosen area to stop, making it a convenient choice strapped to her front. She lit her torch, and slid the straps down to her rucksack, she fumbled through inside, pulling out and putting on leather gloves, as she tucked deeper into the wooden hidden corner of the woods.

Rose's mind captured that horrific night back at the manor, she remembered screening the room noticing the porcelain doll, finding the secret camera along with a bag with her mother's clothes inside, the ones she would have had on before she changed into her dress for Paul.

Rose thought about how quickly her brain reacted to carefully placing the secret camera under her blazer, picking up the bag under the eyes of busy crime scene investigators and rushing off into the bathroom with an excuse for pregnancy sickness. She could see herself back in Sue's bathroom throwing up violently in the toilet, flabbergasted, and in shock, she hid the camera inside her wired bra. It was only a small device, both the camera and the tape she had found, cleverly she changed into the trousers and top belonging to her mother, leaving them on underneath her work clothes. Rose had remembered that night in photographic detail.

She remembered carrying out her own search through the manor, as allowed and expected, grabbing every hour she got given before it came to light that she was too closely connected, too personally involved, in a case she would be dropped from had they found out how connected the families really were together.

She remembered spotting the green-coloured plastic knife her mother had wedged behind the fridge. She remembered going to the sink to throw up as she saw the bloodstains on it, but she had continued to seal the weapon in a concealed bag, she had hidden it along with everything else. She would use a calculating trick to frame Paul: she took another kitchen knife, soaking it up in as much blood of Paul's she could get from the floors. She went back into the bedroom, sneakily able to place it callously on Paul's dead body without a twitch or raised eyebrows from her fellows. She knew she had to see what was on that videotape for herself without the police and she knew she had to make sure all traces of her mother were cleaned up out of that manor. She would act out the investigation and the most anyone would suspect was, if they found out she knew the deceased on a personal level, then even if that meant suspension then that was the risk she was prepared to take.

As she finalised the last little details, twigs crackled on the mudded ground. Of course she had felt nervous but the feeling of doing the right thing overpowered anything else she was feeling, she had texted Eli to say she was fine and Matthew was taking in the news calmly, that she would not be much longer. They were discussing divorce stuff, she imagined she would return back to him, curl up next to him, fall asleep and wake up to Christmas Day, putting all her troubles behind her.

She pulled the hood of her jumper over her head as she removed the knife she still kept in the concealed plastic bag she had put it in.

Rose started digging in a random spot deep into the mudded grounds of earth. After all, no one would ever be looking or searching for a knife they never knew was missing or never knew had even been used. They were looking for no suspects, the case was practically closed, taking care of a huge load of weight from her shoulders.

Now she could concentrate on her own part she was to play,

a criminal, tampering with evidence and conspiring to conceal a murder. She hated every bit of it, she never saw the day coming where she would be that person, that it would be her who was to get rid of evidence useful for the police to use against a person in a court of law. But what had to be done simply had to be done. The first part of her plot was to bury the knife hard and deep, never to be found again. She had felt confident carrying on with her second stage of her plot, out in the dark, the cold, in a rush to get home.

As she bedded down twigs, leaves and paper, as she glared down at the lighter she took from her coat pocket, it was a feeling as though this was it: it was time to say goodbye to evil.

Rose could not think of any better way, nothing more precise than to destroy the rest of the unwanted evidence, a bag of her mother's clothes, the secret camera, a bloodstained hairband, shoes and an acrylic fingernail, all the evidence she knew she could burn, evidence that could neatly vanish to dust, evidence burning in the vicious orange flames of an innocent, burning bonfire…

Chapter 28

Betty Anderson
Middle Sibling

BLOOD IS THICKER THAN WATER

Leaving Lily behind at the hospital on Christmas Eve was an absolute struggle for Betty on that wintery evening. Reluctantly she did so, for all that she'd felt obliged to stay put, having been part of the labour journey from the start. It almost felt inhumane when the midwife spoke of herself and Bran taking over on the situation, insisting Betty should leave so as to be with her own family at Christmas, everything was under control, but was it? The scene she pictured flooded her mind with fear, there were screams of mercy, cries of desperation, to her, if things weren't as bad enough already, having to spend a first Christmas without Georgina Blossom was repugnant, for what more could a human take? If there was one thing for certain it would not just be Florence Anderson's mental health in question, Lily would never recover nor would any of them should they have to act out a cruel and unforgiving thing such as to bury a newborn baby…

David made the drive back a journey of hope and positivity. He never really ever had to say much more than a few philosophical metaphors, accompanied by complimenting music in the car's speakers, he would hear no such thing as Christmas being ruined.

Everything was going to be OK it just had to be, the whole family's well-being was at stake and his wife had been through so much already. Looking at it from a husband's perspective, David could not help feel a little selfish, grateful Bran had arrived just as things got heated, thankful he could take his wife home to their precious sleeping daughter.

The family was always dramatic, as he recalled, they were loud with busy personalities, he had been in the middle of breaking up so many fights, bickers and outbursts from the raging creatures he witnessed in all of them at times, women that looked like screaming banshees, he had seen every crack, every dent and every bit of damage done in his wife's family from the secrets, to the lies, to deceit and guilt.

But with Georgina passing, David had been thrilled that the sisters had all reconciled their differences and he could see the confidence and strength it gave Betty to carry on and fight back from being grief-ridden, maybe she was a little obsessed to become set on taking every call. Maybe she had got caught up in the worry that something bad was going to happen from a bad dream Ruby was having.

David was not half surprised to hear the truth of the girls really being twins, he had always had his suspicions but never a place to say so. Now, all he could appreciate was a good thing that had come from a bad place, sadly, it had taken Sue to write her last words and lose life for the truth to finally come out that Ruby and Lily were twins, they were all now sharing a closeness and bond that should have always been there from the start. It had all brought tears and smiles of joy to his heart. To see his wife so happy, it was guaranteed that himself and Lily's partner Bran would become great friends, making his wife happier still despite bereavement, Betty was doing well and David was going to make sure his wife was going to stay that way…

Magda had settled Ivy down into the master's bedroom as David suggested. The keening infant would want to wait for her mother in her mother's bed that Christmas Eve.

The maid had waited up to hear of any news on Lily and the baby, but by the look of Betty's drained tear-stained eyes there was nothing yet to report. Every second she noticed Betty glance down to check her phone, but after midnight came in, Lily was still in labour, labour that was likely to take her through to early next morning. She thought of how possible it would be to actually sleep, for the remaining hours?

At five a.m. Ivy would surely stir with the thought of her being stamped as naughty or nice wondering if the man in a red suit with a bushy white beard left her all the little treasures she had written a list of, the same little note she had seen her daughter hand over for her father to post to the North Pole. Betty smiled a little, the innocence of a child was a once in a lifetime thing, and as her mother did for her and her sisters and as she still did to the present day, she remembered herself as a once small child, she remembered that Father Christmas always arrived, and there was always one shiny, special, gloriously wrapped gift from their mother to all her daughters. And Betty thought it sacred to have kept the same tradition for Ivy, yes, the little precious child would always have one surprise to open from her mother and father on Christmas morning.

"OK, well I'll be off to my room ma'am, if there is nothing else you need for this evening."

"You've done plenty Magda, thank you, goodnight." Betty's eyes looked in Magda's with warmth, her appreciation of her was more realistic now she could finally see just what a godsent she really was.

"Oh, one thing Magda. Just ignore our little discussion before, of course you would not be leaving our family manor or be thinking about such a thing, would you?"

"Oh, erm, no ma'am, I am here for as long as you need me ma'am." Magda was already red faced, taken aback but delighted with her lady's change of heart.

"Want actually, not need, for as long as you are wanted here, and you are very much Magda, and always will be, just if I was always too busy to tell you before."

David looked on as though it was of no importance to him whatsoever. Whatever conversation had been discussed between the women, all had found its right place, there really was no place like home and he was enjoying everything that had changed in the last few months. Was it so selfish for a loving husband to feel happy? He not only had his daughter in his arms but also his wife's.

There the petite child lay with her tiny feet spread out and out of the covers. She had always kicked any sheet, any blanket, cover away and off from her feet. She had a tiny doll-like frame, at four she could have been three years of age, her beautiful brown skin with a nest of thick brown curly hair sprawled out on their bed, hiding the innocent beautiful sleeping face of Ivy.

It was a perfect moment to see her so perfect, so precious, although it was Betty's first Christmas without Georgina Blossom, it was also her first actual Christmas she would be spending with her daughter and husband. She had never really given much priority before now, her usual Christmas would consist of a dressing-up themed Christmas Eve party where Georgina would insist and persuade Betty to accompany her every single time, and every single time Betty would arrive home selfish hours of the morning, drunk out of her tiny nut, and would still be drunk on Christmas morning. David would always be so kind to let her sleep in at least until midday, waking up instead with Ivy and Magda at five a.m. in the morning, he would open just a few of the many presents Ivy would get to rip and tear open in their bewitching cottage home, yes her priorities had been elsewhere just not so long ago.

That evening was exhausting and painfully petrifying hoping Lily and the baby made it through the labour. Betty wanted to just hold onto to the hope, the excitement of everything being OK, that in the morning everything was going to be just fine.

Right now she would soak up every precious moment of that evening reminding herself just how perfect her husband and her daughter was.

As she lay beneath the covers, different things ran wild, back to feeling that chill down her spine, the baby, Ruby's nightmare? Their ill mother, Sue's tragic death, Paul's up-comings, Rose's erratic distant behaviour, and the new men that had entered the Anderson family's lives.

It was hard to say what thoughts carried her off into a deep sleep, a sleep she tried to fight back in fright, in horror of missing anything about Lily and the baby.

But there in the dark did sleep arrive, Betty fell deeper and deeper into hibernation. And fortunately for Betty Anderson, as she stirred it was only with sweet filled imaginary and thoughts of all things bright and wonderful her dream promised a very merry Christmas, but I guess you could say that's the thing about sleep and dreams. They're not real, or are they?

At precisely four forty five a.m. early Christmas morning when it seemed only three or so hours of sleep had kicked in when a delightful child burst wide awake with a piercing sound screeching, going over the same thing again and again until the opening of one eye from her mother.

"Daddy, Daddy wake up, Santa has come, Daddy!"

Bouncing on the bed knowing usually all too well not to disturb or wake her mother, she would climb over her and onto her father's chest.

"Daddy, Daddy wake up now, Santa has come." But this time as Ivy climbed over her mother, both of whose eyes were now wide open, Betty grabbed her daughter and pulled her close. She tickled her and kissed her like it was her first Christmas, of course David had been awake all along, hoping he would see what he was seeing that Christmas morning: his two most favourite girls, safe and sound and together. With a hundred kisses and a pillow fight David put on his slippers and left his wife's at her bedside. He started dressing Ivy in her thick velvet green dressing gown and it really was beginning to look like Christmas indeed,. It was already a memory made perfect and never to be forgotten by both parents, that special morning.

Their Christmas tree had been standing eight feet tall in snow white fur pines. There was a trail of presents in front, around and behind the delightful tree.

In greed, in sight of the piles of gifts, the small child sat surrounded by pink- and purple- wrapped presents to start with.

Magda was absent in the kitchen, it was far too early to serve food, but she prepared all she would need to do to serve an appetising breakfast when desired. Christmas dinner however, was always at Florence Anderson's manor without fail.

"Is that your phone flashing darling?"

"Oh my God, it is, it must be Bran, she must have had the baby. I'm scared David, I can't look."

David immediately understood his wife's anguish and rescued Betty from her torture. For as long as a good moment lasted this was the news they had all been waiting for. He reached over to the chair the phone was flashing on, his chest was feeling tight and uneasy, he looked into the device, clicked on the screen, putting in his wife's password which was always Ivy's date of birth.

She could see his eyes were dark and serious in those seconds, his frown was unread, it was hard to make out what he was thinking at that given moment.

"Just tell me David. Desperate she begged him to say what he knew.

"The baby has been born, her name is baby Eve, they say she's a little miracle. She's doing well, darling."

"But Lilly."

David cleared his throat.

"They say she's in theatre, they say she's lost a lot of blood, she needs a transfusion. Nobody can get hold of Ruby as she would be a definite match, they can't get hold of Rose, and they've asked if you know your blood type, if you could be a cross match for AB positive."

"I'm blood type A and I know that means I could be a positive donor for her."

Without hesitation Betty rushed to change and pack a bag, calling out for Magda to entertain Ivy and take over Christmas, she knew all the presents would take a good few hours' distraction and thank goodness she knew the satisfaction of presents, girly boxes of treasures her and David would not be missed for long.

David heated the car engine whilst trying to get hold of Ruby. He felt frustrated as he knew she would have been the one who would be giving blood if any of them would.

It was typical for Ruby to be missing in action in the great hour of need, but where on earth was Rose, he thought? And who on earth was looking after their mother, he wondered most alarmed?

David usually calm natured was now outright frantic, but it was only an emergency blood transfusion he was taking his wife to, a common procedure with great results of saving lives and he very much knew there and then, with no time to spare, there was no time to be selfish a second longer. Lilys life needed to be saved and was now in the hands of his wife.

On December the 25th, Ruby and Lily Anderson had turned forty. One was unaware of age and fighting for life, and the other one was missing. It was extremely inconvenient but not out of character, for everyone was always worrying about where or what Ruby Anderson was or doing.

But on that grey, cold Christmas morning if anything had been clear, it was that when it came to family, the brave ones will always go to any of the lengths needed, and that was Betty Anderson, willing, determined and brave. After all, when it really came down to it, what really matters in the end, what always matters and what always counts, is that specific detail you can't change whether you like it or not.

And Lily was her blood, her sister, her newfound best friend.

That blood is always thicker than water.

Chapter 29

Florence Anderson
The Mother

THE BEGINNING OF AN END

When life happens as it so easily does, one could question what
even is a happy ending?
– R. L. McKenzie

It is possible that two events can happen at the same time?

There's also a saying of when a new baby is born a person's
life is taken.

It was Wednesday the 25th of December at four a.m. in the
morning in Florence Anderson's manor. Confused as she was, she
dressed in one of her finest gowns, it was clear she was to dress
for a special occasion, but not quite clear of the indecent time it
actually was when she awoke that morning.

Naively she was not well, confused of most things current,
it was absurd how dramatically and quickly things had changed
with her mental state. It was an awful situation for any family to
witness, with very little they could actually do without her
consent for a medical test.

From the outside looking in, how sad it was to not be
involved or not to have had any clue she was to become a

306

grandmother to her second grandchild,

Awful really, neither did she know one of her daughters would be needing emergency blood, not comprehending another daughter in a few hours was about to save the new mother's life, and so it had been, Betty Anderson had done exactly that, the procedure was successful and each of the women were recovering just fine with the new addition to the family, tiny and fragile, the miracle baby Eve was also exactly that. She had been named, fit for a little miracle.

David had been a saint as usual driving back after Betty's procedure, able to pick up Ivy who undoubtedly was excited to meet her new baby cousin. She was crying, scared at the almost skeleton-like body, stuffed with tubes. She peeped into an incubator not making sense of the wrinkled skin on baby Eve's tiny body.

Ivy had been keen to see her brave mother too, for a moment it had certainly felt like Christmas for whatever Christmas was supposed to feel like.

And so it was on that heavenly December's morning, just as the snow began to fall thick, two women and one newborn were all doing mighty well by the late afternoon of Christmas Day.

Florence Anderson had been none the wiser about the secret being out of the bag, that of her daughters really being twins, or that they had both turned forty overnight. She was very much ignorant to the beastly nightmare Ruby had also suffered in the next room pretty much all through the night that earlier, bitter evening.

How very brutal it was for her to be so forgetful, to possess some mistaken belief that her dearest friend Sue had still been alive and living.

A sad picture it truly was, once again Florence had built up a familiar urge to go round and greet her friend that Christmas morning, to carry out her normal routine.

She imagined she would be opening the bedroom door to a wide-eyed, beaming, beautiful-looking angel-faced woman she had known pretty much all of her life, but well, what a different story that would have been? For Sue was very much dead. And, well, Ruby's nightmare was in fact far from over on that repentant Wednesday, the 25th of December's day.

The elegant woman briskly aimed to step out into the deep quilted snow-covered grounds. The freezing temperature outside would not have been appropriate for the fine gown in which she had chosen to leave.

Before she walked the long wooded lanes out into the main busy roads alone, lost, confused, on foot, considered mad and rightly so, Florence Anderson closed shut the large front double door to her antique manor. With no husband in sight, a sleeping daughter whose boyfriend slept right next to her in love, in hope of what all love could bring to a man's future lay Mark Harrington in the bedroom manor of Ruby Anderson.

Florence Anderson, the once devoted mother, the grateful wife, the once loyal friend, well, she was about to bring Christmas Day to its final end but in great tragedy.

The speed of the wind forced the large heavy doors shut themselves after Florence's weak hands attempted to close them.

With not a wink from Ruby, it was only Mr Harrington who had been slightly ruffled, stirring only enough to roll over and place his arm around the love of his life, but not quite woken enough to come completely out of a satisfying state as he slept so soundly. Her heart beat next to his for a few adored minutes, until his brain became busy, loud with full intent, it was Christmas morning and she had turned forty, something which he knew was massive, a big deal to most women he guessed and all he could think then was had he guessed right? Would proposing to her on this day she had been dreading be what she had wanted? Would joining Lily's engagement news make her scream in delight and say yes, wrapping her arms around him blushing at the thought that she was so silly in thinking any nightmare she was having would actually come true?

How admirable that he so very much wanted to prove he was the man to rescue her as she so very much prayed for, that he would never hurt her, he would love and protect her for as long as he lived, and he knew that for certain.

As he gathered his thoughts together things had seemed a shambles so far, what with every dilemma going on in her family, not only was there not enough time the night before as planned on Christmas Eve to go back to his apartment to pick up the engagement ring, and it had seemed almost ludicrous to be thinking of weddings at a time like it was. Yet when was there ever a right time for anything? And as lovely as their mother was, he clearly thought her deluded. He also knew there was some dark, hidden stuff Ruby had been keeping from him, but it never changed a thing, his mind was set, he was going to ask Ruby Anderson to marry him. He was a fool in love and anyway why would he want to leave her, being the only sister out of wedlock.

He had stared carelessly at her for a few seconds, sorry that she had suffered dearly through the night the way she had, screaming. Had she been fighting at something? Rejecting something? Whatever it was he only hoped she rested well now, he kissed her cheek before climbing out from the bed. He would be quick in his actions, she would be asleep and not notice he had gone, feeling as though her bastard nightmare had done him some kind of favour in making her exhausted enough to sleep through, it would enable him to sneak off. Ruby Anderson was one hard woman to surprise, he labelled her as always paranoid, but a gifted beautiful witch. Sure it petrified him, with all her superstitions and demon-banishing rituals, it would have been enough to have scared off any normal bloke. Yet for Mark Harrington, mostly she fascinated him, he found her magnetic, he craved her electric energy, and he had always known she was who he had always loved even when she was oblivious and never knew he even existed.

The early hours of Christmas morning were ticking by fast, it was early still at five a.m. already an hour had passed by since Florence had wandered out alone into the dark sky clouds. But for Mr Harrington, he only assumed he would pop out to collect the shiny, pretty picked ring. He continued to keep all hope he would get back before she even knew he was gone.

Purposely he muted to silence her ringtone, reckless his actions were, he felt it best not to let any of the sisters disturb her until he was back, at least. With any luck he'd hoped he would make it back before any news on her sister's progress. He checked her phone for any news, but there was nothing, his thoughts were that Lily must still have been in labour. Of course if something so dreadful was to be an outcome he would keep onto the ring and leave the proposal stunt for another time, but for as long as there was hope there was a chance, and he really did think before he left that magnificent manor how wonderful would Christmas and turning forty be for Ruby, if her and her family were all going to be just fine?

As we all know far too well, life shows up with its twists and turns and what one may think is not always what one may know.

Take Florence Anderson's dementia, for an example. Sometimes in a blink of an eye it's possible to miss all the small details that can put together all the lost, shattered pieces and what jagged edges and missing parts there certainly were for this pitied, misfortunate woman Mrs Florence Mary Anderson. In the beginning you could say it was almost blatant that one could be so misguided into seeing picture perfect, if fairy tales existed it did very much once upon a time when she was almost happy, almost safe. On the outside she was rich, belonging as she knew of marriage to be, to a fine, kind man, but inside her heart belonged to another, to a man who fathered her four daughters. She was not bound to have known she would never quite be able to replace that instinctive feeling of true love, a love that would stay part of her forgotten past forever. Yet she did know it was possible to love twice, because she really did cherish her husband Ben for the way he loved her devotedly and consistently.

Now if anybody were to take a closer peep in, they would see how happily married Mrs Anderson was, a woman who never went for anything. Some could see it as disgraceful that she could have been so wrong about Paul, to have been so sucked in to his charm, fall victim to his larger-than-life character, the fiery Jamaican blood she too had once been so familiar with and, all along, at some regretful part of her marriage, she sought, she craved for the thrill and excitement, she craved a little danger of what she thought her dearest friend had married into, the fun Sue once shared with Paul was the fun she desperately missed for herself.

But it had not been so easy to spot the evil, to smell the lies, or be weakened with sorry excuses and promises to change. Not until the idealisation stage had ended. Not until the devaluation stage began and the physical force became a habit.

That man's change of nature was vile once Sue could not bear him a child. The violence was clever, he was a master of manipulation, and not just one woman felt the receiving end of his shoves and fists. For a tiny second in Sue's bedroom manor, before the ghastly moment she was about to surrender to his sexual commands, Florence's brain triggered a flashback. It was a memory of Paul shouting at her ferociously after a usual drunken bust-up between the pair, he had demanded she'd step aside or else. Of course as any best friend would, any woman defending another woman stays exactly where she is.

And it was for that very reason that Florence's life had also changed, feeling the force of his hands as though he was specifically trained to throw women across a room as though they were nothing more than a rag doll. Yet as quickly as she remembered the attack, just as quickly she forgot the crucial part of smashing her head against the side of the desk as she fell crashing down. Yes, Florence had also been on the receiving end of his violent, menacing hands.

But how dreadful he really was, the pain that man had caused was shocking, so very sad how much Sue was yet to bear. It must have been the loneliest place she must have gone to.

That fear once she knew she was just at the beginning of his sordid plan to torture and murder her.

For Florence however, she brushed off the bang on the head as a little accident. It was nothing to be made a fuss of, she was best to have ignored it, because how on earth was she supposed to tell her husband of such a thing? Or even tell her daughters? For they would have wanted to kill him if they had known he had put his violent hands on her, too.

Florence felt a week, defeated scared woman and hadn't that wicked Paul just known so?

So as Florence did all too well she blocked it out with every other sad, hidden secrets she kept stored, and maybe something as a slow bleed on the brain, distorting a particular part causing her symptoms similar to dementia was assumed, missed by her daughters. She was not noticed by her husband who had been convinced she was losing her poor little mind, she being a bored menopausal housewife with daughters who had flown the nest all but one, Ruby of course.

But no one could have guessed Paul was the actual cause. They could not have really understood the nature, dramatic and sudden state of their mother's mental health.

As bleed in the brain can be a slow process which was definitely the case for Florence Anderson but if she was to be left untreated it was inescapable that the rest of Christmas was indeed going to be fatal with deadly repercussions.

As the sky lightened, she walked past, looking into the windows of homes with families oozing love inside of them. She wandered further and further down the snow-covered lanes of Virginia Waters, lost, scared, frozen and away from her family.

Florence Anderson was in great danger…

Chapter 30
Christmas Day

PART 1

In another cottage was a slightly more manic and smaller home where Rose Anderson had felt unsettled. She had never wanted to tell all the lies she had told to Eli, but learning from her mother, evidently she had been taught well. Besides, Eli was too much of a good thing, it was too risky to jeopardise losing it all, she agreed that what you don't know does not hurt you but what you did could change everything? She knew Eli could easily blow the family cover, go to the police should anything go wrong in their relationship later on down the line, she knew all too well now that there were no guarantees in love or marriage, people change and fall out of love as quickly as they fell into it.

Usually she was able to sleep through the night, now she was rattled with insomnia, irritating patterns of interrupted sleeping intervals.

Whilst she lay awake she sensed there was some kind of powerful pathway that came with having a conscience, and Rose had mostly shocked herself with the little one she seemed to have, if any. He had fucking deserved to burn in that bonfire, not literally, she thought, although she did take pleasure in knowing the facts, that he had suffered in his last breaths for sure.

Paul had failed in his plan to inherit Sue's life insurance, deny rape, deny torture, to finally murdering her.

That night before Christmas, Rose Anderson was not thinking about anything else other than she could still smell the thick polluted smoke. She could still see the orange burning flames, watching those last pieces of Paul's demon burn away, burned away with all that may have linked their mother to his death.

All she expected now was for Ruby to keep her mouth shut. If she could keep the secret about their mother's crime from her partner, so could bloody well she.

At five in the morning when Rose Anderson was awake, whilst Ruby Anderson was begging to stir in her sleep, whilst her boyfriend had attempted to sneak off to collect the ring he so very much wanted to put onto her perfect finger, whilst Lily was about to give birth to bay Eve and lose crucial amounts of blood, there could not have been any chance of any secrets spilled as Rose might have feared. With everything going on with her siblings, everything with her mother, impulse ran high, she felt the deep need to go straight over to the manor, wake her sister up and go over all the details, over the story again.

Eli was awake with her at the point he found her sitting up, knees tucked up into her chin looking out into space. He sat up behind her rubbing her shoulders, for himself personally he woke feeling on cloud nine as any new father to be would naturally feel, but it really had felt like pure luck in his case, nevertheless he was a proud, content man and there was nothing Rose could do wrong in his eyes.

"Merry Christmas babes, what's the time?" his voice whispered out to her.

"I'm sorry if I woke you, it's early, Merry Christmas darling." She turned around just enough to meet his lips as he kissed her.

"God, still no messages from Betty about Lily, she must still be in labour. Listen I really must nip round to see Ruby, you can meet me round there this afternoon in your own time if you like, I don't know what kind of Christmas we're all going to be having, but still, thank goodness she's woken up forty with a new man praise the Lord."

"You do whatever you need to do, I'll join you later then, I'm really praying for your sister and her baby, I hope you know." He kissed her again, his relaxed approach made her feel extremely lucky to find the compatible soul she had found in Eli. On that Christmas early morning Rose Anderson had left her boyfriend's cottage en route to her family manor picking up the news of the birth. She was shaken with just how much crazy shit was going on with her family, but what was stirring ahead? What she was about to see next, she could never ever have seen it coming...

Back at the London hospital the bells of St Nicholas rang loudly. Betty Anderson was a soldier ready for discharge, with her dear sister to follow on in the next day or so with her miracle baby niece. It had been dreadful for Lily that Ruby was not there, it had been sickening she had an incline her twin still had not known of the news of baby Eve, nobody could understand where on earth Rose had gotten to either. But no matter what had been going on elsewhere, for Lily, her world was made perfect, nothing could take away the love she was feeling for her baby daughter, nothing and nobody.

At five forty a.m. on Wednesday the 25th of December on a fine Christmas Day morning, a little baby girl had been born. She was greeted and welcomed into the world as a miracle, once the emergency had been over with, waiting proudly was a desperate mother, a begging father, the parents would meet their teeny tiny creation earlier than expected, that special day.

Back at the manor Ruby had woken not long after Mark had left her, hearing the sound of his car tyres splattering bits of stones and gravel up from the forecourt. When she opened her eyes, she had rubbed them hard, she had pinched herself harder but there she was, alive and well. She put her hand to her heart remembering each time the tremors made it stop beating, but now she was forty, and the Wednesday beast had come and gone. Although completely baffled, she felt there had to be some kind of message from it all, quite annoyed she quickly turned to notice Mark was not beside her. It made her smile for she knew he was always trying to surprise her with stuff all the time so she assumed he had sneaked off to perform some sweet display of affection, but whatever it was she knew she would just love it.

The feeling of bliss, hope, being positive was always something she believed in. She reached for her phone oblivious to the muted sound Mark had set it on, she was certain she would only have good news to read, if any. Yet it was still just a bit too soon at the time of the hour it was when she checked, there had been no news, still no birth; and so easily distracted she became, the phone was tossed again to one side and forgotten about.

It was a typical disaster that when the call did finally come in from the hospital, it did so in silence. When the phone's screen had lightened up when it had vibrated, it did so underneath a pillow where it had fallen under and, just like that, Ruby Anderson was out of sight from that situation.

"Happy birthday you old cow," she said to herself… and glared into her dressing table mirror, not seeing much of a change in her reflection just as yet, but she hoped there was a change in her heart. She really hoped she had given it to the right one this time round, that she had picked the man of her dreams this time, she thought, as she waited for his return.

She had wondered what her birthday present would be it had taken over the worry anywhere else for a few short minutes. It was the fact she was so confident why she showed no real fear for Lily, for she had already known, she had already predicted they were both going to be just fine.

She brushed her hair, thinking luck had struck a little, it was quite convenient Mark had done a disappearing act as there was something other than the Wednesday beast that was taking over all the spare parts of her brain. Her breasts were tender, she had an increased appetite and she was late? How iconic she thought it to be, pregnant, another Anderson sister pregnant, never guessing such a thing would happen to her. After all, it was Ruby who had always said she would never have a baby unless she was married, over her dead body would she be a single mum, she would say, but when you looked at her on that snowy Christmas morning you could only see a young woman excited, nervous of course, but a woman who had never wanted anything as badly as she had wanted to be pregnant that morning. She could only hope she truly was and if she was then she could only hope Mark would feel exactly the same way.

She did the normal procedure of weeing onto a stick, she placed the pregnancy test on to the side as she flushed and washed her hands. All there was left for Ruby Anderson to do now was to just wait… Life can be split between two different paths, such as, right time, right place or wrong time, wrong place.

If you saw Mark Harrington driving at steady speed anyone could have seen how happy he was. You would have known that he had felt more alive than ever. You could say it was one of those ridiculous childish moments when you tell yourself to get a grip and calm the excitement down as he had been very excited, of his future, of his promise to his new wife to be, to love, honour and respect her with plenty of added qualities he was sure to bring to her table. Mark Harrington drove that morning as though he was a teenage boy, wanting to get back to her, he drove on his way back to the manor.

Although the skies had lightened a little, it was still fairly dark, there was a mist in his sight that took his full diverted attention for a while. He focused on the road ahead hard, he would be on the long dual carriageway a short while before approaching the roundabout to turn off into a private wooded area which homed just a few of the extravagant magnificent manors, one belonging to the love of his life, known as their mother's antique manor, but it was Ruby's very much loved home as well.

At first he had been unsure by the intensity of her family like all the other spouses, but then he realised the closeness between them all was the most beautiful thing he'd ever seen in a family, he saw the ways they had worshipped Florence Anderson, he had so very much wanted to make the best and biggest impression he could with the woman they had all, in their own ways, clearly looked up to.

Although he did think of the poor dear seeming a little fragile, Mark had passed it off with humour.

"There's nothing wrong with missing an egg from your omelette, happens to the best of us, at least your mum has all you girls," he had said to Ruby in the beginning of it all, when she applauded his comedy and light-hearted spirit.

Something had made him turn down the radio. Not that it had even been too loud, it was just one of those things, as he did, his eyes left the road for not even thirty seconds, but in those lost seconds, something all of a sudden was in his view closely ahead, a figure, a shape of a person? Surely not an animal? A woman it had to be standing there, frozen like a statue, so brazen, perhaps deluded to selfishly jump out into moving traffic, but luckily as Christmas mornings of early hours usually were, it was quiet, there had only been one car in sight, a black Mercedes he had decided to take Ruby's car instead of his own.

Almost immediately there was no time left, it was a split decision between life and death, as Mr Harrington pulled hard on to his brakes, the force of the car tyres slid practically to bursting. As he drove closer, he felt his heart at his feet, he knew it was her, he knew the woman standing still, ahead of him was Florence Anderson, the white velvet hooded gown he had remembered seeing her in one time before, something so distinctive, so demure, he knew it had been her.

His brain collapsed in exhaustion. The choice he had was to swerve out the way to try and save Florence's life or he could drive straight on ahead, in a bid to save his own.

They say we are a fool when we are in love and maybe a fool is what some could say he was. Or maybe perhaps to others he would be more some kind of a hero, either way in a matter of life and death, Mr Harrington decided to sacrifice his own life for his girlfriend's mother's. After all, it would only be him lost, to Florence she lost them all, he had never had a mother or father who had ever given a damn about him and to Mark you couldn't replace a mother. To him he had only come into Ruby's life for a short while, all four of her daughters had needed Florence Anderson.

And so he made the crucial decision to swerve, the impact of the car knocked Florence down to her feet unconscious and there she lay still in the road.

He knew instantly he was taking in his last breaths, his eyes stayed shut but to him he was sure he could see white visions. He was certain he could see himself, he was staring at himself, it was his own reflection who was smiling back at him. He could see Ruby, she looked so beautiful, she was smiling at him too, her beautiful face stayed in his vision until he lost all control and in his last moments of life, in his dying moment, Mr Harrington had only been blinded in visions of love.

He was given no chance at all once the car did swerve, it was too sharp, it had been too difficult to gain back control into the lanes. The Mercedes was nothing more than crushed, crumpled metal when he had landed straight on, smashing into the root of a solid tree.

At precisely five forty a.m. on Christmas Day a baby girl had been born, at five forty a.m. on Christmas Day a man had died instantly at the scene.

Maybe it was destiny? That word we hear and take for granted all so often, but we can't avoid the unavoidable, just like Rose Anderson could not avoid taking the same route. The same road that Mark Harrington had taken when she had been on the way over to her family manor, fired up and feeling impetuous to see Ruby.

Of course it was not just coincidence that it had been Rose to be the next vehicle to firstly spot her mother lying unconscious in the road, she then disturbingly went to go on to spot Ruby's black Mercedes, the adrenaline hit Rose immediately, the taste of fear in her mouth, disgust, revulsion. Rose crept over to the damaged vehicle, desperate to set eyes on what she thought would be the car crash body of her beloved devoted sister. She could not have helped scream in gratitude realising the deceased victim was not Ruby, but as reality quickly kicked in as it did particularly well in her profession, Rose knew regretfully she would be the one having to break the unforgivable horrendous news to her sister that the dead body found was the love of her life, Mr Mark Harrington.

"Ambulance please, I think my mother's been knocked over, she's breathing, but she's not awake. A man is dead, it's my sister's partner, I think he tried to swerve and save my mother's life, please come quickly, I'm off the roundabout to Dalton village, Virginia Waters. My battery is dead, postcode is—" the battery died, but everyone knew Dalton village, it was the most favourable, desired place to live in Virginia Waters, she knew help would be on its way.

She had felt that her mother had a pulse, she waited with her mother's head between her laps, singing to her as she would always sing to them when they had been unwell. She would never say many comforting words, but their mother's voice was heavenly, she sang as an angel would sing.

"Everything's going to be fine Mother. I promise, just rest, and hold on, you've got to, do you hear me Mother?"

Rose felt the baby kick inside of her. She was crying so much she lost all vision, everything became a blur even when the blue lights came flashing, pulling up. She was torn whether to stay or leave, but Rose knew her mother was in capable hands now. There was nothing she could do herself but wait for her mother to come round, and she would, she just had to, but for now she knew Ruby was waiting for Mark and she needed to break the awful news to her sister.

They do say what we don't know can't hurt us and, as much as Ruby Anderson would never get the chance to marry her loved one, she would never know that he was going to propose to her on that fortieth birthday of hers, either.

So sad for Mr Harrington that his dreams and hopes

shattered with life taken. Who knows, maybe if he had known Ruby was taking a pregnancy test, maybe that would have changed everything? Maybe instead of swerving, had he known that little bit of detail, then maybe it could have been his reason to have made a different choice to have carried on driving instead of swerving? Who knows?

PART 2

Whilst back inside the manor, Ruby had spent pretty much most of her time being sick, unaware of any tragedy that had struck.

She slumbered back underneath the covers, curious and suspicious as to how much longer he would take to come back, adamant she wanted to read the test results with him. She became curious as to whether Lily had given birth yet, that she became furious in trying to find her phone to check. As soon as she had finally found the sodding thing she could hear someone thump open the bedroom door. Her bed was away from the door so she knew she would wait a few seconds before she could set her eyes on whoever was bursting in so rudely.

And as she looked into her phone there it was in black and white, the news of baby Ivy at last. Mother and baby were doing well like she predicted.

And in that split second Ruby had felt wonderful. She frowned in shock as she saw her sister Rose, she had not looked like she was bursting in to share baby news, she had looked ghastly, detached, and all of a sudden there she could see that inconsolable state she had seen too many times before.

She had remembered that hellish feeling all too well.

Rose had stood in exactly the same place as she had stood in her dream, crying, trying to tell her something.

Ruby went ice cold. Her body became paralysed in her bed just as it once did as she slept with the Wednesday beast.

She felt this pain at the pit of her stomach. And it was the same pain she had felt from her nightmares.

"Sis, I'm so sorry to tell you this."

"Shut up, get out right now Rose." Ruby denied hearing anything, she tried rejecting any truth she was about to hear.

She rushed to her back doors and slid them open still denying any truth to what she was about to hear. She needed to see for herself, she needed to see that her black Mercedes was parked up in its usual spot but, when she looked, she could only see Mark's BMW vehicle. She had kept seeing her car in her nightmare and every time she tried to see who was inside, her image became flooded with the colour red.

Ruby dropped to her feet, she stopped Rose in her tracks rushing to her aid as she was processing her premonition.

"Ruby, listen to me please." Rose begged her to be strong. she was kneeling, keeping her distance as requested.

Rose herself had no longer been able to stand, gravity was taking her down in a way it had never quite done before.

"Your car was found, I found it, it's Mark, he is dead. Sis, it was Mum, she was in the middle of the road, I think she's OK, but he tried to save her, he swerved, and he never had to do that, I'm just so sorry."

Rose said nothing more, in need of any human response she waited for Ruby to say something, to say anything. Rose vomited violently.

"He told me he would never leave me, he told me he would never hurt me. He can't be dead, he can't be."

But she knew he was, she knew the Wednesday beast had won, she was after all a child of woe, her nightmare had come true, she had felt dead inside, no purpose left to live.

And well, that's the funny thing about life, just when you think you will never have another reason to wake up again, something just comes along and gives you another chance or perhaps it's even another choice? How do you want to spend the rest of your life now? do you want to live or die? Do you want to cry forever or smile again?

Her legs felt weak, her body felt numb. But finding new strength, finding new hope, Ruby Anderson walked into her bathroom and looked into the plastic stick. In clear blue writing, she read: pregnant.

Tears smothered her face, nose sniffling uncontrollably, she looked into her sister's eyes, bewildered, lost and numb in all the pain but they were eyes with new fight in them. She was going to be a mother.

Ruby could do nothing other than pull back the covers to sleep. If she could take something for the pain for her loss then she was not likely to have woken back up, but this baby was going to get her through it all.

Once she had come back around a few hours later she screamed for Mark. She begged for him to come back, she had wanted to see his body, she needed to say goodbye if she could.

All that Ruby Anderson could feel was hollow, it was as though she was lost in another world, hearing information but not processing anything particularly well.

Also hearing about her twins' birth and the miracle arrival of baby Eve, she also learned of the bleed on her mother's brain and that it had not been dementia after all, and of Betty giving blood saving Lily's life.

It turned out that in all the commotion Ben had finally come home, revealing he had built a secret retirement home for

Florence in Mauritius, another magnificent but smaller more practical way to settle down where they could live a fine, ideal and easy life as they were getting older. He had wanted to surprise his wife so badly to show how much he truly worshipped her, to prove what had caused his absence all this time had been worth it, and fortunately for Florence Anderson, well, she pulled through unscathed in the end of her hospital treatment. Once fully recovered there would be no better place in the world she'd rather be, to escape to a place she would be able to put everything behind her, set off into a white-sanded beach with her devoted husband.

For Ruby Anderson the manor was to be left to her after everything she suffered. With her loss and with her sisters married also settled with good men, the house was left for Ruby and her baby with an open door to the family and so it would remain. Florence had agreed under one condition and that was that the manor was never to be sold but handed down in generations.

So for Ruby it turned out that her most favourite place in the world she would get to inherit, was the home in which she would raise her baby, blessed by the man she so very much got the experience and chance to once love, and who had truly loved her. And loving Mark Harrington's child was surely going to be the next best thing to loving him.

With all of the family's lives changing in some way or another, through the hard tragedies that came their way.

There is no easy way to tell somebody to never give up with the fight of life. Do not wait for something to happen to make us remember how precious life really is.

For the Anderson women, well, they all learned some valuable lessons from all that happened to them.

For Lily Anderson she learned:

To trust and believe she deserved good things in life with the man she found to love.

That miracles really did exist.

To always tell the truth for it was the truth what brought them all together in the end.

For Rose Anderson she learned to take a gamble in life, to never settle for anything less than she deserved.

That anything's possible.

Sometimes we lie to protect those we love.

And that sometimes love will make a person do the craziest of things.

For Betty she learned a little thing called kindness, as kindness made her into the fine woman she became in the end.

To be grateful for what she already had.

To love the people standing in front of you.

Because you never know when you're going to need them back one day.

For Florence, well she learned in the end that mistakes can happen and that family and loyalty is everything.

She learned the love of a good man was enough to make all the difference to a woman's life.

And as for Ruby, well, she learned there were worse things in life than just being a single mother.

She learned that the person who you can love the most is still a person who can hurt you the most, intentionally or not.

But she also learned that even in loss we are still capable of loving something or someone else again. For Ruby it would be a beautiful baby girl.

The Wednesday beast released itself free to find another soul to haunt.

But gifted she would always be. She learned some people fear what they do not understand and sometimes you might get called crazy when you really know you're not.

And so left in a huge antique manor, Ruby Anderson took in a deep breath, sucked in the emotions, tears shedding from all directions.

It was still Christmas Day on that Wednesday the 25th of December, it was still her fortieth birthday.

And really, when you do think about it, when life does happen as it so easily does, what even is a happy ending anyway?

The tears of Wednesday.

The End...